DE MOJO BLUES

De Quest of HighJohn de Conqueror

A. R. Flowers

BALLANTINE BOOKS • NEW YORK

Library of Congress Catalog Card Number: 85-13019

ISBN 0-345-33995-9

This edition published by arrangement with E.P. Dutton

Manufactured in the United States of America

First Ballantine Books Edition: January 1987

**Dedicated to those folks
who have put up with me
these long years of creation**

and the delta clan flowers

And the Shark said: Shine, Shine, you doing fine,
but if you miss one stroke
your ass is mine.

SECTION ONE

~~~~

DE CALL

CHAPTER 1

〰〰〰〰

THE FREEDOM BIRD GREW FROM A SILVER SPECK IN THE sun and landed with a jarring shock and the stink of rubber. The gleaming plane carried the Oakland Army Base's last load of Vietnam returnees for the year 1970. It taxied to a stop and two soldiers in starched green fatigues pushed a ramp up. The door opened. Tucept HighJohn stepped out and blinked, thick sunlight glinting off his dark skin and accenting the deep wrinkles in his khakis. The wrist of the hand held up to block the sun was handcuffed to the other wrist by a short length of chain.

Mike and Willie D, also in chains, stepped off the plane, followed closely by a big ruddy MP with a holstered sidearm.

Back to the world, Tucept muttered.

The three black soldiers started down the ramp. A line of unchained returnees in sundark bodies and medallioned khaki uniforms filed off behind them. At the bottom of

3

the ramp Tucept hesitated before moving toward a door with two GIs standing beside it. The two GIs tried not to stare at the three handcuffed Blacks and the MP walking behind them.

At the door, Tucept glanced at Chambliss. The MP nodded and Tucept went into a large room bare but for a podium and rows of chairs. Chambliss nodded them to the front row. The rest of the GIs from the Freedom Bird filed in and took seats behind them. Tucept kept looking over his shoulder, having people behind him made him uneasy.

Willie D leaned across Tucept and put his chained hands in front of Chambliss.

Chambliss fumbled in his pocket, pulled out keys and unlocked them one by one. Tucept rubbed his wrist with little sense of gratitude. He wouldn't really feel free until he was out of the army and had the papers to prove it.

A major walked in and mounted the podium. A short man drawing height from his military bearing, he waited for the pack to silence itself.

Welcome back to the States, he said, in the monotonic of a script run too many times, Your country is proud of you.

Tucept felt Willie D shift beside him.

They were the brave and the proud, the major went on, they would be paid after changing their summer khakis for warmer winter greens and having their orders cut.

Tucept only half listened. He walked through emerald green jungles and golden bamboo gardens. A brood settled on him, a deep malignant mood.

On the podium the major finished his presentation with a grand flourish, . . . to show its appreciation, your country is treating you to a free steak dinner.

Vulgar noises greeted the offer of a "free" steak dinner, in the messhall no less.

Ignoring the yelling, the major stepped down and walked off.

Chambliss stood and Tucept, Willie D and Mike followed him from the room. The other GIs filed out behind them. They went through a cursory customs check and left their duffelbags on a thick greenline that went into a huge warehouse room off to the side.

Chambliss left, I'll wait in the locker room, he said.

Tucept followed the greenline into a huge warehouse. The room was huge, with roofbeams shrouded in dust-moted cobwebbed shadows. Bins and bins of dressgreen uniform issue made the big room damp wool musty. Tucept went from bin to bin, receiving issue and moving down the line like a product on an assembly line.

In the locker room he showered and dressed slowly. Still in summer khakis, Chambliss sat on a bench smoking a bent Winston.

Their eyes caught for an uncomfortable moment and Chambliss cleared his throat, Okay you guys, let's get this over with.

Mike came out of the shower toweling himself, fair skin Nam burnt a stringy brown, torso carved lean and covered with a wet plastering of fine hairs.

Relax Sarge, he said with a smooth smile, don't get strac on us now.

Willie D grunted, a low sobering note that caused them to dress quickly. When they were ready, they followed Chambliss from the room and down busy halls until they stood in front of a closed door. Chambliss knocked. Hearing a response, he pushed the door open and stood aside to let them enter. They came to somewhat casual attention in front of a redheaded captain sitting rigidly behind a desk. Little American flags on the walls, army commendations, a picture of the captain jump-harnessed in the door of a C-131.

The captain looked up.

DE MOJO BLUES

Sergeant Chambliss sir, Chambliss said crisply, Escorting three prisoners to the States, Privates HighJohn, Brown and Daniels.

Recognition hardened in the captain's eyes. Without taking his eyes off them the captain held his hand out for their orders. Chambliss handed over the packets, stepped behind them and stood to attention. Tucept sweated in his heavy dressgreens, thin rivulets running down his shoulder blades. He wanted to scratch.

The captain's mouth tightened as he read through their orders. He looked up and through them.

I'm required, he said, still not quite looking at them, to ask if you have been counseled, if you understand and accept the sentence of your courtmartial. Do you understand the nature of your discharges and the fact that this might be held against you in some phases of your civilian life?

He paused for their nods of acknowledgment.

As soon as you give us these papers, I will be out of the army, said Willie D, that I understand.

The captain soured visibly. He looked at them for the first time since reading their orders. He started to say something and changed his mind, reaching instead into his desk and pulling out three packets. He threw them on the scarred wood of the desk top.

Their pay and their orders Sergeant Chambliss, lock them up and escort them to the gate. Dismissed.

Excuse me sir, said Chambliss, but I was only spose to keep them restrained until we got to the—

The captain stood, his body rigid, his voice controlled, Sergeant, I said chain them and keep them chained until they are off my post.

Sgt. Chambliss snapped to crisp attention.

Yessir!

The captain remained standing while Chambliss re-

6

chained them. Tucept watched tensely until Willie D let himself be chained again.

Chambliss picked up their papers, Alright you guys, he said, let's go.

Mike and Tucept turned to leave. Willie D came to attention and saluted the captain, one chained wrist following the other to his forehead.

The captain's face blurred, but he made a tightwristed motion to his forehead that passed as a returned salute. Willie D about faced and walked.

They followed Chambliss to the gate, returning power salutes given by brothers they passed. A double beat to the chest and the upraised fist, chains jingling faintly as if they wore bells.

At the gate Chambliss unlocked the handcuffs, this time fumbling. He got them off.

Okay, you guys, he said gruffly, . . . take it easy . . . uh, good luck.

Mike and Willie nodded. Tucept looked away.

They watched him go.

He was alright, said Mike.

Fuck him, said Tucept, a beast is a beast.

They caught a bus to San Francisco, each sitting apart in a seat by himself, riding with their private thoughts. Tucept watched the passing scenery, the cars, Chevys and Fords and buses and women, even billboards, hungrily drinking in the sights and sounds of the World. He brought the image of Ruby to his mind, the way he had done a thousand times in Nam.

He hadn't called her. He hadn't called anybody. They didn't expect him for another month. Called himself surprising folks. The anticipation of seeing her clawed through him. Ruby. The memories of her that had faded over the past year were sharp again and emotion rose to his chest. He reached into the breast pocket of his dressgreens and felt the shallow bulge of her last letter.

By the time they reached San Francisco, he was itchy and wanted to get off the bus, move around some.

At the San Francisco bus station excitement caught them. San Francisco. The World. Damn, look at this. Sight, sound, movement, things happening. They walked up to Market Street and sat on a sidewalk bench. After life in an olivedrab world of jungle green and dirt brown, San Francisco's rainbows of sight and sound were intoxicating. They just sat and watched, Tucept perched on the bench back, Willie D sitting with head bent back on the backrest, Mike stretching long legs into the sidewalk.

A sister in a curly fro, fat bow legs and a soft limegreen dress outlining arrogantly swaying hips, stepped off the opposite curb and started across.

Chooiii, whispered Mike, that is fine. Beaucoup dap wa.

Willie D and Tucept's appreciative silences agreed.

Mike sat up, straightened his tie, patted his hat cocky.

I'm going to get some action, he said.

She crossed the street and stepped up on the curb.

Hubba hubba, said Mike.

Hubba, hubba? echo'd Willie D.

Tucept and Willie D laughed so hard they fell off the bench. The woman looked at them curiously as she passed. Mike grinned sheepishly. He turned to the still laughing Willie D and Tucept after she got out of hearing range.

Look what you two clowns did, you made me blow it.

Wasn't us blood, Tucept said through bubbles of laughter, You wanna hang with us, you got to do better than hubba hubba.

So I'm rusty, said Mike.

Ruefully he watched the swaying hips walk off.

You think I ought to catch her?

They pushed him after her, Go ahead blood, beaucoup dap wa medin, numba one, bic. You owe it to yourself.

Mike resisted them, indignantly brushing their hands off. He had to laugh in spite of himself. It has been awhile, he said, maybe I need to start off with one that isn't quite so impressive.

Tucept and Willie D fell out, unseemly howls indicating total loss of composure.

Not that funny, said Mike and sat beside them, eyes still on the swaying limegreen hips.

I can't do anything as long as we in these monkey suits, said Mike.

Let's get a room, said Tucept, we change our clothes and hangout some before we go home. We can get a bird out tomorrow or whenever.

Beaucoup dinkidou, said Willie D, I'm not spending all my little money on a hotelroom. Never happen GI.

One of us gets it, said Tucept, the others become visitors.

Now that I like, said Willie D.

They found a hotel and Mike went in. Twenty-five minutes later Tucept and Willie knocked on the red door of Room 750. Mike opened the door. He had showered and was standing barefooted in the pearlgray pants of one of his Hong Kong suits.

Hubba hubba, said Willie D. He walked in and bounced himself on the bed.

Tucept looked around. A square little room with a big double bed, flat white walls. A pay TV, a faded hotelroom landscape.

Tucept showered and trimmed his army issue beard, occasionally stopping to glance at the face that stared back at him. He turned it this way and that. Tucept HighJohn. The wide clan HighJohn nose, a high forehead and tight stingy eyes. Lines that confused rather than exposed. Willie D's impatient knock on the door jerked him out of the mirror.

About an hour later, stupid off wine and some herb

they had brought from Nam, they hit the street in Hong Kong specials from Vietnam's ever present Hong Kong tailors. Tucept sported a black 3-piece with matching overcoat, Willie D was in an offwhite suit with white gators, and Mike in a shimmering pearlgray 3-piece.

They hit Market profiling. Up and down the street. Up and down. In a barbershop on a sidestreet a high-pockets brother smelling of aftershaves and hair lotions convinced them that the blowout was the latest thing.

See, the brother said, the hair was blownout with a hot comb and then shaped to style. Everybody's doing it.

They walked out of the barbershop with huge afro halos and strode Market again, up and down, shiny suits and afro halos gleaming in a midday sun. Unconsciously they stride in cadence, side by side, left right left right left right.

Hey soldier boys!

Whoever that was couldn't be yelling at them. They march on. Left right left right.

Hey you, three soldier boys, bloods in the suits!

They turned. A wide brother, wide grin framing a gold tooth, broad face spiked with a pencilthin mustache. He stood in front of a military ring store, hundreds of little rings sparkling in the window front beside him. They had seen these little stores near every post they had ever done duty on.

He waved them over, Over here, he said, give me a minute.

They hesitated, offended that he had peeped them as army. Or even ex-army.

He waved more insistently. They worked their way through the sidewalk traffic to him.

Aint trying to sell you nothing, he said, gold tooth winking like a little sun, Saw you were just out the war and thought to blackinize some.

They grinned and their suspiciousness evaporated.

Number one brother blood, You was in the war? Tucept held out his fist to be dapped.

Cut it short, the brother said. They went through the basic Namwide dap, fists slapping in the elaborate handshake ritual of black Vietnam. The Black to Black salute.

Willie and Mike dapped him. They all dapped round.

Who were you with? asked Willie D. His long head weaved as he spoke, absently monitoring the flow of the crowd around him.

3rd Marines, up near the DMZ in the north. Where were you stationed?

In the delta, said Willie, Firebase Sin Loi.

How could you tell we were vets? asked Mike.

I recognized the Hong Kong suits and seem like every brother that get off the bird get one of those damned blowouts.

You recognized the suits, nice huh?

The brother looked amused and dipped his head noncommittally.

I'm Bennett, he said.

I'm Mike Daniels, from Atlanta.

William E. Burghart Dubois Brown, from Fayetteville North Carolina by way of Fort Bragg, folks call me Willie D.

HighJohn, Memphis.

You from San Francisco? Willie D asked him.

Bennett shook his head, grinning through the gold tooth, I'm from the best part de hog brother, Birmingham. Came through here when I got mustered out and knew I had found myself a home. He winked, More freaks per square inch here than anywhere in the continental United States.

They laughed and dapped again. It was good to see a brother from the war doing well and enjoying himself. Must not be that hard.

DE MOJO BLUES

A young soldier walked up in a dressgreen uniform without patches or ribbons, a trainee's bald scalp still gleaming.

Excuse me, Bennett said. Following the trainee into the store, he motioned for them to follow. The dark little store was ringed with glittering showcases. Bennett showed the young soldier some rings, something nice for the lady, he said smoothly, or maybe for your mother.

How many times had they heard that rap? Tucept looked at the rings in the front showcase, twinkling eyes in little black coffins, reflections in the window a skyview of little stars. He watched people passing by outside. Noticing the vague outline of his face, he refocused, the people outside sliding into blurs while his face, marred by twinkling stones, became clear. He looked at himself. Out of the army. Free. Could do what he wanted. Could go where he wanted. A free man. Just an hour ago he was Spec 4 HighJohn. Correction, Private HighJohn. He watched his face smile wryly.

Bennett sold the trainee a ring for himself, a cheap bracelet for his mother. He solemnly stood behind the cash register until the trainee left. Then gold twinkled and he walked over.

It's a living, he said.

We didn't say anything blood, protested Willie.

Bennett shrugged and glanced at his watch, a thin gold piece contrasting sharply with the junk he sold.

Say look here bloods, there's a party in my building tonight, a friend of mine is leaving town. I'm going right after work, what it look like?

A party sounds good to me, said Mike, that's the way to come back to the World.

This a throwdown? asked Tucept, a sho nuff boogie?

Any other kind? said Bennett.

They laugh and their hands flow through dap.

Tucept checked his watch, We'll be back then man, about five.

They left the shop and cruised San Francisco. They rode the trolley cars, shaking up and down the hills, tourists, staring at the bridge, at buildings. At women. Women, walking around, talking, all over, being normal, just being. Chinatown was fascinating, Oriental and familiar after a year in Nam but still American, a bridge between two worlds. At the Wharf they sat with shoes off, toes wiggling.

Mike squinted his eyes at the sun off the water, A nice little town, he said.

What you going to do when you get home? asked Willie D.

Willie D had joined planning to make the army a career. Brought up in the shadow of Fort Bragg and the 82nd Airborne, he had wanted to jump the big iron bird like most kids wanted to learn how to drive. The court-martial had destroyed his dreams of being a lifer.

I guess I'll be going back to school, said Tucept. He didn't sound convincing.

School for me definitely, said Mike, my pop will pitch a fit if I don't go ahead and get that law degree.

Mike's daddy was a big man in Atlanta insurance. When Mike got drafted Mike Sr. pulled strings but Mike Jr. went anyway.

They sat in a reflective pause. Over the last year they've become accustomed to leaning on each other, Blood, Brother me, Brother Black. Now they're back to the World and preparing to go their separate ways. They are suddenly uncomfortable, the salty breeze chilly.

Let's go to this party yall, said Tucept.

Bennett closed up shop early and turned in the receipts down the street. Walking distance, he told them. They left the busy Market area behind, following him into a residential area, quiet and somber, with rough, wornout edges. The sky darkened as dusk fell. Feeling like he was on patrol back in Nam, Tucept scanned around him wary for boobytraps and ambushes. What if this was an ambush, a soldier's scam, setting them up for the old ripoff? He relaxed. He was with his boys. Wasn't nobody taking off him, Mike, and Willie D.

At Bennett's highrise, they rode up a slow elevator scrubbed a defiant clean and stinking of ammonia.

At the door they hesitated, suddenly selfconscious. Would everybody at the fucking party be able to tell that they were brand new vets too? They looked at each other's worried expressions and broke out laughing. Bennett took that as his cue to open the door and the muted sounds of a party pulled them in.

About 20–25 people wandered around a large apartment in various stages of party. Good mixture. Attractive women. Easy ambience. A large apartment well but sparsely furnished. A thick white rug.

Bennett shooed them in and detached himself, You dudes mingle, he said, it's a good group of people. No problems.

They stood in a selfconscious little knot, feeling as if they were still in dressgreens. Tucept didn't notice too many blowouts. Maybe everybody here is a square.

Good thing we changed, Mike whispered though no one was near enough to hear. They angled over to the wine table, got some glasses of wine, something to put in their hands. For all their cocky talk they felt out of place and intimidated. They heard Marvin Gaye coming out of wall speakers, talking about what's happening brother, he was just getting back from the war and wanted to know what's going on.

Tucept listened, realized that it was Marvin Gaye talking about coming home from the war. Sent tingles down his spine.

Hey yall, he said excitedly, that's Marvin talking 'bout coming home from the war.

They listen closely, eyes closed, faces dreamy.

Yeah? Marvin's new piece, I heard about it, said Mike.

They split up, Mike beelined for a lady, Willie D bogarted himself into a group smoking a joint, and Tucept claimed a big easy chair by a window. He sat down and placed Mike and Willie D from habit.

He absently pulled a little leather bag from his pocket and handled it in his hand. From inside came a faint muffled clanking. Marvin sang on, the party ebbed and flowed around his still figure. No one tried to pull him into the party, they accepted his brooding demand for privacy.

Nam had changed him. Already he thought, something so alien to him that he only knows it as restless anxiety. Explosive imbalance. He watched the party with a strange sense of distance, as if standing off and watching himself watch the others. His distance surprised him. His contempt. Plastic people with plastic concerns. He grew suddenly angry. His eyes misted and Jethro's green fatigued back walked slowly through the jungle foliage. A gold bamboo forest loomed in front of them, stretching as far and as deep as the eye could see, mean and primal with tall stern stalks draped in vines and drenched with a gold shimmer so rich it tainted the air around it.

Jethro hesitated at the edge of the golden garden and looked around. He entered. The gold air tinted his barkbrown skin and his green jungle fatigues a gold alien tone. Suddenly concerned, Tucept hurried to cut down the space between them, lugging the heavy M60 machine-gun cross his hip.

He bounded up to the bamboo garden and was close enough to see the AK rounds when they smashed into

15

Jethro's body, when they flung Jethro ragdoll limp into the bamboo stalks. The M60 roared in his hands and bamboo stalks shattered in a sunglinting rain of gold slivers. Tucept ran up raging, firing and crying.

He burst into the gold garden, the pig tearing a huge golden swath before he dropped it. Jethro was impaled on a broken shaft of bamboo, a bloody crowpicked black scarecrow, eyes wide open, guts ripped from his open belly, the side of his head bloody ruin, his left arm shredded away.

Please man, Tucept muttered over him, please don't die on me man.

He lashed out savagely with his foot at the impaling bamboo stalk. The stalk cracked and Jethro's body swayed drunkenly before falling to the bloody golden ground. Tucept dropped, cradled Jethro's head and wept, ignoring the firefight raging around them as the unit caught up. No man please, he cried softly as he stuffed Jethro's filthy guts back in his belly.

Oh God please. He almost laughed aloud. He hadn't called on God too long to think he could call on him now.

Take the bones, said Jethro.

Willing to believe, Tucept shook him and Jethro's bloody guts flopped on his uniform. He was still shaking Jethro when Mike and Willie D pulled him off the body. He fought them and they had to talk him down, It's alright man, be cool Tennessee.

With his back to a leaning bamboo stalk, he watched numbly as medics stuffed Jethro's body into a used bodybag. When finally he rose he saw with revulsion the blood and bone fragments stuck to his uniform and slapped viciously at the spot.

Tucept? Tucept?

Tucept opened his eyes.

Willie D sat beside him, You alright man?

DE CALL

Willie D's tone was casual, but when Tucept didn't answer Willie D looked him in his eye. Tucept focused momentarily on the crisscross grids of Willie D's facial scars. A fragmentation grenade had sliced Willie D's walnut face into so fine a pattern that you had to look hard to tell why the symmetry was marred.

I'm fine, said Tucept.

Mike walked over and stood next to them.

Just thinking about Jethro I guess, said Tucept.

Mike put his hand on Tucept's shoulder, Number ten GI, don't bring Nam back with you. Com bic?

Bic. I'm cool.

Mike and Willie moved back out into the party like birds of prey, falcons on the wing. His cronies. He felt a wave of emotion. He became aware of the leather bag in his hand and put it away. More people arrived and the party pace picked up. Someone passed him a joint and he held onto it, smoking it slowly.

Tucept sat out the rest of the night in the easy chair, eyes focused far away, a half-smoked joint in hand and a mind full of golden bamboo gardens.

ON NEW YEAR'S DAY 1971 A BLACK AND YELLOW CAB PULLED up in front of the Memphis Tennessee residence of Dr. and Mrs. HighJohn. Grinning foolishly, Tucept climbed out of the backseat and put his duffelbag down in front of a long, lowslung yellow brick house with a ring of shrubbery moating the front yard. Home.

He shouldered his duffelbag and started up the long sloping driveway. He noted new shrubs. Momma's been working on the yard. The thought was warm and gave him, for the first time, a sense of really being home. Out of the war. He hadn't called from the airport. Still called himself surprising folks.

His daddy's blueblack Cadillac and his momma's skyblue Toyota were in the carport. A row of bricks had

17

been set around his momma's garden. A bewhiskered little yapping dog ran out at him. Tucept kept a wary eye on it while he rang the bell.

His momma opened the door and peered through the heavy metal bars of the screen. She held up her hand to block the sun silhouetting his bulky uniformed figure.

Momma, he said excitedly, happily. Momma, it's me, Tucept, your long lost baby boy, carrying my sword and my shield.

Tucept? She squinted, already unlocking the door, broad attractive face shifting into a smile. Tucept came in the door and hugged her.

What's happening old gal? he said, playing with his momma like he liked to do.

Why didn't you call us, she said reproachfully, full-fleshed mouth trying vainly to be serious, Why didn't you tell us you were home?

Pleasure etching familiar lines deep, she started laughing again, excitedly slapping his shoulders. Spastic with pleasure he held her back and looked her over, his eyes soft. She had put on a little weight, a rounder face, wearing her hair straight again, new and deeper crinkles around the eyes. A deep brown woman, built solid from the spirit up. Half fending her excited slaps off, he looked around the den. It was different, a brown-gold carpeting, chairs redone in a soft brown fabric, more plants, paintings.

You didn't even tell us. James Henry! Caldonia! she sang out to the back, Come out here and see what I've got for you.

Her head dropped to the side quizzically, What are you doing home so early?

Tucept cleared his throat, I got a early out Ma, cause of Mr. Nixon's troop withdrawals.

The little dog yapped frenzy around his ankles. Tucept dodged out of his way.

That's Rascal, his momma said, Shut up Rascal.

Tucept, dancing out of Rascal's way, grabbed his momma and danced her around with him. She tried, not too hard, to escape his grasp and both tried not to step on the frantic dog dodging underfoot. Laughing wildly, she slapped at his shoulder until they both almost fell. He let her go and backed out of the way of her slapping hands. The little dog followed him, nipping at the trouser leg of his uniform.

His father, Dr. James Henry HighJohn, stood in the door to the kitchen watching them, a small amused smile on his heavy face, a paper in one hand, a white shirt unbuttoned.

Tucept walked over and stood in front of his father. He stuck out his hand, and said, almost shyly.

Hey Daddy.

His father nodded, a small smile fighting the hard lines of his jaw. Standing together like that, wrapped in their shynesses, their likeness was spitting image. Two big head men with wide faces dominated by prominent noses and foreheads, Dr. HighJohn's forehead highlighted by a receding hairline only just yet hinted at in Tucept's blowout.

Good to see you boy, James Henry muttered.

Tucept nodded.

Della HighJohn watched their homecoming with fond amusement. Long married to one, mother of the other, long forced to monitor rigid shells for emotional clues. Memphis knew Dr. James Henry HighJohn as arrogant, she knew him as shy. Tucept had the same rigidity, the same fear of expressing anything deeper than an orchestrated front. They stood, shook hands still held and tempering smiles too broad for their respective comforts.

You two ought to quit, she said, shaking her head and laughing aloud, as she brushed past them to the kitchen.

Caldonia! she yelled, her voice singing the word, Caldonia? Tucept is here.

Caldonia HighJohn yelled and rushed into the den. She and Tucept hugged and chortled.

Tucept, you're back? asked Caldonia.

What does it look like to you?

Watch out now, she said, Don't get smart. I'll send your black ass back to Vietnam. What are you doing home so early man, you weren't due back from Vietnam for another month or so. How you feel? You alright? What are you doing here? Tell me.

Her questions run up one on the other, not waiting for answers, impatient, always in a hurry. A big woman, tall and robust with a round symmetrical head highlighted by a short fro. She too was fuller than Tucept remembered. The HighJohn nose on her looked good. She was a year younger than he was and probably knew him better than anyone else.

What are you doing home so early? she demanded.

I got a early out, said Tucept, glancing at his father standing in the doorway, glancing away when he caught his eye, They're letting folks out a month early to make their troop withdrawal quotas. I'm out.

Tucept felt a pang of guilt, there was no reason to have to tell that lie. But he had done it now, he didn't want to admit to a lie.

Dr. HighJohn left the door.

Where's JB? Tucept asked Caldonia.

In the back, she said, sleeping. Come on.

Let me put my stuff in my room.

He shouldered his duffelbag and they went to his room. He stopped at the door. Piles of fabric and spools of thread littered the room. A sewing machine sat authoritatively in the middle of the room. Spiraled planters and clothes and strange evocative canvases lay around in various stages of completion. Thread hung from hooks and lay in ungainly piles. A loom sat majestically in a corner. The room smelled fresh instead of the close musty smell it had when he lived there. And where was his stuff? His model airplanes, his books, his pictures, his clothes. Everything.

Momma uses this room now, said Caldonia, realizing why he had stopped at the door, Come on. I want you to meet Jabbo. I call him JB most of the time.

Tucept dropped his bags and followed Caldonia to her room. The baby lay in a wood crib. Asleep. Still waters. His nephew. Blood. Family. Tucept felt a quick fullness at the thought. A little wrinkled brown face with eyes tightly shut. A mobile made of twigs, leaves and red flowers floated around the head of the crib. Tucept felt the flowers. Plastic.

The real ones kept dying, said Caldonia.

Tucept stared. JB had been born while he was in Nam. They had sent him a couple of pictures of the boy but that didn't tell him much. He hadn't even known she was pregnant until right before he left. He had forgotten the father's name.

What's his name again, asked Tucept, his surname?

He's a HighJohn, said Caldonia coldly.

Hell that sounded good to him. Another HighJohn.

Hey you named him HighJohn, he laughed, Jabbo HighJohn. Git down.

His daddy denied him.

Oh, he looked to see how she felt about that, You going to court?

Fuck him, she said, picking the boy up, Fuck him.

What's his name?

Jabbo HighJohn.

I mean his daddy's name.

I call him JB for short.

Check.

She gently woke the boy up. He came awake with a

21

jerk and a whimper. Caldonia put him to her neck. Tucept moved around in front of him, playing with his fingers. A HighJohn for sure. The HighJohn nose, forehead. Tucept brushed his fingers against Jabbo's cheek. The baby jerked away from him and made a sour little face.

Tucept laughed, Hi there boy, he said, I'm your Unca Tucept.

Caldonia held him out, You want to hold him?

Not me, said Tucept, backing up, He's too little for me.

She laughed and thrust him at Tucept. Tucept almost stumbled backing up.

You oughta stop, she said, just like their momma. She laid JB down and felt his diaper.

You wet yourself, didn't you boy, she said in tones that Tucept'd never heard before. He watched her change the boy's diaper and realized that his little sister wasn't 7, 12, 15 anymore. She was, he frowned, subtracted a year from his own 21, damn, Caldonia was 20. It was hard for him to think of her as a woman, much less a mother. He grunted.

I'ma go finish unpacking, said Tucept, talk to you later Cal.

Back in his room, he started pulling gear out of his duffelbag. Hey MA, he yelled, boots in hand and wondering where to put them, Alright to use my, uh, your room?

Della came to the doorway.

Move all that stuff to the backroom, she said, if I had known you were coming it would already be back there.

She picked up a pile of bright print fabrics and balanced the material on her forearm.

He took it from her, I'll do it Ma, I just wanted to make sure that it was alright.

She watched him empty his bag. Fatigues. Another

set of green and black jungle boots. A dented canteen. A web belt. A photo album. Two floppy boonie hats. A small leather bag.

You want something to eat?

The smell of spaghetti cooking in the kitchen. His momma knew that was his favorite.

Thanks Ma, I guess I will.

You see Jabbo?

Yeah, aint that something?

I'ma Granma, she said smiling, thats what I want to be called. Granma.

You got it Granma.

And you're an uncle now, she said, leaving the door, You be careful with my loom Uncle.

Tucept pushed her equipment to the side of the room. Tomorrow he would borrow her car and run down to Nashville's Tennessee State University in Nashville to see Ruby. Right now he wanted sleep. He yawned and stretched cracking bones. A thick gold quilted bedspread covered his bed. He folded it back and lay down on the brown blanket beneath it. Kicking off his shoes he worked his feet a second before relaxing, feeling his body drain itself of tension. As he drifted into sleep, he looked around the room, only his eyes moving. Home.

Familiar sounds stroked him. His father left for work about noon. Tucept listened for the remembered screech of the Caddy's back fender hitting the curb when it pulled out of the driveway because his daddy drove a car so hard. His momma walking around the house humming snatches of Billie's God Bless the Child. Backwoods North Carolina by way of Striver's Row NewYork, Della HighJohn kept much grit tucked snugly under a thin mask of sophistication. Taught him his first blues back when he was a liddle biddy boy, *hear that lonesome wailing, whooeee, my momma done tole me*. He heard her and Caldonia talking. The TV. A radio. JB cried once. Twice. A flushing toilet. Long ago growing up years welcomed him back. Caldonia put one of his old Lou Rawls records on the box.

*When I get home in the evening heres what I'm gonna
   do
Going straight to my room and think an hour or two
I know I got the will but it's the way I got to find
To stop breaking my back and start to using my mind.*

When Caldonia peeped in on him to tell him that the spaghetti was ready, he was out of it, snoring with his mouth open. She closed the door and turned out the lights.

THE RECEDING BLUE RIDGES OF TENNESSEE'S SMOKY MOUN-tains lumbered sluggishly along the side of the highway. Tucept had made this Nashville run a million times but this time the scenery was new and narcotic. Smoky blued mountain ridges lined with scrub trees, muddy lakes and blue crystal streams. He drove slowly, less careful than stalling. He hadn't called her. Another surprise. What if he was the one surprised? What if she was with somebody? His almost relieved mind ran through the scenario, forced her to choose, him or me, or them, dammit, choose.

He felt for the ragged scrap of a letter in his pocket. The last one he had received from her before leaving Nam. He didn't get them regular like when he first got incountry. He had gotten in the habit of carrying the latest with him, reading it whenever he got a chance, dogging it until the next one came and he would put the tattered one away.

What if she had found somebody else? The thought that had haunted him in Nam, lying in some godforsaken ricepaddy trying to figure out what time was it back in the World, what was Ruby doing now, out partying, in school, fucking?

When he reached Nashville he sped through the tiny winding streets to the Tennessee State campus. Nashville's narrow little twisted streets always depressed him. Student apartments up on the Hill. At her door he hesitated, took a breath, rang the bell.

A tall pretty boy answered. It was a few seconds before Tucept could say anything.

Uh, is this Ruby's address?

Yeah.

The brother stood, waiting, tall, well formed, pretty petulant lips, smooth brown skin, a frat cap. Qs. He stood in the door with the proprietary air of a man who feels that being a woman's lover gives him sayso in her affairs.

Is she in?

Who wants her?

Tucept HighJohn, said Tucept flatly. Voice grating, jaws tight, pissed.

Just a minute.

He closed the door. Tucept fumed. He wanted to get in his car and go for home but he would be damned if he would just walk off. Fuck this mothafucker.

Ruby came to the door and threw it open. Tucept! she yelled. They came together and hugged. Tucept's tension unwound like a taut spring sprung.

The feel of her body next to him was heaven and her breath on his chest sent tingles up and down his spine. Ruby Ruby, been gone so long. She made him breathless with pleasure, an effect that she had had on him since he first met her, when he was a practicing college militant, when she was a senior graduating from high school and he was her ideal of what college was about.

He saw the brother watching and closed him out. Her hug was his claim. Her hands in the small of his back pulled him to her and the smell of her was in his nostrils. Damn she felt good next to him like this. He could feel her against him, her breasts against him, her hips and legs, wisps of her hair tickled his nostrils. He grinned. He had not hugged in over a year. He couldn't believe it was really happening. Finally.

Hey baby, he said, choking, How you doing?

What are you doing here? she pouted. You didn't tell me, what are you doing home, are you alright?

I'm fine, he said, feeling good.

They went to the living room. Two more dudes sitting in front of the TV. A college apartment, a TV, Day-Glo prints and textbooks. White lace lampshades. Bright red throw pillows on a beige rug. The sharp bite of incense.

Ruby had Tucept about his waist, hugging him. Oh Tucept, she said, its so nice to see you, you should have called me though.

This is Tucept HighJohn, she told everybody, He's the one that I told you about.

Tucept, this is Joe Dyer, you met him at the door, and this is Sam and Ramon.

He shook the other brothers' hands. Joe Dyer nodded at him and they shook, not bothering to hide their animosity.

Ruby sat him on the couch and asked him if he wanted anything to drink.

He just wanted to look at her, short, firm, fine, a pixie face with a bird's nest of a fro, glittering eyes that looked right at you wide and questioning. Cocoabrown woman with big eyes and bigger ideas. He sensed a difference in her, in the way her eye fell on him with a new directness.

She sat on the couch next to him and he realized that he was perched on the edge. He sat back, suddenly conscious of the field jacket and the floppy boonie hat he wore. Relax, he told himself angrily.

On the little black-and-white screen a newscaster spoke of Nixon's troop withdrawals. Clips of Vietnam. Ruby stared at the screen. He watched her surreptitiously. He wished these boys would leave, specially this Dyer fellow. Wonder what his role was. Tucept glanced at him. Dyer was watching him. Held Tucept's eye just long enough to be a challenge.

Ruby stroked his shoulder,

How long have you been home Tucept, why didn't you call me?

I wanted to surprise you.

Well, she said laughing, okay, I'm surprised.

It embarrassed Tucept to be going through all this in front of the other 3. Why doesn't she tell them to leave? He hasn't seen her in a year.

How are your folks? she said.

Everybody's fine, how have things been up here on the Hill?

You know the Hill, she said, it keeps you going.

Hey Ruby, said Joe Dyer, you hear about Tadpole?

They laughed, an insider's joke. Tucept smiled uncertainly. He should pack up and get the hell out of here. Instead he sat uncomfortable but determined to last it out. Ruby stood and fat nipples traced erotic designs on her blue blouse. Tucept glared at the brothers, daring them to look. They looked.

A chopper *whopwhopwhopp*ed across the screen. Vietnam. Tucept's eye was drawn to the newscast.

You just got back from Vietnam didn't you man? asked Joe Dyer.

Ambush, Tucept thought and nodded slowly.

So how was it man, tell us about it.

You know, basic garden variety war, he said in a low mumble of shrugged shoulders.

Joe Dyer leaned forward, face sharp and alert. Smelling blood.

Tell me about it, he said, I didn't go, they tried to draft me but I told them what they could do with that hokey shit.

Sho did, didn't he? said one of the frat brothers, Tucept didn't remember names.

And kept on telling them, the other commented.

They hooted and slapped five.

So tell me, asked Joe, what was it like?

Tucept shrugged again.

Like on TV? asked Ruby, still looking at the newscast. The newscaster gave a bodycount.

You got drafted? asked Dyer.

Tucept considered lying. No, he said finally, I volunteered.

Dyer leaped on it, spinning his chair around to face Tucept, Hey, Hey, Hey, he said, Gungho. Sergeant Fury and his howling commando.

The room laughed

You volunteered for Vietnam? said Dyer.

Well you know, said Tucept, I didn't really think about Nam when I volunteered.

Which was a lie, he had wanted to war.

Oh, said Dyer, you thought maybe they were going to send your black ass to the Pentagon. Doesn't sound like you were thinking period.

Shamed, Tucept could only shrug.

So tell me about it man, said one of the frat brothers, My main man he went to Nam and he came back wasted.

I hear the brothers went on a funny trip, said Dyer.

Tucept fumbled it. We, uh . . .

He remembered a blues that Jethro sang one guard duty night in a perimeter bunker.

Me 'n my brothers, we had to throw down
We went to the war, we caught hell all around
And now I've learned to watch my brother's back

28

DE CALL

Aint nothing we can't do if we be bold and Black
We learned how to throw down, We learned how to
*   throw down*
On Firebase Sin Loi

How could he explain it? A brother looking out for another brother's back.

You know, we learned that, uh, the brothers, you know, uh we stood together. Tucept stumbled and lamely finished . . . we survived.

Wait a minute man, said Joe Dyer, what you trying to tell us is that you felt like a man cause you were over there playing soldier for these whitefolks, a nigger killing gooks for crackers.

Tucept flushed. Smash this mothafucker. Empty a M16 clip into this mothafucker's face. Watch it shred away in a red angry spray.

That's not what I was saying, said Tucept angrily, I was just trying to . . . fuck it.

He wasn't going to keep playing Dyer's game. He wasn't walking into an ambush with his eyes open.

Ruby leaned forward, her face lit with a sudden question.

Did you ever kill anybody Tucept?

Ruby Ruby oh Ruby . . .

Tucept looked at her blankly, running the words back in his head, feeling the texture of them for booby traps, pungi sticks, bouncing bettys that strip a man of his balls.

Dyer grinned, Sure you did, didn't you brother, I hear some dudes get to nutting off when they get to killing gooks.

Joe! said Ruby sharply.

Tucept withdrew from the conversation, eyes narrowed, face closed attention to the TV screen. Like he was watching the movie. Sensing his discomfort, Ruby shifted the conversation back to the randy fool Tadpole. The screen threw restless shadows across their faces in the dark and they spoke of school while Tucept watched golden memories. He wanted to leave but he was determined to be there when these other motherfuckers left. Finally Ruby put them out. The frat brothers told him welcome back and goodby. Tucept and Joe Dyer didn't even try to be civil.

As soon as the door closed he turned on Ruby, Don't you ever go against me again woman.

His voice was nasty and dangerous.

Surprised, Ruby took a minute to respond, Wait a minute, she said, I'm sorry if you got your feelings hurt, but it wasn't my fault, it wasn't Joe's either.

She was defending that mothafucker. Yeah, well fuck her too.

You fucking him? he asked.

She hesitated only a minute but that was all he needed to hang her.

He's a friend Tucept, and I do date, she said, her voice saying that she could do damn well what she pleased.

So what's the deal, he insisted, him or me?

Oh come off it Tucept, she said, getting up and sitting on the couch where she didn't have to face him, There isn't any you or him, I'm concerned with me.

Her voice patronized an unruly child. His voice grated ominously, You saying he's more to you than me.

Her face soured, Oh be real Tucept.

I thought you were my woman, he said, I thought you were waiting on me.

He sounded like a fool and knew it.

I'm just tired Tucept, she told him, that's all.

She sounded like she was tired of this shit. He was blowing it. He caught himself, nodded and acted as if

30

that really was all that was wrong. Yeah, he said, I guess I'm tired too. He yawns, It was a long drive.

She busied herself picking up items in the living room, putting them into stacks and places.

Are you staying or are you going back to Memphis? she asked without stopping what she was doing or looking at him.

His insecurity radar told him she was saying go back to Memphis. He started to cop an attitude and go. The strong move. But he couldn't do it. That would be it, all over, and he wanted her. He wanted to be with her tomorrow and next year, forever.

I'm leaving in the morning, he said assertively, casually adding as if an afterthought, if that's alright with you?

That night she came to bed in a blue nightgown, thick, cotton and functional. Silently she lay beside him and their tentative caresses grew cautiously into passion.

Soon her palm was fever on his skin and his tongue was full of the taste of her heat. But his dick stayed soft. He became aware of it. Panic seeped in as he sent urgent messages downriver. What the hell was happening down there? Lets get on the job gang. Everybody has to do their part. Sweat popped out on his forehead and he took a moment to wipe it off, like that might be the answer. God, she would think it happened all the time. Tucept concentrated on a harddick, didn't feel even a twinge. Damned thing felt like it was curling up on him. He concentrated on her firm breasts, her wet tight sheath. Not with Ruby, not now. Her warm heated palm circled his dick. He could feel the passionate pressure of her hand turn questioning. He felt her firm lips slacken under his. Her eyes opened and she looked up at him.

He wanted to explain it away, but what could he say, his dick was saying it all. He wanted to cut the motherfucker off, what good was it.

You don't want to? she asked him.

I want to, he said, attempting levity, my dick doesn't.

He rolled off and lay down beside her, disgusted with himself. Driven to distraction by the feel of her warm, still undulating flesh, anguishing silently, This has never happened before. Why now, why with Ruby?

Don't worry about it, she said.

I don't know what's happening, he said, it's never happened before. I swear.

He picked the limp dick up in his hand and studied it, as if he would be able to see the problem.

Don't worry about it, she repeated. She pecked at his cheek and went to sleep. He lay there, pissed at the world long before sleep came. Nothing was going right, he thought with real anguish. How many times had he thought about Ruby, about seeing her again, how many scripts had he run through his head. His scripts had gone fine. It was life that was perverse.

His sleep was restlessness. She felt it and woke in the night. A contoured brown breast settled sensuously as she flicked on the bedside table lamp. She studied him under the lamp's lit circle. Her matted fro threw uneven shadows on his back. He lay on his belly, facing her, lips slightly parted, beads of sweat dotting his forehead.

He twitched and moaned and she leaned closer, trying to listen.

CHOPPERS FALL FROM A LEADEN SKY AND SPIT BUFFALO soldiers into a muddy gold ricepaddy. Puppets on a string, buckdancing minstrels dodging slow motion bullets to the tune of Yankee Doodle Dandy. You dance on gossamer strings sometimes seen sometimes not. They move your arms like jerky windmills and buckdance your feet, you fight and strain but still you dance, what a dance do they do.

*   *   *

TUCEPT SHIFTED, HIS HEAD LEAVING A DAMP SPOT ON THE pillow. She frowned and placed her hand on his back. His skin was damp, the rhythmic rise and fall of his deep breathing pleasing to her touch. Her hand stroked his back in small concerned circles. She frowned, her smooth brow furrowed in thought. When he was in Nam she had used him to keep others at an emotional distance, her man in the war. She didn't really feel anything for him. There had been a certain glamour, a sense of romance about her man in Nam, her soldier boy, but now that he was back, making demands and being a problem. Well. It just wasn't fair for him to act like she owed him something. To make her feel for him. She stilled herself to see if she could detect something in her for him and shrugged.

She had felt for him once, loved him even, but since she'd been on the Hill she'd already loved others.

SEVEN LITTLE YELLOW PUPPETS IN BLACK PAJAMAS AND conical black straw hats walk into the bright gold killing zone. Seven little puppets in black pajamas tell jokes and laugh and dance and sing. Tucept empties an automatic clip from his M16. They die laughing, jerking grotesquely on strings suddenly cut. After lying dead, they pick themselves up and laughingly dust themselves off. A joke by Mattel. They begin again, string jerked back into position. This time they get to wear the whitehats. This time the Americans get ambushed. Tucept's strings jerk him onto the trail. Tucept tells the man behind him a joke. And they walk into the killing zone.

THE MUSCLES OF HIS BACK KNOTTED SPASMODICALLY AND she jerked her hand back. Lines bunched on his forehead and moved in fitful twitches. He cried out. She reached for his shoulder. At her touch, he jumped up, arm flung out and knocking her back. His eyes snapped open. She scooted out of range. Tucept registered the move and focused. He lay back down on the bed.

What happened? he asked.

A dream? she ventured.

He didn't answer. It wasn't until she heard his breathing regulate itself that she realized he had fallen asleep.

That morning their conversation was plastic, bland, uninspiring. Neither spoke of last night, yesterdays or tomorrows.

Coffee?

Please.

Weatherman said it would be nice today. Not too cold.

Good.

Tucept watched her with a certain regret. He'd blown it. He'd lost the slightest semblance of confidence and in the harsh light of morning his defeat could only irritate her. He watched her eyes focus on everything but him and he realized that he didn't know her. A year of dreaming about her in Vietnam had warped his idea of who she was beyond all sense of human possibility.

Finally he said he was leaving. At the door he stood for a moment of uncertainty and hope unrealized.

She could have been his he thought bitterly. All the plans he had made were cold and sour. He felt like a fool for dreaming, a fullness threatened to rise up in his throat but he's cool. He locked it back and smiled a lopsided aint no big thing smile. He studied her face. He had learned in Nam the value of having clear well-etched memories of people you wanted to remember. They kissed and went through the motions of I'll be in touch, come back soon, please do.

He rode home hard, pedal to the metal, bogarting cars in front of him, creeping up bumpers, evil red eyes challenging drivers when they glanced in their rearview mirror. He almost lost a curve, tires screeching for traction, the back of the Toyota fishtailing the highway. He pulled over to the side of the road and calmed himself. Standing beside the car, he kicked tufts of the dirt from the gravel covered roadbed. He wouldn't be going back to Nashville for awhile. Moisture gathered in the corner of an eye and wiping at it angrily, he got back into the car and drove home.

CHAPTER 2

∿∿∿∿

MEMPHIS TENNESSEE SITS PERCHED HIGH ON THE bluff of the Mississippi River. South Memphis, bordered by the forest of Riverside Park, sprawls alongside the river. About four months after he got out of the army, winter broken and spring in full flower, Tucept was driving down Riverside Drive when he looked across the expressway at the park. He saw a house high on a hill in the park. He looked closer, eyes squinting. Dark clouds passing slowly behind a skyline jagged with trees and hills. In the gathering dusk he couldn't tell if it was really a house or just a more solid bunch of shadows.

Curious, he drove to Person Ave. and across the bridge over the expressway into the park. He followed the little winding road deep into the park but he couldn't find the house. Had he actually seen it? He had wandered this park as a boy before the expressway was built when it had really been wild, his personal playground, he didn't remember any house over here. He pulled the car over and got out, stretching and breathing deeply of the spring-wood freshness.

He leaned against a tree and thought about it. The house had been high on a hill. Which way was high-ground? He needed to go down the road a little ways here and cross that old dead tree bridge. He thrust himself into the brush. When he got to the bridge he crossed it, arms out and balancing himself where he used to just run across it as a kid. He worked his way up and found it, sitting in a clearing at the top of the hill. Grinning, he walked up on it and looked it over.

A strange little house, three stories high on a patch-work lattice of thick wooden stilts. A rickety set of stairs ran up the side to a door. The moist delta air had weathered the original ivory coat to a peeling steel gray. The long flight of stairs swayed in the high wind and he hesitated before finally starting up, balancing himself to a sway made even more ominous by the sound of the wind whistling through the stilts. Upstairs, he pushed open the door and walked in. The house was musty with the oldsmell of long unuse. Grime and leaves were backed up in the corners but the 2 rooms were large and highceilinged. From the backroom he looked across the river to Arkansas under the setting sun.

He stood at the front window and smoked a joint. From the living room he could see what looked like all of South Memphis, he could see kids playing, folks walking around, mowing lawns, going to the store on the corner of Person and Riverside Drive. Looked like he could see them a lot clearer than he should have been able to see them from this distance, the damned window was like a big television screen. To the north he could see the new highrises thrusting arrogantly into the sky above downtown Memphis. He looked over South Memphis and as far as he could see he claimed. My town.

A strong wind blew off the river and he felt the house

sway faintly on its stilts. He liked it, liked the feel and the drama of it. He watched the sun fall below the horizon and felt the darkness settle in around the house and the wooded hill.

He took the agent's name from the door and followed a little dirt road outside back to the main road so that he wouldn't have any trouble finding the house with his car. Then he drove back to the house just to make sure that he could find it again. Good thing he did too, because when he drove away he looked back and the treefringed hill looked bare.

He rented it, 50 dollars a month and utilities. Only those he showed how to find it could. Caldonia, his folks, Marva, his cronies. And even they had to call sometimes for more explicit directions.

Once he moved in he spent a lot of time wandering around Riverside Park and walking along the riverbluff. That's how he found the highbacked driftwood chair.

The day he found the chair began bright and sunny, the sun gleaming off emerald trees. He went to the river, smelling the dusky riversweat long before he saw it. He got to the bluff, pleased as always when the muddy river came into view. Across the river the jagged edge of Arkansas rasped against a darkening sky. He sniffed the air. A storm coming.

Tucept scrambled down the bank to the edge of the water. He could hear the gurgle now, soft, slow, easy. He squatted on the bank, the toes of his jungle boots sinking into the muddy bank. The sun slid through gathering grayblack clouds, burnt orange sunstreaks deepening as the day waned. A log floated by following the curves of the bank and a small bird flapped its wings furiously in an attempt to gain altitude.

Tucept cooled out, lulled by the slow crawl of the river, the water lapping softly at the banks. Old man river. He pulled out Chancelor Williams's *Destruction of*

Black Civilization and was soon deep into the ancient glories of Mene's Memphis. Old Memphis on the Nile. Ptah's city, the Egyptian god of scribes. He who thought the world, said it in a word and then it was so. Something drew Tucept's attention and he looked up just as the chair was floating by in the water. A monster of a wood chair, with thick armrests and a high carved back. It got caught in downstream shallows. He put his book down and worked his way down the bank to it. It had obviously been in the river for awhile and river artistry had carved it into flowing driftwood lines. The setting sun threw the grooves into deep relief and Tucept could almost see movement in the chair's fluid surface.

He looked at the muddy brown water warily, testing it with a stick. No telling what's squiggling around in there. He kept telling himself to forget it but finally he stuck a cautious foot in and reached out for the chair. The water was curiously warm, the sensation not unpleasant. He had to struggle to dislodge the wet slippery chair but finally he worked it loose and to the bank with a grunt of satisfaction.

He congratulated himself, running his hands down the grooves in the wood. Clean it up some it would make a nice chair. Carved into the back was an *X*ed circle. He looked into the sky, he wanted to get the chair in before the rains started.

By the time he got it home and up the stairs it was dark, the winds whining and whipping a faint spray into his face. He worried about getting the chair wet until he realized how foolish that was, it was already riversoaked. Upstairs he put it in front of the front window and put some newspaper in it so he could sit down and check it out. It felt good, solid and substantial. Comfortable. His hand stroked the grooves in the armrest.

The rains started and Tucept's tower swayed gently.

That night he started working on the chair, playing Lou's Breaking My Back while he worked.

He spent the next two years working on that chair, playing Breaking My Back until the record jumped and skipped.

> *Getting up early in the morning cause I got to beat*
>   *the man*
> *Can't afford to let nothing bother with my plans.*

He used sandpaper to accent grooves already carved in by the river, cleaning away the deadwood in long rhythmic strokes. He became obsessed with it, marveling over the twisted rivergrooved ridges, the grain coming to life beneath the dead wood. He cleaned and regrooved the crossed sun in the high back. He found a rusty nail on the riverfront one day, drove it into the side of the chair and hung the little leather bag that he brought back from Nam on it. Often he would take a break from laboring on the chair and just sit in it handling the little bag in his hand before starting again with the sandpaper.

It gave him something to do, school bored the shit out of him. Bor-ring. He spent just enough time in class to keep his grades up and keep his Vietvet check coming, with which he paid rent, brought herb, books and food, in that order. Occasionally a class interested him and he would attend until he had milked it for all the information that he thought he could get out of it, most bored him after a couple of weeks. Instead he spent his time chasing the gals or in the game room playing doubledeck pinochle and discussing life's little profundities with his cronies, a bunch of good old boys from the good old '60s days. But that chair he worked on daily with a fine and growing obsession, shaping and carving to Lou's rhymes.

DE CALL

I know I got the will but it's the way I got to find
To stop breaking my back and start to using my mind.

When he wasn't working on it he was sitting in it, idly handling the little bag. Finally it got on Marva's nerves. Marva was his woman. Supposedly. Couldn't prove it by her.

Foot tapping she watched him through slitted eyes. God she hated to admit a mistake. A handsome fatcheeked woman, a sleek brown, streamlined, always crisp, she had chosen him and gotten him. She was accustomed to getting what she wanted. What she wasn't accustomed to was not being vastly more important in the lives of her men than apparently was the case here.

Her tapping foot gained momentum as she watched him sit and brood, face closed and distant, that damned bag in his hand. It relaxed him, he told her before. Say it did? She didn't see any sign of it. He spent enough time with the damned thing for her to have detected any improvement. What was she doing here? She slid a small gold ring up and down on her finger, the tapping foot of her calflength boot accelerating. She didn't have time to waste like this. She had tried treating him nice, being blasé, making him jealous, tried making him anxious, she had tried some of her best moves on him, but he hadn't noticed. He was so much into that damned chair and that damned bag that he hardly had time to live. She was doing all the work in this relationship. She grimaced. That's what she got for going after what she wanted rather than what wanted her.

Tucept.

Hmmmm? he murmured, not really focusing.

Tucept.

What?

Irritated and grumpy. The fucking nerve.

I'm leaving.

41

He nodded, still not really listening. The gold ring's motions became abrupt and hard, leaving a lighter brown trail of hampered blood on her finger.

Will I see you Friday?

Right, he murmured noncommittally. She was furious. She didn't like being thwarted by man or god.

She draped a bright gold shawl on her neck with a note of finality and went to the kitchen.

Lost in a deep brood of golden bamboo gardens Tucept barely noted from the corner of his eye when Marva came into the room from the kitchen with a knife in her hand. She swung at him. Not close enough to cut him but enough to get his undivided attention.

He leaped out of the chair and backed up from her, still not quite focused eyes on the knife waving bright arc bright in her hand.

He tried to be cool about it, What do you think you doing? Put that knife down woman.

Look at me, she yelled, a strident demand for attention, What's my name?

What the fuck are you talking about? He stopped backing up and tried to bluff her, Now give me that knife!

He made to reach for it and she swung at him clumsily. He jumped back and almost fell, but no way. Dying in a domestic squabble lacked dignity. Violence was a no-no. You could get hurt on a zoom.

Come on now woman, you better give me that knife.

She advanced on him, Marva baby, not woman, Marva remember?

Look—Marva—cut it out okay, enough is enough.

She swung at him. Fuck cool, fuck dignity, he turned and ran into the bathroom, slammed the door and locked it. She struck at the other side of the door with the knife, gouging the wood. Again and again the knife bit wood. Tucept knocked at the door from his side. Good solid wood.

If you don't put that fucking knife down I'ma whup your ass woman! You just wait till I get my hands on you.

He listened through the door to see how she was responding. He didn't hear anything but he wasn't opening that door.

Rattling the doorknob, he called her name, Marva?

The knife bit the wood and he jumped back.

Resigned, he sat on the toilet seat and considered using the time wisely.

He thought he heard her leave and went to the door to listen. He heard her going down the steps and peeped out.

The knife was stuck in the door and he worked it loose with a curse.

From the front window he watched her walk down the stairs and get into her car. He stood far enough back in the shadows so that she wouldn't be able to see him if she turned around to look. He was disappointed when she didn't.

The angry spray of her tires left trenches in the black dirt on the side of the road.

What the hell got into her, he wondered, what brought that on?

He frowned, eyebrows drawing together.

He had been blasé about her he had to admit, half aware of it but not really caring. He had gotten comfortable with her after he got her. Now he felt vaguely dissatisfied. He fucked up, he thought dully while he watched the car drive down the road and across the expressway.

He looked at the knife in his hand with a frown and flipped it into the corner. It landed point first but didn't stick and fell over on its side. A regret nagged him. Fucked up. But the thought was already an absent one without force. The nagging dulled as he sat back in the chair, fingering the bag still in his hand and listening to the muffled sound with unfocused eyes.

TUCEPT PUT A BILL WITHERS ALBUM ON THE BOX AND Withers's guitar leaped into the silence of the room. Tucept sat back. He loved him some Withers. Lean on me when you're not strong. A good old country boy singing good old country blues. Look like everytime he open his mouth he say something real. Painting pretty pictures with a song.

A knock on the door. Lost in the music he missed it at first. It got insistent and he went to the door growling, Just a minute, I'm coming. Goddamn.

Took you long enough, said Caldonia, brushing past him when he opened the door, JB asleep in her arms.

That boy getting too big to be carrying around like that.

He fell asleep out there waiting on you to open the door, she replied testily.

She put him down and he started stirring.

You were probably in here sitting in this chair day-dreaming again, she said as she plopped herself down in it, I have had a day, a day, do you want to hear about it?

Not really, he said, You want something to drink?

I don't blame you, she said, but listen anyway. I'll take tea thank you, and a joint if you got one.

When he came back, lit joint and teacup in hand, she was pacing.

He put the cup on the armrest of the chair.

Your chair is coming along right nice, she said, sitting back down and running her hands down the grooves before picking up the cup of tea. I didn't think it would look so nice when you first started working on it.

Got a lot more to do, he muttered, not really wanting to talk about it. He sat with his back against a facing wall and sipped on his tea. They sat in relatively comfortable silence. A finger tapped impatiently on the armrest. He could see that she wanted to talk but he figured she would when she felt like it.

She noticed the bag on the nail.

What's this? she said picking it up.

Don't open it, he said sharply.

She looked at him curiously, What is it?

Belonged to this brother I knew back in the war. His mojo bag he called it, he was into that hoodoo shit.

Momma told me that hoodoo run in her family. That half of the family won't make a move without a consultation and the other half make a damn good living.

Damn, said Tucept, Momma into everything.

I was talking to her the other day, said Caldonia with a loud embarrassed laugh, She thinks we're failures.

Who, Momma, he asked, she told you that?

Well no, said Caldonia, she said that her life was over now that we were gone.

Awww, Just empty nest blues, said Tucept. Momma don't think we failures. Not the way she always comes through whenever we in need.

But that's just it, she's wondering now if she did the right thing giving her life to us. Like I'm doing. She laughed, a wild and wooly laugh that grated his nerves wrong.

I'm not giving up my life, she said with sudden vehemence.

Nobody asked you to, Tucept protested, hands up, palms out.

He does, she pointed at the sleeping JB, He wants my whole life. Everything I do has to be built around him, she whined, I don't have time to do anything with my

life. Between him and that bullshit job, I don't have a
life, I don't like living like this.

A whine in her voice irritated him.

Cal, I don't want to hear all this whining, he said
harshly, Whatever you got to do to enjoy life just do it.
You want to talk about plans and dreams, cool. This
crying shit no. If you choose to be weak and go down I
don't want to hear about it. I aint gon help you be weak.

I don't need your help to be shit, she spit at him.

And I don't need you over here crying either.

Fuck you.

What brought all this on anyway?

All what on?

I don't know, all this failure talk.

I told you, I was talking to Momma and—

And she didn't say shit about us being failures, he
interrupted.

She held the bluff for a minute, then deflated, like hot
air escaping from a balloon, I don't know, she said, I
guess I'm just afraid I'm gon blow it. JB I mean, I mean
I'm it for him, you know, it's all on me. His daddy don't
own up to him and I aint asked him for a dime. Ever.
Fuck him. But you know, sometimes . . .

Her voice trailed off.

Hell, said Tucept, you can do it. If other folks have
done it then I know a HighJohn can.

She laughed, wild and wooly, slapping her thighs.
That laugh bothered him and he looked at her closely,
noticing when he did the haunted look in her eyes,
tension in her shoulders. He felt for her. His sister. She
reminded him so much of himself, hardheaded and determined to fuck up in my own way thank you. If she
went down, he thought, he would be the last of the
HighJohn line. He would be alone. The thought scared
him. A lot.

Caldonia started putting on her sweater.

DE CALL

You can let Jabbo stay here for the weekend if you want, he said.

She thanked him with a smile of warm surprise. It was the first time he had ever volunteered.

Thanks, she said, but I promised to take him to the zoo. For that he would even pass up a chance to stay with his Uncle Tucept.

Okay, he said, I'll carry him down for you. No need to wake him.

He pulled money from his pocket, counted 42 dollars and passed 20 to Caldonia.

What's that for? she asked.

Uh, for Jabbo, I'll try to do what I can when I can.

Oh come on, she said, pushing his hand away, You know you can't afford it, you don't have to do it, seriously Tucept.

I know what I don't have to do. I'm his uncle aint I? Aint he a HighJohn?

He stuffed the money in her skirt pocket, Here, buy him some Pampers or something, or else I'll just have to.

She stuffed the money on into the pocket, He's too old for Pampers, she said.

Tucept smiled and picked up Jabbo. She held the door open for him.

Just don't be giving my money to no hardleg, he said jokingly.

Aint no hardleg getting shit of mine, she snarled.

Tucept wasn't going to touch that one. He carefully followed her down the stairs, JB in his arms, and thought about Marva. Others. He had done a little thinking on the new assertiveness by black women. His cronies considered him soft on the woman question. He approved because he believed in folks being the most that they could be and he could see where some women might feel that they get limited horizons and rawdeals. Like the one Jabbo's father was putting on Cal. Fuck him. Tucept smiled cynically, he was probably doing his bit to embitter sisters too. He decided that he would try to be a more progressive man in the future, whatever the hell that meant.

He put JB in Momma's Toyota. Cal hugged him and drove off. He sighed. She had interrupted his day with problems that he couldn't tune out. She was family and he was an emotional punk. He started wearily up the stairs. Being emotional was tiring. But hell, who knows when I might need somebody to lean on.

〽〽〽〽

Tucept met Jethro his first day in the army, Fort Campbell Kentucky, summer of 1969, basic training. A tall heavyset smoothskinned brother with a little point of a Mississippi chin. Tucept sat next to him on the bus from Memphis.

Get off the bus assholes!

Startled, Tucept scrambled off the bus with the other new trainees. Soon they were shaved, scalped, dressed in ill-fitting fatigues, assigned bunks, footlockers, webgear, ID, dogtags and a new name. Assholes.

Lineup assholes! screamed the drill instructor, Fall in!

Trainees scrambled into ragged formation and stiff uncomfortable attention. The brother from Mississippi leisured into formation.

You, glamour boy, the DI pointed the Mississippi brother out. His new breast tags named him: TREE   U.S. ARMY.

You, Tree, knock out ten.

Cursing under his breath Tree got down and started counting out pushups. The DI stood over him profiling his best snarl.

Tree counted ten and stopped.

48

I didn't hear you, the DI yelled down at his back, Try it again asshole.

Still in place Tree grinned and said, Your momma's a asshole, asshole.

The DI's face froze rigid with anger and Tucept laughed before he caught himself. They both pulled KP. First day army. Dropping spuds into the big metal potato peeler, Tucept decided that he was going to do easy army time. He glanced over at Tree at a big sink busting suds. Obviously this brother is to be avoided. But when they got back to the barracks at the end of a long messhall day Tucept found that he and Tree were bunked top and bottom.

A talker too. Talked long into the night. Didn't like tomatoes or television, didn't like the army, didn't like Fort Campbell, didn't like sergeants and officers and brownnosing negroes.

What you think Tennessee? It's better than home though, Taproot Mississippi, ever hear of it? Aint much there cept my daddy's little farm. He think I'ma let it kill me like it's killing him, wore him down all stringy and mean you know? They call me Jethro back home, Jethro man, you just call me Jethro.

Their friendship was awkward. Tucept at 19 was already a pompous moody man, already weighed down with the need to know all the angles before he could make the simplest of moves whereas Jethro was spontaneity incarnate. Tucept was fascinated with him.

Tucept attacked the army like he did everything, trying to master and max it. He bucked them but he always tried to cover himself, to look like he was playing by the rules. Jethro wore his role of company badman openly. Jethro bucked the army and didn't give a damn who peeped it.

Even so the company was surprised when Jethro trotted out to the physical training field one Friday morning, about their third week basic training, in a bright red nylon T-shirt. The DI stared for a moment as if to make sure he had all the details right and with a chestheavy sigh of resignation he walked over to face Jethro.

Tree, what the fuck are you doing now?

Jethro looked innocent, You mean my silk T-shirt Sarge?

I mean your pretty red silk T-shirt Tree.

It goes with my drawers Sarge, said Jethro, pulling down the waistband of his fatigue enough to show red boxer shorts stuck to his skin by a thin layer of sweat.

Gimme ten Tree, said the disgusted DI, No, gimme fifty.

Arms strong by now, Jethro knocked off 50 pushups without adding a wrinkle to his smooth babybrown face.

Look at him good, the DI admonished the other trainees while Jethro pushed up and down, up down up down, Look at him real good, this is one fucker that aint going to live a month in Nam cause he just won't listen.

Up down up down.

When Jethro got back to the barracks from KP that night Tucept was lying in his bunk reading one of yesterday's letters from Ruby. He had gotten two more today and had to catch up. Jethro stalked in and flung himself onto his bunk, obviously pissed.

Don't see what you got a attitude about, said Tucept, you knew they weren't going to allow that shit. You know the rules. You gotta at least look like you going for the okey doke.

My T-shirt don't hurt nobody, said Jethro. Look a here Tennessee man, what if I should run up on a woman right? Pretty gal right? And we go to her spot and we take off our clothes right? And her drawers look better than mine, how that gon look, right?

Tucept peered over the bunk at him and muttered, Fuck you man.

Jethro took a shower. Tucept watched him put the red shorts back on.

Dressed in his civilian clothes, he came over and shook Tucept's bunk, Yo Tennessee, you up? Lets go over to the PX and look at some *Playboy*s.

Tucept gave his most cutting look, Spare me, he said.

You don't ever do nothing Tennessee, said Jethro, walking out the door, How can you live like that? You missing life boy.

Jethro stayed gone 5 days.

The 5th night Tucept was awakened by an insistent hand. He mumbled that he was getting up and blearily eyed the grinning Jethro. The night around them was dark and the barracks muttered with the nocturnal sounds of 147 sleeping men.

Here man, Jethro stuck a warm bottle of soda in his hand and took the top off with a bottle opener, Have some of this here red soda water.

Tucept peered at the bottle, then at Jethro.

The MPs are out looking for you.

Went to get me some red soda water.

The MPs are out looking for you.

Had to go to Clarkesdale to get it.

Jethro climbed into the bottom bunk with his clothes still on.

You not gon tell the orderly room that you here?

They'll know when they see me in morning formation.

Tucept took a sip of his soda. Warm. Sweet. Strawberry.

Tennessee?

Yeah?

These Kentucky women like my red drawers.

Go to sleep.

Tucept resolved again not to hang with the brother.

Tennessee?

What? muttered Tucept sleepily, irritably.

When we get to Nam we got to look out for each other right? I keep your back you keep mine, right Tennessee?

Tucept hefted up and looked under his bunk. Jethro lay on his bunk fully dressed, working his thumbnail into a triangular tip with an ivoryhandled nailfile. Tucept's eye caught a small leather bag trimmed with red flannel that Jethro wore around his neck. His conjure bag, he claimed, his mojo hand. Tucept stared at it for a second before focusing up to Jethro's face.

Nam? he muttered.

He hadn't really thought about going to Nam. For some reason he hadn't even considered the possibility. Nam was just too unreal to take seriously. He tried to visualize what could war be like.

How you know we going to Nam? he asked doubtfully.

Just stick close man. I'll make sure you get through. You got things to do.

Tucept snorted and lay back on his bunk, looking at the ceiling and listening to the snores and occasional grunts around him.

Weeks pass. They grew army.

Everywhere they went they doubletimed. They knew when to knock out pushups from a DI's glance. Straining their bodies into an olive drab competence, they began to know the army perspective as their own. They spoke the same language and salivated to the same bell.

I can't hear you assholes!

KILL! KILL! KILL!

Faces contort, mouths *screaaaaaam,* a sea of bayonets stab the sky in a vicious coordinated grid.

If one of you assholes fuck up, you all fuck up! No weekend passes asses!

KILLLLL! KILLLLLLLLLL!!! KILLLLLLLLL!!!!
KIIIIIIILLLLLLLLLLLLLLLLLLLLLLLLLLLLL!!!!

The DI pushed his Smokey the Bear hat away from

his forehead and rubbed the red line it left there, idly choosing the ones that he thought would die.

Like Dofunny. Dofunny never got it together. Fat brown body never did tighten up, couldn't do a pushup, couldn't hit a target on the rifle range, never remembered rules and regulations and slept with his eyes half lidded.

Every morning he got run over by the 2nd Platoon.

Most of the brothers in the company were in the 1st Platoon while the 2nd Platoon was a Tennessee hillbilly haven. The DIs encouraged the two platoons' rivalry in everything, including the morning run. So nothing was done when every morning Dofunny would start weaving and gasping, fall out of the 1st Platoon's ranks and under the thudding boots of the 2nd.

One morning Dofunny came back from sick call with his head bandaged and Jethro freaked. Muttered and paced the floor all night long, I don't believe this shit, he said, aint taking this shit, not in 1969, fuck this . . .

At 9 PM Tucept thought it was funny, by 2 AM he was snarling from the top bunk for Jethro to go to bed.

The next morning, after watching the nimble 3rd Platoon dance around the smoking wreckage that was Dofunny, Jethro called the brothers to meeting behind the lowcrawl pits and they stood in awe of his performance. He yowled and cajoled, his body weaving and dipping and speaking in tongues, exciting them as much with the body language as he did with the rap.

He demanded.

They agreed.

Something had to be done.

So we fall back right? said Jethro, We fall back and we see if they can kick all our black asses together as easy as they do one fool on his own.

The sun ate dew early that morning. The DI's cadence was a lashing whip, 3 platoons of boots hitting as one:

The DI called the cadence:
> *If I die in the combat zone*

Three platoons answer as one:
> *Box me up and ship me home.*

The DI called:
> *Tell my people I done my best*

The company answered:
> *Then lay me down and let me rest.*

DI:
> *Am I right or wrong?*

Company:
> *Right.*

DI:
> *Are you gon be strong?*
> *Right.*

Sound off
> *One two*

Sound off
> *Three four*

Bring it on down
> *One, two, three, four, one two, threefour.*

Dofunny broke stride. The brothers eyed each other as Dofunny started falling back through the ranks, fat brown face once again desperate.

Tucept and all the brothers were in the last two ranks. Tucept and the brother to the other side of him grabbed Dofunny by his arms and half drug him along. Tucept screamed furious angry curses at him. Deadweight mothafucker! Making us carry your black ass! Weak mothafucker! Keep up damn you! he screamed at the gasping, weaving Dofunny, Keep up! Tucept felt the hot breath of the 2nd Platoon. Heard the relentless thudding of their boots.

> *Shine Shine you doing fine but if you miss one*
> *stroke your ass is mine*

DE CALL

Shine Shine you doing fine but if you miss one
stroke your ass is mine
Shine Shine you doing fine but if you miss one
stroke your ass is mine

Tucept laughed, dry and selfmocking. He let Dofunny's arm go and they heard him impact the wall of the 2nd platoon. THWAAACK!!

Tucept stopped running and spun on his heels. He lost his balance and the green wall of the 2nd platoon smacked him to his knees. They piled on, yelling and swinging. On the bottom of the pile, Tucept swung wildly. The 2nd Platoon collapsed around the hole in their center and the desire to get a lick in. Tucept got kicked in the jaw and cursed soundly, he was going to look like he got brutalized down there. He freaked, swinging biting kicking and clawing. Berserker. The 3rd Platoon ran into the stalled 2nd. Frothering DIs reached into the pile and pulled him out. Being marched to the orderly room Tucept saw it was just him and Jethro. He muttered something under his breath about colored people. Won't stick together for shit.

~~~~~

EARLY IN SPRING '72, IN OLD LEVIS AND AN OD ARMY T-shirt with the sleeves cut out, Tucept HighJohn came out of his place in the woods and hitchhiked to his folk's house. He had a key and let himself in. His momma was in the backroom, humming a blues over her loom. Tucept watched hypnotic brown fingers weaving a fine emerald cloth into existence.

Hey Ma, Tucept kissed her cheek, I came by to clean up the attic.

Good, she said without looking up from the piece

between her hands, It's been waiting on you. There's some hot lemonade over there for you.

He smiled warmly, Thanks Ma. His throat had been feeling sore and he wondered if he was coming down with a cold. Hot lemonade was his momma's favorite cold recipe, her mother had given it to her whenever she felt a cold coming on and she had given it to him and Caldonia. He drank it and felt better immediately.

Sit awhile before you go up, she said without looking up from the cloth between her hands, You have a lot of work ahead of you today.

She sounded like he was going to be laboring, wasn't that much work up there in that attic. Still he sat. It always felt good to be around his momma. Something about her refreshed folk, made em feel good.

Hey, he said, bending closer to the cloth and tracing out a black web. A web so fine it was hardly visible, That's really nice Ma, he murmured, You getting better and better.

I'll give it to you when I'm through with it.

You gon be through with it by the time I get out of the attic?

She shrugged, Depends on how long it takes you to finish.

He watched her nimble fingers for awhile before climbing the stairs to the attic. The attic was hot and steamy, slanted roofbeams and dark cobwebbed corners of dusty old memories, bulging boxes, bags, piles of old clothes, busted toys, lawnmowers, furniture, bicycles, lumber, boxes of papers, photos and records and the scattered pieces of 4 old ice cream machines. Homemade ice cream. Ohboy. His mouth watered but he couldn't find enough pieces to make a complete one. He found the box that he stuck his army gear in when he got back from Nam and pulled out a couple of fatigues and a pair of jungle boots to replace the ones wearing out on him. He placed them on the steps so he wouldn't forget them.

Finally he really started, methodically working his way through by section, throwing away stuff that had been sitting up there forever. He left papers alone. Most were his father's records from when he first started out making house calls to scattered farms in Arkansas. Tucept remembered sharing the back of the old beatup Plymouth station wagon with Caldonia and medical fees; crates of greens and cabbages, sides of meat, bushels of corn and mason jars of red, grape, orange and yellow preserves. On holidays they would get homemade candies, fudges and brownies. Tucept found records of the many offices his father had before he and some friends built the new medical clinic on the South Side.

In one box, taped and reinforced against time, Tucept found letters that belonged to his granma, suitors who referred in flowered script to his granma as My Dearest Jewel. He visualized his granma as a My Dearest Jewel. His momma's notebooks from Fisk. Her old essays. *The Effect of Religion on Community. Power and the Negro Worldview. The Blues and Hoodoo as Negro Psychology and Treatment*. Damn. His eyebrow raised. Momma was deep. The attic was deep. He put her papers with his stack of booty, to be read later. Wonder what else was in the attic? Hell this was fun. And hot. Sweat poured off him as he worked.

Finally he got up and stretched, wiping the sweat from his face with his T-shirt. He sat at the little triangular back window and smoked a joint, blowing the smoke outside. Once he was thoroughly high, the steamy attic became a world of its own and he worked it like an automaton, lost in his rhythm and old comfortable memories.

Bruuuuhhhhhh.

Tucept, his momma yelled, Would you get the door please?

Tucept came down from the attic into the cool air downstairs with a cramped sigh of relief. He hadn't realized he had been up there so long.

Through the door glass he saw two dashikiclad brothers talking. Tucept didn't recognize either of them and he opened the door with a questioning slowness.

The shorter brother, stocky and glowering through a bearded face, asked if Doctor HighJohn was in.

No, Tucept shook his head, he isn't in.

The brother looked at him without warmth, Are you Tucept HighJohn?

Tucept nodded.

We'd like to talk to you if we could.

Tucept stood aside and asked them to enter.

He stepped briskly inside and introduced himself. Shukim, he said.

The name rang a bell and Tucept played with it for a moment until he remembered why. Shukim. One of Martin Luther King's lieutenants. Had stayed in Memphis after King was shot and had become involved in local community activism.

The tall brother with him nodded greeting.

Shukim sat in a den chair and glared at him before pronouncing abruptly, People around here say that you and your daddy are two of the smartest bougie in this town.

Shukim's head bobbed as he spoke, as if he were listening to a music no one else could hear. Tucept frowned and waited.

We want to know, said Shukim, what you doing for blackfolk's freedom. We want to know what your plan is.

Tucept looked at him blankly, totally wacked.

Uh . . . uh, I don't understand, he said, playing for

time, struggling for clarity. The high that had been so great a minute ago turned on him. He couldn't think and struggled to clear away fluffy mental clouds. Condition red, man the defenses. Sweat beaded his brow as he forced himself to straighten up.

Shukim stared at him, head bobbing, impatiently waiting and not expecting to hear anything he didn't already know. Tucept glanced at the tall brother. His obvious sympathy only angered.

Sweat running down his face, Tucept's mind finally began to kick the high and move into gear. His plan for blackfolk's freedom? What the fuck? He didn't have the faintest idea what this fool was talking about.

He switched tracks. Why me? Who sicced this fool on me? The last time he had seen Shukim, he was still in highschool, back in '68, down at the Temple the night before they got King. The night before they brought him down.

> *We've got some difficult days ahead*
> *but it doesn't matter to me now . . .*

On a humbug him and his cronies had decided to see King since he would be speaking over at the Temple. Irrelevant local militants, Levi jackets faded to uniform perfection, they had helped break up King's first parade for the sanitation strike and forced him to try again. And now they came to jeer him.

> *I may not get there with you but I want*
> *you to know that we as a people will*
> *get to the promised land . . .*

A big storm that night, thunder and lightning rippling around the Temple to the cadence of his words. They had to admit the boy could preach, his black moonface sweat slick and gleaming as he called down power under the stained glass windows of the Temple.

I'm not fearing any man . . .

Tucept had been moved. Tear tracks trickled from his eyes. And when he saw the way the blackfolks in the audience stood up with a longlost pride and dignity he left with a lot more respect for the King.

The next day the 30-06 bullet sang into his neck and Tucept and his boys hurled themselves through floodlit streets and brick warfare with the National Guard in a rage contained by tanks, Cointelpro, and the Great Society. A rage that finally settled into slow relentless anger falling rain on stone. A rage that made college a scowling beard, a ragged afro, strident anger, a .50-caliber machinegun shell necklace that looked symbolically photogenic on the nightly news and a freckled redhead on the side that didn't.

Tucept looked at Shukim with hard unfriendly eyes. He had been like Shukim in those days. Before the war. Looked like him and acted like him. But he had been playing a role, strutting the stage. Shukim was sincere.

You bougie Blacks are all alike, said Shukim suddenly, head bobbing with the suddenness of his assault, People tell me that you and your daddy got some sense, but I can see you aint doing nothing for blackfolks.

Tucept remembered his first class accusation. Hurled against him when a brother from his old neighborhood said, in front of witnesses, You wouldn't play with us because your father was a doctor. A bougie opportunist.

Who me? Tucept remembered wailing, shocked, shamed and shrunken in front of his activist peers, What are you talking about man? I thought we were cool. Are you serious? You talking about me? My daddy? My daddy aint beating nobody. Fuck you.

Intimidated under Shukim's ungiving eye, Tucept started blustering, Hey man, he said, I did my bit, I went through the Sixties too man. I was there. I been beat and teargassed and busted, I was there man. I marched and I fought. And I know all about talking and posing too. Now you want me to talk some more. No more talk man, I'm willing to work with anything that's real, something that's concrete, but I aint got nothing to talk to you about, I aint got to sit here and convince you of some plan I got for blackfolk's freedom, what makes you think I'm going to tell you about it?

A strange sensation of standing back and watching himself, watching too swift too angry words tripping over themselves.

So what are you doing? he said finally, I'm willing to work with anything that's concrete.

Contemptuous pity mingled with Shukim's earlier belligerence. He stood next to a shelf of trophies Tucept's folks had won playing bridge. He grunted and picked up a gold hand holding a spread of cards. No trump. He looked at it disdainfully. Tucept looked around the den selfconsciously, its very comfortableness an accusation. Shukim put the trophy down, letting it fall on its side. Tucept righted it.

We're working over on the Franklin projects, said Shukim, as if he were on a podium giving a boring lecture, his voice even and modulated, We're helping them build a truck garden, teaching them how to be selfsufficient, grow their own foods, we're trying to organize them for survival.

That's cool, said Tucept, I can deal with that. I'll come down and help you with that.

That's good brother, the tall brother spoke for the first time, We can use all the help we can get.

Tucept nodded at him, cautiously grateful.

What days and hours you working? asked Tucept,

knowing as he asked that he wasn't down for working in no garden. He was good for a couple of days maybe, max a week. Jiving again.

It was like Shukim knew it, contempt obvious in the brown lemon of his face, his drawn-together eyebrows. He just didn't have anything more to say to Tucept, studiously ignoring Tucept as his eyes continued to sweep over the den. As if calculating how many blackfolks had to suffer so that Tucept HighJohn could grow up comfortable.

The tall brother said he had heard Tucept was in the Nam, how was the herb, how were the women?

Tucept's eyes slitted, he certainly wasn't admitting to no herb, or women. Probably bougie traits. How do they know all my business anyway? Aint I got no privacy? I'm living in a fucking fishbowl.

Tucept's attitude reached for the threshold of anger.

Shukim stood, We're leaving.

Tucept walked them to the door and down the driveway.

Where's your car?

The tall brother answered, Don't have one.

How you getting way over to the other side of town?

Shukim turned on him, belligerence once again riled by this display of privileged naïveté.

We hitchhike, he said tersely, Look man, we want the good things in life too.

Shukim's dashikiclad arm swept gracefully, green cloth billowing behind it. It encompassed his folks' house, the large, well kept lawn.

We want cars, said Shukim with a false patience, We want a nice place to stay too, but these things aren't as important as blackfolk's freedom and they will just have to wait.

Tucept didn't say anything. Sucker was determined to bust his chops.

DE CALL

They caught a ride and Tucept HighJohn walked back up the driveway fuming and muttering curses. Back in the attic, sweat rolling down his body, he worked with a vengeance that placed everything in precise strict alignments. His plan for blackfolk's freedom, he muttered through lips beaded with sweat, what kind of shit was that to put on somebody?

CHAPTER 3

〰〰〰

JUST LIKE BEFORE THE WAR, TUCEPT HUNG OUT ON THE fringes of the movement through the low profile '70s; a body for demonstrations, community work, passing out flyers, making meetings and programs, trooping it until the day Gail called him down as an intellectual, the ultimate activist putdown.

All I'm saying, Tucept held up the document they had just worked over, is that this doesn't say anything new, just a bunch of rhetoric that folks have heard a thousand times already. Old news. We gotta be a lot slicker than this, otherwise blackfolks gon be suffering forever.

Gail looked at him smugly, You're saying it isn't intellectual enough?

Tucept's eyes looked to heaven. An intellectual par excellence herself, she followed the party line like the puritan Marxist-Leninist she was. He had always dug her but activist women demanded you be either superblack or downtrodden. He aspired to neither. Cool was his game.

He should have kept his mouth shut. He knew better. He wasn't considered seriously political by his nationalist and Marxist-Leninist cronies because he didn't participate in their political dialogue. As far as he was concerned, the choice between a five state bantustan and being cannon fodder for the latest set of good white folks was as bad as assimilation.

Feeling unaccountably mischievous, Tucept harrumphed until he had everybody's attention and made so bold as to suggest that there was only one legitimate goal of political activity: Conquer and Hold.

As he said it, a strange sensation surged through him, a quick chill as quickly gone. It left him dazed and confused, unfocused. They smiled indulgently. HighJohn again. Think he HighJohn de Conqueror they laughed. He amused them. After all they were serious political activists, HighJohn was just a halfass bougie nationalist.

He laughed it off with them, his ha ha hearty claiming to have just been kidding anyway. They went back to yesteryear's plans. Yesterday's battles. HighJohn sat back, shut his mouth and watched through veiled eyes. It wasn't wasted time. Keeping his finger on the pulse you know. Just hated to see them wasting good effort. He respected them. Warrior clans.

The sensation lingered, a memory tingling with significance. He savored the remnants, it had felt great. The discussion went on but Tucept was long gone. What was his contribution to blackfolk's freedom? He was only one man with a limited little time on the planet. One shot. He wouldn't waste it on no bullshit.

DE MOJO BLUES

THE HOT BALL OF THE VIETNAMESE SUN HAD JUST BARELY fallen below the horizon when an openbed truck pulled up to a squat sandbagged bunker on the perimeter of Firebase Sin Loi, a sprawling American basecamp perched precariously on top of a high mountain peak. The truck braked to a stop and a cloud of dust settled around it. Tucept and Jethro climbed from the back with an M60 machinegun, 2 M16s, an M79 grenade launcher, ammo and C-rations. They waved at the rest of the GIs to be dropped off on guard duty and bundled their stuff up to the bunker, a square hole dug deep into the ground with sandbagged sides and a sandbagged metal sheet top resting on four poles. Chicken wire kept out grenades.

Down the perimeter to the right was another bunker, to the left a guardtower rose on stilts into the rich-toned sky, the falling sun behind it etching its lines in dark powerful strokes. One of the two GIs in the tower raised his fist and pumped it twice in the air. The second followed.

Tucept returned power. The fist, two pumps.

Jethro walked up wiping sweat from his face with the green towel around his neck.

Brothers in the tower, said Tucept, pointing.

Jethro gave power. The fist, two pumps. The brothers in the tower returned power.

They went inside the dark little bunker, Tucept blinking at the sudden change in light. A damp and musty hole. Jethro laid on a bunk running against the dirt-packed back wall. Tucept sat on one of the two stools facing the jungle and made sure the claymore mines were hooked up. Then he placed the heavy machinegun in its bracket and fed it a belt of ammo. Outside a moody sky dropped swiftly into dusk. A bright red flare went off and momentarily shared the sky with the last rays of sun. The darkening world around them was gradually reduced to their bunker and the tangled blackgreen jungle on the other side of a perimeter belted with barbed wire and studded with the irritable little claymore mines.

I'ma take a piss, said Tucept.

He ducked his head and stepped outside. The two brothers were silhouetted in the tower.

He peed into the wind, taking off his bush hat and enjoying the breeze against his forehead. Lazy birds glided through a sky of such rich tone that he felt like he was in a painting. Back inside he sat on the stool and watched the nightgreen jungle turn black.

What time is it? mumbled Jethro from the bench.

Don't worry about it, said Tucept.

Jethro lit a joint and passed it. Then he turned to the wall and slept. Tucept took a long hit on the joint, his eyes scanning the jungle. Wonder if they were being watched from it, the observers observed.

Behind him a jeep roared by on the little dirt road that connected the perimeter points. Night crept on. Tucept's sense of time slowed to pace and he daydreamed about the world. Sometimes this was all so unreal and he had to forcibly remind himself this was real, no daydream, no TV, this was Vietnam. In the flesh.

A chill in the early morning woke Jethro up and he sat on the stool next to Tucept.

What time is it?

Don't worry about it.

Sorry it's brothers in the tower, said Jethro, pointing at the tower with the two brothers in it. Profile too high, he said, like being the point man but what can you do when you the point, you can't let folks walk into the ambush. But then I spec a man called by HighJohn know all about that.

Jethro's tone changed, How you come across a name like HighJohn anyway? he asked.

Tucept shrugged, According to my family, my greatgrans choose it after the Civil War, the Surrender my granma calls it when she telling the tale. Named after some root. Some HighJohn de Conquer root.

Not some root, said Jethro, The root. The serious mojo root. That's ole HighJohn de Conqueror himself's root.

Jethro reached into the deep side pocket of his jungle fatigues and felt around until he came up with a twisted little blackbrown root and passed it over to Tucept. Strange little grooved thing. Tucept got right up on it, fascinated with its strange gyrations. For some reason it made him uneasy.

This is it huh, he asked, HighJohn de Conquer root. He had always wondered what it looked like.

Jethro nodded. Tucept looked at it for a long time before handing it back to Jethro.

Keep it man, said Jethro, it's yours anyway.

Uh thanks man, he said cautiously, unsure if he should accept the gift. He fingered it reflectively before putting it away in a chest pocket. He fastened the flaps and patted the little lump, What do you know about this HighJohn de Conqueror? he asked.

Little bit, said Jethro, probably not as much as you do.

Tucept snorted, I don't know nothing about him man, he said, except that he was a slavery myth about some tricking man.

HighJohn de Conqueror is more than a slavery myth, said Jethro heatedly, it's just that slavery was the last time blackfolks needed him, but his spirit rest right there in that there root of his and whenever blackfolk's backs are pressed up against the wall, then ole HighJohn he get to walking this earth like a natural man, kicking ass 'n taking names, overcoming all obstacles in his path. Blackfolks just can't lose when the spirit of HighJohn is walking with them. Hell ole HighJohn might get to walk-

ing over here in Nam, tough as it's been 'round here.
According to the Lost Book of Hoodoo, the spirit of
HighJohn gon be walking soon. I been reading the signs
and blackfolks is sho backed up enough against the wall.

Got much about HighJohn in this, uh, Lost Book of
Hoodoo?

Everything is in the Lost Book of Hoodoo, said
Jethro with a sly grin, Dat's de black book of power. De
mojo book number one.

Never heard of it, said Tucept. He pulled out a little
notepad he carried and jotted the title down.

Who's it by, who published it?

Don't know all that, laughed Jethro.

Where can I get it?

Jethro sang a blues ditty:

> *Go back to where the blues was born.*
> *Go back to where the blues was born.*
> *Ask old man river to blow his horn.*

Jethro laughed loudly, the sound carrying out into the
jungle. Tucept put the pad away and turned back to the
perimeter.

Fuck Jethro with his wild riddle-talking ass.

Fuck you man, he muttered.

Jethro laughed again, One day that mojo gon start
talking to you boy, you remember what I say, the birth
of the blues, the man with the horn.

Uh huh, said Tucept, Check. He was through with it.

Jethro pulled out his ivory nail file and started working his nails. Moonlight glinted off the triangular tipped
pale squares.

Don't matter if you listen or not, I was told to wake
you up.

Wake me up? asked Tucept in spite of himself, By
who?

Jethro shrugged the question off, You aint ready.

Tucept was halfassed amused, You saying you were assigned to me, that you knew we were going to hook up?

Jethro shrugged a yes.

Gimme a break, Tucept snorted and turned back to the stone quiet jungle. Another jeep gunned by on the little road behind them. The bunker was silent except for the little *screech screech* of Jethro's nail file.

The sound irritated him. Tucept got off the stool, lay down on the bunk and looked at the moon. The golden orb yawned at him, a bright hole in a midnight sky.

Tennessee been good hoodoo ground, said Jethro from the stool. But them Delta boys now, they be known for working with both hands. We got another Tennessee boy back home name LaBas. He do good work but he shy his left hand. But now them Delta boys they just come naturally 2-headed.

Tucept grunted and closed his eyes. Grunting usually satisfied Jethro that he was listening. As he drifted off to sleep, he vaguely heard Jethro singing a blues:

> *Me 'n my brothers we had to throw down.*
> *We went to the war and caught hell all around.*
> *And now I've learned to . . .*

The roaring machinegun woke him up with a jerk.

He popped out of the bunk onto the stool in the front of the bunker in a smooth fluid motion.

Jethro fanned the 60 in short bursts, lips locked in a tight grimace as he bounced behind the chattering gun. Bright red tracer trails leaped from the jungle and punched angrily into the sandbags around the bunker. Bullets *wheeennng*ed past them. Tucept ducked hot shells thrown off by the bouncing M60 ammo belt and fired bursts from his M16 at the tracer trails. The post siren screamed and deadly Cobra gunships dipped out of the sky, blades chopping the night air and nose guns spewing death into the jungleline. The night roared and the firing died away. The siren ran down and the choppers left the sky and a thick ringing silence behind them. Tucept scanned the quiet smoking jungle, still hyped, willing his heart to slow down.

Yo Tennessee? said Jethro, You alright?

Tucept grunted to the affirmative.

Jethro pointed at the tower down the road. It had taken a direct hit and was down and burning, a red torch of war in the blacknight sky.

ᘓᘓᘓᘓ

TUCEPT SAT POISED AGAINST THE HIGH BACK OF HIS DRIFT-wood chair, the little leather bag he had brought back from Nam working in his fingers. Outside his window the air was still and moist, silent and waiting. A hurricane was expected in the gulf. Memphis braced itself for the agitated fringe. In the distance he heard the low rumble of thunder and the sky darkened abruptly. The winds rose and the old house swayed gently on thick wooden stilts. Whispering trees bowed in swaying homage as the winds gathered force. A gray rain wall leaped from the sky, heavy drops drumming the roof and splattering against the window. He left the window open, letting the fine mistspray wash him and run rivulet down the rivercarved grooves of his chair.

He watched the storm silently, still but for the leather bag in his hand, its faint muffled clicking audible in a silence intensified by the rain outside. The drumming rain insulated his room from the rest of the world and the gray rain wall reduced even the closest trees to vaguely swaying shadows. The woods around his tower disappeared. Surrounded by his books, his works and his fetishes, he was in his own world.

He looked at the bag in his hand and frowned. He hadn't opened it since he left Nam. Three years now he had been afraid of it. He worked open the drawstring and slowly poured small grayivory fragments into the palm of his left hand. He brought them up to his face, peering intently. Bones? Little pieces of bone. I'll be damned. Fighting a surge of revulsion he forced himself to look at them, shadows fluid in the raintainted darkness.

Jagged lightning threads glowed briefly in dark distant clouds. Spray from the open window washed across his face and the bones in his hand. Tucept looked at them long moments before dropping them with sudden impatience to the hardwood floor.

They fell in a circular, symmetrical pattern. The shouldered cross. Resisting an urge to sweep them up, he stared at them, lulled by the rains drumming his roof, splattering the big heavy drops against the window, the swaying house and the wind bluesharp whistling through the creaking stilts.

Lightning crackled, tagged almost immediately by an angry wardrum of thunder. It lit up the dark room with a bright jagged flash, momentarily etching the pattern of the bones in a sharp abstract afterimage in Tucept's eyes.

A vision slid into his mind. Clear and distinct. Crystal. A bright sharp image of a dead and dying universe, of dulled suns old and cold. He sensed great age and desolation in the starless skys of dead galaxies, once teeming human and alien species now only myths and memories. He saw a people marching. Tired and worn lean by survival's demands, yet still they marched, even danced, an elegant graceful dance of survival. Survivors. A sensation of strength and power flowed through him as he watched the vision flicker into an existence just as quickly gone. The moment passed. The vision died, leaving him with that tingle of significance. He frowned and tried to recapture it but it was gone. Outside, the storm. He stood and began to pace reflectively. It had been different from any dream or daydream he had ever had, more vivid, more real. He had felt it. Felt it. He shivered. For a quick moment he had known power.

MEMPHIS. AN OVERGROWN RIVER TOWN SITTING ON THE tip of the delta and magnet for Blacks throughout the blackmud Mississippi delta lands. Memphis. Where country blues first try on city airs. First stop on the trek upriver to St. Louie, Chicago and Detroit, to the promised land and the cold concrete of the northern cities.

Beale. Just a little ole strip of a street rising out of the river and cutting deep into the black heart of Memphis. Beale. When Tucept was a boy, it had been a last gasp delta fastlane, gamblers, joints, pimps, whores and sailors. It had been street musicians and oldmen playing checkers. Country blackfolks from all over the delta out for a Saturday night howl in pink pants and yellow shoes. Lansky's and Pape's clothing stores, Culpepper's BarBQ and the Harlem House, the New Daisy Theatre and a line of pawnshops full of old blues, horns and guitars pawned until the day the blues walked again.

The spring day in 1973 that Tucept came to Beale it was a ghosttown. Urban renewal had bought up the stores ten years ago and torn most down. Those stores left standing empty were boarded up. Tucept walked down the deserted little street absently. Schwab's Department Store. Boarded up. He had bought a derby here once. He had liked that derby. He ran his hand over the rough grain of the winterpeeled wood and moved on, moving slow. Jethro had said to seek the birth of the blues. Had to be Beale. Tucept walked up and down the empty street, his mind open for sign. He was soon depressed by the empty little buildings, the riverwind whining through blank boarded-up spaces.

An oldman sat in Handy Park on the corner of Beale and Third. Tucept nodded as he passed. He remembered when the little park would be packed with oldmen sitting around the gunmetal statue of W. C. Handy, playing checkers and talking about the good old days when Beale was really hot, before Boss Crump closed it down, when the blues walked and talked like a natural man.

He looked at the oldman sitting in the shadow of Handy's statue and frowned. He hated to make a fool of himself but hell he was down here now. The nagging memory of the quick vision had finally driven him here. Beale Street. Where the blues was born. Ask old man river to blow his horn. He went to the small park and sat on a bench across from the oldman, under the shadow of the Handy statue. Working up his nerve, Tucept looked at the oldman surreptitiously. A deepwrinkle barkbrown man in a black suit and a clean white union shirt.

Around them, downtown Memphis bustled with Saturday commerce, gleaming new skyscrapers towering around Beale's old boarded-up 2-story pastel buildings. Damn shame about Beale, he thought, gone, just like the blues.

Don't you worry about the Beale none, the oldman said, blues neither boy, Beale 'n the blues both will live again when the folks need em. Aint never died, just moving through transitions with the folks. The blues like to keep up. Been a unbroken line son.

Tucept frowned and looked at the old man closely. Was he talking to me?

The oldman grinned and snapped red checkered suspenders, Aint nobody else around here to talk to is it, he said.

He walked over and sat on the bench next to Tucept. The Handy statue threw half of him into deepshadow.

He smelled faintly of ancient forests thick with sweet rotting foliage and damp pinecones, gnarled oaks and deepchested maples. His eyes stared through Tucept, intimidating him. Tucept blinked.

The oldman took a penknife from an inside pocket and began whittling slivers from the nails of gnarled treebark fingers.

You can still feel em blues can't you? he said to Tucept, Cause they riding the wind, in the concrete here. The oldman looked out on the deserted little street and smiled crookedly. Blues been around long as blackfolks have. Got us over many a hump. The blues is a living blues. Been a unbroken line boy, we aint got too many of them.

Tucept didn't answer, half resenting his train of thought being broken. Oldmen always had something to tell you.

Damn right, said the oldman, and you do well to listen.

Tucept looked at him harder, eyes narrowing and shielding his mind.

The penknife the oldman was using to pare his nails caught Tucept's attention and tugged at his head. Then he remembered. Jethro, filing his nails down into the same triangular cut.

Excited, he looked at the oldman closer.

Do you know a brother from Taproot Mississippi? Named Tree? Jethro Tree?

The oldman frowned, Can't say I do.

Why do you cut your nail like that?

Seemed like the thing to do at the time.

The oldman looked up at him, amusement shining through walnut eyes.

Tucept realized he was being played with. He started getting an attitude. Something was going on here.

Who are you?

Most folks call me Spijoko. It'll do.

Do you know of a book called the Lost Book of Hoodoo?

Spijoko looked at him, eyes scraping the back of Tucept's skull. Tucept blinked.

You interested in hoodoo son?

Uh, I don't know, shrugged Tucept, I would like to read the book. A buddy of mine told me about it.

Spijoko frowned, treebark wrinkles of his face rearranging themselves. He put the penknife away, pulled a flask from a pocket, unscrewed the top and libated, By the tail of Moj.

Tucept thought it curious.

So you do know of the Lost Book of Hoodoo or don't you? Yes, no, maybe?

Patience puppy.

Tucept's lip twitched and he sat back with an effort.

Spijoko took a drink from his flask and offered it to Tucept. Tucept passed.

Spijoko insisted. Tucept took it reluctantly, wiped the flask top with his hand and drank. A tangy tea. Cool and refreshing. Invigorating. He drank deeply before returning it.

Thank you, he said, that was nice.

Mike and Willie, said Spijoko.

Tucept's eyes widened, slitted.

Mike and Willie? he asked.

You want to read the Lost Book of Hoodoo, go see Mike and Willie.

What do you know about Mike and Willie?

You want to read the Lost Book of Hoodoo, go see Mike and Willie.

Spijoko shrugged. Conversation over.

Tucept stood. He didn't like not knowing what was going on, he didn't like feeling played with. Hey give me a break, he said angrily, all this mumbo jumbo aint necessary. I aint to be played with. How you know my business anyway? What do you know about Mike and Willie?

Even as he wolfed he wondered. How did he know of Mike and Willie? Something was going on here that other folks knew that he didn't know and he didn't like that at all.

Spijoko looked at him with an oldman's amusement at the drama of the young. He slowly screwed the top back on his flask. Tucept tried to hold his eye but threatening depths made him pull away. Spijoko looked away, dismissing him.

Fuck it, said Tucept. He got up and stalked off down the deserted little street toward the river. At Main he looked back. Spijoko sat in the shadow of the statue. Tucept cursed and crossed Main.

TUCEPT GOT OFF THE DUSTY SILVER GREYHOUND AT NYC'S crowded Port Authority terminal and looked around for Willie D. He spotted him almost immediately, a tall brother in a faded army fieldjacket, standing still in the milling crowd. Willie D saw him, raised a hand and pumped twice. Tucept put his bag on his shoulder and walked over. They embraced, Willie D bearhugging him.

I was afraid I would miss you, said Willie D, shorn of the North Carolina accent Tucept remembered, Do you have more bags?

This is it.

Willie D's hair was dreaded, thick snaky locks peeped from under a blue baseball cap. He smiled from the depths of a thick beard.

How you get your hair to do that man? said Tucept, touching a shoulderlength strand lightly.

Just don't comb it, said Willie D.

Don't it get dirty?

I said I don't comb it brother, not don't wash it.

Just don't comb it and it does that?

You got it.

Willie D reached for Tucept's bag, Well come on man, the family is waiting to see you. My lady don't believe half the stories I tell her about The Ghetto. Whatever she asks you about you just agree, whether you remember it or not.

He laughed, head back, dreads bobbing.

Tucept shouldered his bag, I got it, which way.

Infected by Willie D's bubbling camaraderie Tucept stepped sprightly as he followed Willie D through the crowded bus terminal and onto a racketing subway car. With both of them standing at the door in their fieldjackets they looked like matching bookends. Head steady swiveling, Tucept was fascinated with the press of people and the spastic pace.

Mighty public town you got here, he said.

Totally lost, Tucept blindly followed Willie D as they got off this train, on this one, switched to that one. At Willie D's signal they got off and went above ground. Finally.

The Bronx, said Willie D, weaving surely through bright streets paved with both English and Spanish, through densely populated urban canyons bracketed with tall brick buildings.

Soon they moved into no-man's-land, burntout hulks and deserted streets violated by an occasional purposeful pedestrian.

They turned up an alley and followed it halfway down a block of deserted buildings. Tucept felt hedged in by the emptywindowed buildings towering on both sides of the alley. Here and there a dark window had a flowerpot in the shadows of the alley and he wondered if the sun ever reached down to the ground.

They turned into the back door of one of the buildings. The lobby was a shambles, the front door hanging off its hinges, huge pieces of the wall missing and grass growing from the cracks of a buckled-in floor.

Fire and water damage, said Willie D, in response to Tucept's stares, Pipes have been gone and we had a fire here recently.

They started climbing broken stairs, dark and cluttered with debris. It was a huge building and the floors disappeared into imposing darkness. Tucept was spooked. Willie D can't live here can he?

You live here man?

Yeah.

Yeah?

Some other people too, two new families last week.

Willie D laughed at him, the sound carrying hollow echoes in the deserted building.

Heavy huh? We're reclaiming it, rebuilding it and negotiating with the city for it. Willie D shrugged, But we have to live here to do it.

On the 5th floor they went down a lit hall. At a door about halfway down the hall Willie D worked open three sets of locks.

A spindly little brown babygirl waddled at them and into Willie D's arms. Hey Daddy, Daddy.

Willie D lifted her up and she squealed, This is my little girl, aint you little girl?

Daddy, Daddy.

Abeki, say hello to Tucept HighJohn.

She turned shy, Who is he?

He's a friend of daddy's. Now get it girl, don't you keep daddy waiting for you to be polite.

Hello daddy's friend, she said, laughing quickly at her play on words.

Willie D laughed and swung her into the air. Tucept, girl, he said, Tucept HighJohn. From Memphis Tennessee.

She giggled wildly. He put her down, locked the locks, dropped the deadman's bar. Tucept went through the foyer into the apartment. The space was large but crowded, a big sound system against the wall, African art and sculptures scattered haphazardly amid books, plants and records. A shotgun and bat leaned against the wall beside the door. The walls were covered with political posters, some framed: *One People, One Struggle. If There Is No Struggle There Will Be No Progress. People's War. Forward Ever, Backwards Never. Martin, Malcolm, Marcus and Maurice.*

Linda came into the room in jeans and a white blouse, dreaded hair tied back with a blue leather ribbon. A fine woman with a vibrant spirit that made Tucept smile immediately.

Linda, this is Tucept HighJohn, my old buddy from the Nam.

They shook, Nice to meet you, she said, Willie's told me a lot about you. Just put your bags down anywhere.

I asked Willie D how you get your hair like that, said Tucept, All he told me was by not combing it.

That's it, she laughed, running her hand over her dreads and smoothing stray strands.

That's all? I figured he just didn't want to tell me the secret.

He told you.

Tucept stone cold enjoyed the evening. They made him feel right at home, fed him a real good dinner and left him full. He and Willie D told every tale they had about Vietnam.

So there we were at the party with these blowouts on our heads, said Willie D, we looked like clowns.

Tucept howled, It was those Hong Kong special suits that did it Willie D. We were a year behind.

What do you call him, asked Abeki, you keep calling him, what, Williedee?

Huh? said Tucept.

Willie D, laughed Willie D, Everybody around here just call me Willie man.

Oh, we used to call him Willie D in the war.

Oh that's too cute, laughed Linda, Willie D? What else about him do I not know? Like Hong Kong for instance.

Willie D and Linda laughed a long, drawn out old friends laugh. Tucept laughed with them, greedily sharing their pleasure. He felt a pang of loneliness and wished he had somebody that he knew like they knew each other.

A sudden knocking on the door cut their laughter abruptly short. Willie went to the door and asked who it was.

From behind the door, a muffled murmur, Me man.

Willie threw the door open. A tall excited brother stood there, Hey man, Mrs. Murphy heard noises in the apartment below hers.

A thick stocky dude stood in the door of the apartment across the hall. He darted in his apartment and back out with a pistol. Willie grabbed the shotgun and a heavy flashlight from beside the door. He stuck the flashlight in the tall brother's hand, Here man!

The three of them took off down the hall.

Damn, muttered Tucept the Cowardly. He darted after them, thought about it, went back for the bat and ran to the dark mouth of the stairs. He heard them running down the steps below and went barrelling down the stairs trying to catch them, moving so fast he would've run past the floor if not for their voices and a sudden commotion.

He ran down the hall and into a room lit by the big flashlight. With the pistol and the shotgun, Willie and the other two tenants covered two black dudes with their hands up in the air. Between them sat a can of kerosene.

As Tucept walked in, Willie jammed the shotgun into one man's stomach. As he fell, Willie D went upside his head with the stock.

We caught this motherfucker here once before, he grunted as the man went down. We warned him then.

Hey man, I didn't know, his partner whined, I didn't know.

Shutup motherfucker, you didn't have to know, the tall brother with the flashlight growled, you knew people were living here.

I—

The tall brother kicked him in his balls. He doubled over and spouted vomit as he fell.

Bring him over here, said Willie, dragging the repeat offender over to a waterwarped stool.

They arranged his legs on the stool and Willie asked Tucept for the bat.

Tucept's eyes went wide but he kept his mouth shut, he didn't live here.

The bat arched. *Craaaaacck!!*

Bones cracked and splintered through the dark flesh.

The man woke up screaming, a thin wail that pierced Tucept's every nerve.

The man whimpered and begged as they put the other leg up. He struggled and they held him down. Willie D raised the bat and it came down a blur in the light of the flashlight.

Craaaack!!

The man passed out. His buddy was whimpering and begging, Please let me go, please, I won't come back, I swear.

The dark room stank with fear and hostility.

You take him out of here, said the brother from across the hall, and you tell him that next time we see him on the block we'll assume he's hunting.

The man looked at his moaning buddy, How I'm gon get him out, I can't carry him.

I don't give a shit what you do with him, snarled Willie, I know you better get him the fuck out of here.

The tall brother kicked the broke leg man again, bringing a new whimper of pain,

Lowlife mothafucker, a kid died the last time we got torched. Here mothafucker, take this back to the sucker that hired you.

He kicked the screaming man again. And again. Again. Agai— Willie grabbed him, That's enough man.

Get him out of here, he said to the other.

But how—

Get him the fuck out of here!

The man scurried over and after a moment of trying to figure out how best to do it, he put the whimpering man around his shoulders. They escorted him out without helping him with his load.

Tucept was sober for the rest of the evening. Willie didn't bring it up, like it happened all the time, like picking up his mail. After the dinner Tucept stood at the window looking out at the darkening street. A moody bombed-out landscape. The empty row of buildings across the street were burntout hollow shells, some nuke movie, silent, brooding sentinels of a dead civilization. Tucept was impressed with Willie's heart, he couldn't hang.

Willie D came up beside him, Rough huh?

Yeah man, this is heavy, how long you been here?

Not long, we may not stay, we have a chance to get a place in Harlem. We'll probably take it. We hate to leave after we've put so much into it. Check this out.

Willie showed him where they had plastered the walls, replaced the plumbing and wiring, showed him a gaping hole half fixed in the wood floors.

Linda's doing this one, she should be through with it in another week.

Ha, more like a month, Linda said from a thick chair in front of the TV. Since we've moved here we've become competent carpenters, plasterers and handyjacks and we thought we were activists before. Workers.

They laughed. That old friends laugh.

Linda and Abeki went to bed. Tucept and Willie sat around drinking wine, smoking herb, swapping memories. In the quiet of the wee early hours the street outside looked softer, easier, slower. Willie enjoyed himself immensely, talking about Sin Loi, The Ghetto, their courtmartial. Ole Willie D still a believer, realized Tucept, serious about being a vet. He knew how Willie felt. He still wore his fieldjacket too, thought of himself as a vet, nostalgic for the time when they had felt strong, powerful, brotherme, brotherblood, brotherblack.

Say man, Jethro ever say anything to you about a Lost Book of Hoodoo?

Naw, said Willie.

He thought on it some more, face frowned up in thought, the old fineline grenade scars accented. Naw, he said finally, I don't remember no book to speak on. Lost Book of Hoodoo? Sounds interesting. What is it?

I don't know, Tucept shrugged, It's this hoodoo book that Jethro spoke on a couple of times. Black secrets of power or something like that.

All this in a book, Willie started laughing, expecting Tucept to join in. Tucept's chuckle was forced. He was halfass defensive about the whole thing.

Yeah well if you find it, get me a copy, said Willie, I could use some power.

You don't remember him saying nothing about no books of no sort, asked Tucept, never heard of it?

Naw man, sorry.

It's okay man, no problem.

In the morning over waffles, Linda asked him if he would like to go see the Nigerian art exhibit at the Met.

They had tickets but they had already seen it once. He could have hers, he and Willie could go.

Tucept wasn't that thrilled about it but he had a little time before his train left. He told her yes and thank you, he appreciated the offer.

He and Willie stopped by the museum on the way to Penn Station. Tucept checked his bag and they strolled through the place. Tucept was fascinated. The stuff was heavy, intricacies and techs that astounded him and filled him with a new appreciation for the African genius.

He felt a strange sensation as he moved through the room, a vague uneasiness that he couldn't identify, a sense of unseen activity. As he walked through looking at the work, the sensation grew, drenching him. A charge. He started sensing it as strength. He defined it. Power. Force. The room seethed with power. The mojo was strong. The pieces themselves became insubstantial, merely focal points of the power throbbing through the huge cavernous museum. Willie D and the milling crowds faded into the background as Tucept bathed himself in waves and eddies of power. As if led, he found himself eventually in front of a little piece sculpted of stone. Two hands broken off at the wrist held a small creature. He stood and stared, greedily drinking the power emanating from it and exalted with the intensity of the charge.

He noticed the nails on the stone hands and looked closer. Blunt triangular nails. Riveted, he looked at the information plaque. An African sorcerer making a sacrifice, nails delta cut in the tradition of some African sorcerers since before recorded history.

$$\mathscr{S}\mathscr{S}\mathscr{S}\mathscr{S}$$

OUTSIDE A CHOPPER *WHOPWHOPWHOP*PED THROUGH THE thick Vietnamese sky. In the distance they heard the familiar faint firecracker pops of a firefight somewhere.

We didn't do it, said Tucept.

The young JAG officer sighed with pent-up relief and sat down, brisk now, professional. He flipped his yellow pad to a fresh page. The sergeant, I believe his name is Gill, said it was a Black he saw that night, you were the only Blacks in the area.

He waited for a response. Mike shrugged, We didn't do it.

You didn't do it?

We didn't do it, said Tucept.

Lt. Lawrence frowned. He wasn't reassured.

You wouldn't make a ass out of me would you?

We didn't do it. We were in The Ghetto when it happened. Folks saw us there.

A knock on the door. Lt. Lawrence put his papers together and stood. Well, he said, this is it. He was tempted momentarily to shake their hands. Instead he nodded and followed them in, wondering if he was about to help the guilty walk away. A man was dead. Was he a traitor to his own? He put the thought from his mind. In the little courtroom three colonels sat as judges, strac, military, impassive. Already mad. Tucept could practically hear them thinking. The courtroom was still and hot. Tucept could feel that Viet sun even here, seeping through the wood walls and the tin roof.

He barely listened as the charges were read. The U.S. Army against Brown, Daniels and HighJohn. Murder.

※※※※

TUCEPT GOT OFF THE TRAIN AT THE RAGGEDLY ELEGANT Washington D.C. Amtrak station and followed the crowd up the front drive. It was a nice day and he unzipped his fieldjacket. As soon as he walked up, a little red Benz scooted up and braked. Mike leaned out of the driver's window and waved at him.

DE CALL

Grinning, Tucept shouldered his duffelbag and walked over to the car. Mike leaned over and snapped the door open. Tucept hopped in. A little boy sat quietly in the back. Mike and Tucept gripped hands and Mike whizzed off.

What's happening HighJohn? What brings you to our fair capital city?

Just passing through.

Mike's laugh was manicured, Just passing through? he said, Man who do you think you're talking to? This is Mike Daniels, I went to the war with you remember? That's my boy in the back. Mike this is Tucept HighJohn.

Tucept looked at the little quietfaced boy sitting in the back.

Hey champ, he said, and held out his hand to be fived. The little boy looked at it an uncomfortable minute before fiving him listlessly and settling back into the seat cushion.

I'm dropping him off at his mother's, he's been with me this week.

Mike's thick black hair was sculptured, his sand tan skin smooth and pampered. Dressed in soft, well cut casuals, he looked fatcat satisfied.

You looking good man, like life's been treating you right, said Tucept.

Mike opened the sunroof, I'm doing alright. Making a living.

The wind eased in, moving around Tucept's head and neck. Refreshing. Tucept watched the huge edifices of the capital city pass by. He felt more at home here than in the fastpaced too public too crowded New York City.

They pulled up in front of a large Georgian house.

Won't be but a minute man, Mike's smooth face was suddenly troubled waters, I'm just going to give him to his mother and I'll be right back.

The little quieteyed boy opened the back door and slid down to the sidewalk.

Say goodby to Tucept, said Mike. The little boy waved.

Mike boosted him up on his shoulder and they walked to the porch.

Tucept sat back in the ride, wondering again if he was just wasting his time. He expected no more from Mike than he had gotten from Willie D. That damned Jethro had him on a wild goose chase.

Mike got in the car, sitting a moment before starting it up.

What's wrong blood? asked Tucept.

Mike shrugged, Nothing. Where to, any place special you want to see?

Naw, just figured we could shoot the old shit.

I know a nice bar.

Mike pulled out into the flow of traffic, talking as he shifted into gear, Nice to see you man, It's been awhile since I even thought about Nam, what, three, almost four years since we left Nam.

Mike shook his head. Feels like yesterday.

They pulled up in front of a nice bar. The Pit Stop. In the parking lot Tucept hesitated, conscious suddenly of his fieldjacket.

Say man, I won't feel out of place will I?

Mike looked amused, Of course you will.

He rummaged around in the backseat and pulled up an attaché case.

Take off the fieldjacket, he said digging into the case, and put this on. He pulled out a loud but tasteful designer tie. Green.

This? asked Tucept. He held the green tie next to his beige corduroys and frowned at the clash.

Man just put the thing on, laughed Mike. Who cares if it doesn't match? Certainly not a couple of old boonie rats from Firebase Sin Loi.

Tucept took off his fieldjacket and tied the tie loosely around his neck.

The little place was nice, mellow halflit ambience, tailored men and glittering women draping the bar. As they walked in the door, a vivacious woman passed them, leaving behind her a faint teasing trail of perfume and gay laughter.

Nice, said Tucept about the place.

Isn't it, said Mike about the woman.

They eased into a couple of spaces at the bar.

Screwdriver, said Tucept

Kir, said Mike, sweet please.

From their position at the bar they could see the entire crowd.

I see you know the right spot, complimented Tucept.

I learned a little something in basic training. So how have you been my man, said Mike, what's the latest news? Run the pedigree champ.

Samo samo, said Tucept, I'm alright, back in school, looks like I'm destined to be a professional junior. Just ain't serious enough about it, get bored too easy or something, I got more incompletes than I got grades. How about you?

I'm in school over at Georgetown Law, said Mike. Went there after I left Howard. Working in the firm of a friend of my father's. He's going to get me a position at Acme as soon as I graduate.

Acme Industries?

Acme.

Damn boy, you starting right at the top, they've got fingers in everybody's pie.

Right. And I've got a finger in theirs. Big bucks my man, the corporate joyride, some nice golden handcuffs, the whole bit. So I'm in the books.

As he spoke, his chiseled head swiveled around the bar to spot likely ladies. He held his drink up to the light and toasted, On the fast track my friend, ready to leap to the money track and a quick lick at the power track. Basics. I got to have it.

Mike shrugged, But you didn't come here to ask me about me or my career. Not HighJohn, he who never makes a move unless he has at least three good reasons or five so-so ones.

Tucept grinned.

Mike gave him a cynical smile, raised his glass again in toast and drank.

It goes without saying that you're welcome to bunk down anytime you're in town. So how was Willie D, how's he doing up there, is he taking care of himself?

He was fine man, got a nice family and all.

Willie D? said Mike, Now isn't that something. I'll have to get in touch with him. Always planned to get in touch with the both of you but I never did. Same with you. Always one day.

The band played softly in the background, a sax, guitar, piano and traps. A buzzing cocoon of soft voices from others around the bar insulated them. Tucept dipped chips in guacamole on the woodgrain bar, Mike ordered another kir, sweeter this time please.

Mike stirred his kir and tasted it. He smiled and drank it straight down, set the empty glass down and turned to Tucept. Again, he said, What brings you to Chocolate City?

I'm trying to hunt down this book that Jethro used to speak on, the Lost Book of Hoodoo. I was told, or rather, I wondered if you ever heard of it, or if Jethro ever told you anything about it.

Mike thought, closing one eye in concentration.

Lost Book of Hoodoo? he muttered repeatedly.

Lost Book of Hoodoo?

Lost Book of Hoodoo?

He shook his head slowly, then with conviction, eye opening slowly.

No, I don't think so man. Sorry.

Tucept shrugged, I didn't really expect you to. Just a hunch. Figured it'd be fun to play it. And see D.C.

Did you try the Library of Congress?

Right. And a couple of rare book dealers. They never heard of it.

You got me boss, said Mike.

Tucept's eye roved the bar, alighted on a cherrybrown sister with long hair swept to the side. Her hands were graceful, the occasional eyes she gave him curious.

Anything happening tonight? My bird doesn't leave the airport until ten-thirty. Can you give me a lift?

My time is yours my man. You tell me what, you tell me when, I'll tell you how.

I don't have anything particular in mind. Something refreshing.

Mike thought about it, snapped his finger. Bob Marley, he said, is that refreshing enough for you, in a lowclass nocount dive on the other side of town. How about that for flavor. Come on.

They relocated. The new place was a dive, bad light, bad sound, cramped, no food and weak drinks but packed and seething with energy. Marley was hot. Wildman, shaking his dreads, bounding all over the little stage, electrifying his audience, stroking, pulling, moving em. He started the set with War: a declaration of war taken from an old Selassie speech, telling folks that this is war but don't worry, our victory is as certain as good over evil.

He went to One Drop, chanting:

They make the world so hard, that everyday the people are dying.
They make the world so hard, that everyday we got to keep on fighting.

Mike and Tucept sat right up on him, felt the crowd's pulsing throb as Marley charged them, feeding them power. Tucept's heart beat reggae bass and he felt good. He felt damned good.

Near the end of the set Marley did his signature piece, the last one to be issued before he died, Redemption Song, his small voice huge, his guitar his only accompaniment. The rowdy crowd stilled and listened while he sang his redemption songs, the only songs he ever had.

Some say it's just a part of it, we've got to fulfill the Book.

Tucept jerked alert, rising excitement almost choked him. He knew before he looked at the small delicate hands in front of his face. There it was, fingers tipped in triangular points. Delta-nailed.

Bible or the Lost Book?

After the set Tucept approached Marley and asked him if he knew of the Lost Book of Hoodoo. He got a string of Jamaica style geechie talk and his question ignored. But even as the man ranted and turned to walk off, deep within his eyes, he spoke.

Before Marley left, he did an encore. We're the survivors, he said repeatedly, hypnotic, incantoric, The black survivors.

HANDY PARK, EARLY ON A DEWBRIGHT MORNING. BEALE rested under a warm autumn day and cool riverbreezes. Tucept let out a great sigh of relief. Spijoko was there in faded overalls and a red checkered shirt, feeding pigeons from a 25-cent bag of popcorn. A monstrously big black flathead tomcat walked up to him and arched its back against his leg. Tucept smiled and bent down to rub it behind its ears. It purred and popping its tail it followed him over to Spijoko's bench. Clouds moved swiftly through a sunny sky and lapping riverwave shadows rippled over Spijoko's face. He nodded at them.

Tucept sat down beside him.

I want to read the Book, he said.

Spijoko looked at him, amusement as always bubbling in his brown eyes.

The hoodoo path aint no easy road son, bigger men have fell. The water always deeper than it look.

HighJohn replied, I wanna know power.

SECTION TWO

Drama

SECTION TWO

~~~~

DE QUEST

CHAPTER 4

〰〰〰

TUCEPT MEDITATED, HIS BODY MOTIONLESS BUT FOR THE rhythm of his breathing. He let himself relax further into trancestate and tried to bring the vague image in his mind into sharper focus. *His room, the high ceilings, books and papers, batches of herbs, concoctions, fetishes, the green couch and the spool table, himself sitting in the highbacked chair by the front window, in T-shirt and Levis.* Vague though. No detail. He let himself sink deeper, opening himself to the world around him, trying to see it as if his eyes were open, trying to touch, feel and hear it with his senses yet not his senses. He could focus in on specific details but that wasn't what Spijoko had him looking for. That was more memory than awareness. He should see it in his mind as he did with his senses. It had taken him awhile to detect mental images. His image work exercises had suffered until, by studying the ones that came unbidden, he realized that mental images were different from visual images and he quit looking for visuals. He resisted a desire to force it, to quit, to twitch, to do anything other than just sit here. Even still the image was hazy, details fading in and out. He was aware of air from the open window. He was aware of the sound and snap of the flapping curtains, of an open book on the floor beside him. He tried to read the page. Squibbles.

The big black flathead tomcat walked into the room, sat on the book and stared at him. Tucept watched himself open his eyes to stare back. He opened his eyes to stare back. Tucept was almost afraid to really open his eyes and look but he did. The cat stared curiously at him from slitted catgreen eyes. Tucept grinned, Well I'll be damned. He had known when the cat walked in, he had seen it in his mind.

He tried to put himself back in his exercise but he was too excited and couldn't compose himself. He looked around the room and it felt almost spooky to see it as he had seen it in his mind.

He shook himself awake and began functioning. He looked at his watch, he had to make today's lesson. Today's lecture rather. Old dude could go on sometime, get as tedious as these exercises. He had almost quit this one after doing it daily for God knows how many months. But Spijoko knew when he didn't do them. Wait till Spijoko heard about the cat. He glanced at his watch again and went for the door, the flathead tom darting between his feet when he opened it. Stepping outside felt strange. The sun was warm on his skin. He took a deep cleansing breath and stretched while standing at the top of the stairs. He had a strange sense of dislocation. He hadn't been outside for a couple of days, hadn't seen or talked to anyone. Sometimes after he had spent a couple of days immersed in his studies and the world in his head, it came almost as a shock that the realworld was still functioning, that folks had other concerns than his. He spent a lot of time in his head. He could see how the mystics got off on living in caves. He wondered if he was just wasting himself. Would all the time he spent programming his head ever mean anything to anybody else, much less the struggle, or was he just a bullshit bougie on a personal after all? He checked his watch, he would be late. Antidiscipline. He bounded down the stairs. The big black flathead tom took the stairs two at a time.

He strided his woods with long sure steps. The tom was kitten frisky, racing off after squirrels that didn't move fast enough and batting at windblown leaves.

Had he really known when the cat walked in? Tucept frowned through his eyebrows as he tried to sort out the thoughts running through him. Was reality as fluid as it seems? Just what is reality?

Spijoko sat on the bank of the river. His weathered face cracked in greeting. Tucept sat on the grass beside him, trying to formulate the questions in his mind so that they wouldn't sound too wild.

Spijoko looked amused. Reality is what you will it to be, he said before Tucept spoke. As you define so shall it be. That's what makes you the sorcerer. To bend reality to your will is the essence of magic. The rest is parlor tricks to impress the impressionable. Genius alone, he said, don't guarantee you an audience. But the power, the power boy is in the will. The Will, the Word and the Way is the whole of sorcery.

Will? What will? Just will? Tucept asked dubiously.

Spijoko laughed, Not just will boy, sorcerer's will.

Tucept's mind chewed at the concept but he wasn't quite getting it.

Discipline? he asked.

Raise your arm, said Spijoko.

Huh?

Raise your arm.

Tucept lifted his arm and let it drop.

What did you do?

I lifted my arm.

You willed your arm to lift and it responded. It took no discipline to raise your arm. You didn't even have to grit your teeth none. You simply willed it, the muscles and nerves responded and it was so. It's the will that initiates the responses in your controllable space. Most folks can will little, some body functions, efforts at goals. The sorcerer on the other hand is a creature of will. The will of a great sorcerer is law in the world. You use your will to tap the mojo boy.

Spijoko tapped Tucept's knee. What's the mojo? he asked.

Uh, said Tucept, A mojo hand is a item of power that folks carry to do their bidding.

That's low hoodoo, Spijoko snorted, his gesture one of contemptuous disdain, All that other low hoodoo, bush wizard stuff too. Love potions, voodoo dolls, getting rode and all that, nothing but small tools necessary to focus small wills. We talking masterwork here, a master hoodoo needs no tools other than hisself, his will and his mojo. But even low hoodoos understand that the mojo is the power boy, the lifeforce of all things. Other traditions call it different, ki, mana, prana, the force, etheric, even god or laws of nature, on and on, all kinds of names for the power. Different traditions approach it different too. Some looks for nothingness, or to be one with the cosmos, or the perfect existence, all kinds of things. The hoodoo thing is to be a conduit of the power. The Way is to align yourself so precisely in the dynamic of the natural laws that you become one with the power. You are the power. The strongest force on the board. De mojo. The center of the universe and thereby its rulemaker. A Master of Destiny. Adept at applying your will to the destinical points of balance that determine the way of things. Conjuration boy. Conjuring evolving reality. Aint nothing like it. Even reality must yield to the hoodoo will.

Tucept nodded excitedly. He was game, on with the program.

Three more months radar training exercise, said Spijoko.

Three months? said Tucept, excitement evaporating.

Three months.

Three months? he asked petulantly, Why?

To see what is not seen, to know what is not known.

I saw the cat. Did I tell you? My cat walked into the room while I was meditating and I saw it.

Good, said Spijoko, should be a productive three months.

Then what? Tucept sulked.

More exercises, more disciplines. Patience puppy. There'll be plenty more to bore you, no need to be in such a hurry to get to them.

Tucept pouted.

Bad attitude HighJohn, make it four months. Do you wanna be a hoodooman or don't you?

CALDONIA WHISTLED WHILE SHE WORKED. SHE STUFFED the wet rag down the gas tank of the red Buick Electra 225 with short stabbing pushes to the tune, Caldonia, Caldonia, what makes your big head so hard. She stopped pushing and judged what was left hanging out. That ought to do it.

The night was cool and she drew the hood of Tucept's old fieldjacket over her head. It was chillier than she had expected. She had drug the jacket from their folks' attic and put it on tonight with some idea of camouflaging herself but damned if it wasn't comfortable, especially tonight. After all this was war wasn't it?

She laughed aloud and a woman walking by with an

Irish setter looked at her curiously. Cal started going through the deep pockets of the fieldjacket like she was looking for her keys and the lady went on with only one quick peek over her shoulder. Better get this done and over with girl. She wiped the oily film from her hand while judging the length of material hanging from the gas tank. High heels, dammit, she had on high heels, high damned heels, real smart girl, real smart. So much for your great planning skills. She took off her shoes and stuck them in the deep breast pockets of the fieldjacket. She liked these pockets, she might keep the jacket. Of course she had on pantyhose too. Gravel rocks beneath her feet made her curse and shift around on the asphalt as she used a stockinged foot to push the 3 sloshing cans under the car closer together.

Stepping back and making sure her hands were dry, she lit a match. She was almost surprised by the sudden flare in the dark. It flickered and flared out. She lit another.

She lit the material, spun around and started running. The material went out before she went three steps. She glanced at the modest yellow brick home with the white picket fence bordering the spacious lawn. No lights had come on. Relax girl, if you gon do it, do it right. She held the match until the material caught and then turned and walked off, swiftly but with, she thought, priceless dignity. She felt like a model on a runway she was so cool, a movie scene, a drama, she had the lead role and nobody here to see the performance. I should have held a news confere . . .

WHOOOOSSSH!

The car went up with an explosive bark, bright flame in a night come suddenly alive with barking dogs, lit windows and Caldonia's wild and wooly laughter.

She felt great.

When she got home that night she came through the

door whistling, Caldonia, Caldonia, what makes your big head so hard?

Jabbo was at the dining room table.

Hey boy, she said cockily.

Hey Ma, he said sullenly.

Sullen little bastard, she thought, affectionately kissing the top of his head before he could protest.

Ma, he protested, embarrassed yet pleased, having decided at 6 that being kissed by his momma was mushy and for little kids.

Come on Ma, I'm a big boy now.

He tried to look stern and she laughed and traced the scar on his forehead, from cracking his head on the steps and the car broken down three blocks from the hospital. She remembered a hysterical 2-block run carrying him limp and bleeding before a bus driver stopped his bus and picked her up. Liked to kill yourself didn't you girl. It had got her back on an exercise schedule, she wouldn't be caught short like that again.

Well I'm a mushy mom, she said kissing the top of his head again, And you'll just have to put up with it. Where's Gloria?

In the back.

That's a good one, she pointed at the drawing he was working on, What is it?

A spaceship landing on Mars. See, he pointed, that's me coming out of the door, on spaceships we call them hatches. And this is the command module, these are the solar reflectors.

Do tell, she said, a little intimidated, you know I don't know anything about spaceships, you'll have to teach me.

Command modules and solar reflectors. Where did he pick up all of this stuff? He was forever shocking her with the strangest bits of information. She went to the back to pay the babysitter and he followed her, drawings in hand.

Have you eaten?

I ate good.

Something's wrong with that phrasing, she said, I ate good is not right, think about it.

She would. I ate well didn't sound right either but probably better than I ate good, she would check it. She paid off the babysitter and took a long bath in thick bubbles and hot scented water. The memory of the explosion warmed her. I ate good too, she thought grinning.

She was in a good mood all evening and JB got away with not having to do as much homework as he usually did. That put him in a good mood too and the house was warm full that evening. After he had gone protesting to bed, she took another bath, long, leisurely, and languorous, soaking away the lingering smell of gasoline.

Tucept woke her early the next morning. When she opened the door he greeted her with a laugh as wild as hers.

She shushed him, JB's asleep.

Tucept followed her into the kitchen and sat while she brewed strong coffee. She could tell he knew from his sly grins. She didn't say anything

So how does it feel? he finally asked.

Wonderful, she said.

Everybody knows you did it. I've had a hundred people tell me my sister burned up some dude's car.

I didn't burn it up, she said, I blew it up. There's a difference.

They howled, bringing a sleepy JB to the kitchen.

Go wash up baby, she told him, get ready for school.

He stumbled out, still too sleepy to protest being excluded from the festivities.

What kind of car was it?

Deuce and a quarter. Fire engine red.

Do it Cal.

It did feel good, she said, sitting across from him, whistling with the coffeepot, Caldonia, Caldonia, what makes your big head so hard?

You think he'll figure out you did it?

He will when he gets the letter.

The letter? said a suddenly horrified Tucept, You wrote him a letter telling him you did it.

I couldn't help it.

Daddy aint gon like that, said Tucept, he don't mind you blowing the dude's car up, but writing a predated confession, that he aint gon like.

Why I got to worry about what he like?

Who's going to pay for your lawyer? I can't. Who's gon get you out of jail when they arrest you for terrorism? Not me cried Chicken Little. In case you don't know it, blowing up folks' cars is against the law. You, sister mine, are in trouble.

I just don't care, she said, unassailable, her face lit up like the first sunrays of morning. I feel great. And don't have time to worry about it either. You see before you a new entity, I'm alive dear brother, and I'm going for the gold. I intend to enjoy life buddy. She laughed and slapped at her thigh, All I did last night was ring life's doorbell.

Tucept hadn't seen her this loose since he got back from Nam. Her mood was infectious and the kitchen rang with their laughter.

Jabbo came into the kitchen already grinning and ready to have a good time too.

Caldonia put out grits, eggs, toast and cereal.

You eating? she asked Tucept.

He was too excited to eat.

You better be careful how you treat your momma

kid, he told Jabbo, She a tough cookie, just blew up a dude's car. Blew it up buddy, Babbabbabbbooooom!

Jabbo's 6-year-old eyes were delighted, already embellishing the story he would be telling his friends.

You blew it up like on TV Mom? Babbababooom! he said, spastically mimicking Tucept. Why Ma? Was he a badguy?

He wasn't a badguy, he just owed me a debt. Eat now, you have to go to school, I'll tell you all about it later.

Today.

Today. Remind me. Eat. If you ate *well* yesterday I expect you to eat as *well* today.

Yeah man, she blew it up, laughed Tucept, And stamped it debt paid.

Yeah Ma? asked JB, Tell me about it now Ma.

Later, right now you eat. Your Uncle Tucept is leaving before he gets stamped debt paid.

She waited until Jabbo started eating and escorted Tucept to the door.

Well look he said, Come by after work and we'll celebrate with a bottle of cheap champagne before they come to take you to jail.

She had to laugh, Okay, okay. Just get out now so I can get Jabbo to school and me to work.

Wait, he said at the door. You aint told me nothing, come on Cal gal, give me some dirt for when folks ask me why you did it.

It was the color, she said, fire fucking engine red. That was three years of my support payments sitting out in front of his nice comfortable house, no, his home, in fire fucking engine red. She laughed, Everytime I saw that car it set my alarms off.

And now? asked Tucept.

Now I feel great.

Gotta go with those feelings, said the grinning Tucept.

He hugged her, You too wild for me Cal gal. Babbaba-
booooommmmm!

Well you know how it is, she said, whistling Caldonia
Caldonia as she closed the door on him, A man gotta do
what a man gotta do.

HE FIRST SAW HER ON THE CROSSTOWN BUS. SHE AND
this lame got on and sat across from him. Tucept was
impressed. Their eyes caught and threw both of them
off, split second time stop. He watched her surreptitiously, trying not to stare openly. She was so vibrant,
practically glowing. Dressed in bright golds and yellows,
skin a sweet caramel smooth and a triangular face alive
and framed under an umbrella afro parted in the middle.
He always did like that hairstyle. Made him think
Wildwoman. As she spoke her body emphasized points,
a nod of her head here, a quick dramatic slash of her
hand there. She glanced at him repeatedly, her interest
apparent. Conscious of staring and trying not to show
the brother too much disrespect Tucept turned to look
out of the blued bus windows at the passing streets of
South Memphis. He saw her reflection and feeling her
eyes on him even in the glass, he stared at her reflection,
feeling the draw of her even there. His eyes kept easing
back to her in longer and longer intervals until he was
staring openly, practically drooling. She looked back
boldly, occasionally stopping her conversation. Excitement surged through him and his groin tingled tight. He
heard himself growling low in his throat. At his stop he
considered staying on. Maybe she would get off without
the dude. Cockblocking chump motherfucker. He shrugged
and got off, convinced that he would see her again,
and promising himself that when he did he would get
her.

*　　*　　*

DE MOJO BLUES

RAINING AND DRIZZLING, A WEEPY DELTA NIGHT. AN OLD blackwoman with still thick ginger hair sat on the covered porch of a small comfortable home on Riverside Drive. She sucked on an unlit pipe and shifted for comfort under a thick patchwork quilt that covered her lap and shoulders. A cup of herb tea warmed her large arthritic hands. The slight spray of rain that made its way under the deep roof of the porch felt good to her, the old quilt was thick and warm and the tea was strong. She watched the rain mist the trees across the expressway and remembered when she first came to South Memphis from Mississippi this whole area was woods. She looked at the house on the hill and quit rocking. There was a light on. She smiled enigmatically, a quick twitch of thick lips.

Momma, her daughter called from inside, it's raining.

I know that, she muttered to herself.

Her daughter came out onto the porch trailed by her grandson, both of them also gingerheaded. The oldwoman's daughter came out chipping her teeth. A big woman, 38 and already old, she wiped her hands on her dress and looked across the park.

Aint no house over there Momma, she said crossly.

Her mother didn't answer and again daughter chipped her teeth. A lot of folks in the South Memphis neighborhood that ran alongside the park said there was a house in the park, see, they would point it out to those, and there were many, who swore there was nothing there. See, those who saw would say, there, on top of the hill.

But, said the doubters, why can't it be found? Tell me that.

Some old folks, toes still clotted with Mississippi and Arkansas mud no matter how many years they had spent on Memphis asphalt, would just nod politely at the doubters and say, Meat for adults, milk for babes. The woman went to the edge of the porch and peered into the weeping evening. Sometimes on drizzly days like this one, she thought she might have seen a vague outline of what could be a house on the hill. Her eyes squinted into the rain before she shook her head at her foolishness. Old folks' tales.

Nobody lives in the park Momma, she said.

The oldlady stroked her daughter's thick hip. She was a good daughter, never made her feel unwanted or a burden, but a rigid woman, thick like bittersweet chocolate. The old spirits shied away from that sort. It's a wonder her son-in-law had sense enough to choose her.

De hoodoo man live in the park Momma, said the little boy who had come out on the porch with her, We seen him.

The kids of the neighborhood used the park for their playground. They had come out of the woods lately with stories of a redeyed bluegummed blackbearded black man who walked the woods with a big black tomcat. Those who swore they saw a house on the hill just nodded knowingly.

The old woman's daughter grabbed her son's arm with a thick hand.

Junior, the woman said through chipping teeth. I told you to stay out of that park.

I wasn't in it Momma, he said, I was just passing by it and I seen him Momma, I seen him, ask Jerry or Ishala, they seen him too.

He looked at his granma to back him up but she wasn't going to get into this one.

You see Ma, her daughter said anyway, You see what you done, those stories you always telling him got him full of that hoodoo shi—she caught herself and shook Junior by his shoulder—mess. Well she may not mind but you will young man. Inside you, out of this rain.

Junior darted inside and stood just on the other side of the screen door.

Thunder rumbled deep bitter base in the distance and the oldwoman muttered something around the pitted stem of her unlit pipe.

What did you say Momma?

The oldlady repeated herself, I said the old gods are angry.

I DON'T REMEMBER YOU FROM ANY BUS, LYNN TOLD HIM, lying naked beside him, her hand slowly caressing his sweated chest, The first I remember of you is the night I met you at Alunga's party.

Tucept hadn't been in the least surprised when he walked into Alunga's party that Saturday night and there she was, sitting against a wall talking to another brother with that same vibrancy that he remembered from the bus. His heart walked into his mouth and he told himself to relax. Be cool man, this one is mine.

He saw his man Daniel leaning up against a wall and eased over to stand beside him.

How you doing man?

Dan nodded. The party swiveled around them. A July sweatbox party. The dancefloor gyrated under a steady bass beat and summer funk. A pleased little grin sat on his face as he watched her from his wall. Finally he made his move.

Are you dancing? he asked her, his low voice carrying over the crowded buzz.

She looked him over, her eyes speculative. She nodded and got up. On the dancefloor they fall easily into the rhythm and heated play between them. A shifting gray tent of a blouse danced around her torso and his interest rose naked to his eyes. He danced up on her and put his lips to her ear, I knew I would see you again, he said, but I didn't think it would be this soon.

She laughed and twirled away from him. He followed her, stalking, his dancing hips rhythmically erotic.

After the record he thanked her with a fleeting touch to her shoulder and went back to the wall beside Dan.

I'm in love, he said.

Dan looked dubious.

Tucept watched her dance, pleased with himself, this woman was his. He finally pushed himself off the wall and went after her.

I swear the party was the first time, she said and laughed, a multicolored melodic scale playing with his ears. She got out of bed and stretched, muscles rippling sensuously under her taut skin.

And then you scared me, she went on, coming at me so strong like you did. Truly I didn't know what it was, I just felt so good. I said I wonder if it's this man that's got me feeling this good. I wondered if I just felt good because I wasn't with Boyd anymore, because that was the first night that I had gone out by myself since Boyd and I had been living together and I was just ready to party. So I came back and talked to you and I felt good and I said, it is this man, I'm going to look into this.

She kissed him and went to the shower. He watched her, admiring her body with a lazy satiation. He lit a joint, listened to the patter of her shower and savored a cool night breeze on his still sweating body. He felt good, real satisfied. Damned if he didn't like this one.

She came out of the shower and he watched her put on translucent bra and panties. A satin slip caressed its way down her body. He fucked her with his eyes and she felt the heat, preening with perceptible undulation as she fingered through her closet looking for today's wear, head held off to the side as she spoke of things fantastic and fabulous, truly they were.

I should have known you were a theater woman, he said, from the way you carry yourself.

Wait until you see me onstage, she said, I don't play

any creampuff women, I play only stone bitches. Women with character.

She went through silks and satins and soft pastels. He came to the closet and fingered one, a soft beige shift.

These pieces are definitely you.

From thrift shops most of them, she said, others from my mother and my aunt. See, she said, reaching into the closet and pulling out a bright gray silk flapper's dress with padded shoulders and countless tiny linked sequins.

They were truly grand, she said, holding the dress across her arms for him to see before carefully putting it back in the closet.

You kinda grand yourself.

Oh no, she protested, breathlessly serious, not like my mother.

As she spoke she absently stroked her breast. He walked over and cupped the small firm mound. Here, he said, let me do that for you.

He squeezed her breast rhythmically, gently hefting its weight and watching her eyes glaze. Her nipple hardened in his palm. His hand squeezed a low moan from her and he slowly slid her slip off. He unsnapped her bra and let the weight of her breast settle into his hand. When he slid into her it was slowly, she opening to his hardness inch by yielding sucking inch. Come on baby, he murmured in her ear, let me in. She growled in the back of her throat and her walls opened to him. They fucked like minks, a rollercoastered night bathed in sweat, moans and passion.

God that was good. Spreadeagled on the rumpled sheets, she laughed her approval, You know men have called me frigid.

Bullshit, he drawled, well-fucked and drowsy with satisfaction, stocky dark body etched naked on the white sheets.

I don't know what it is, she said, her hand clutching and stroking his dick as she talked. Petting it. Kissing it.

It must be because I'm comfortable, she said, because I'm relaxed. Before I thought something was wrong with getting hot.

He didn't care what got the credit as long as she liked the loving.

He stroked her, handling her, as if reassuring himself that she was his, that she was real.

Why hasn't somebody claimed you? she asked, purring under his touch.

He shrugged, Just luck, I guess.

You're a young man, she said approvingly, Young and flexible. That's good. Older men are so set in their ways.

I'm progressive macho, he said, pleased with himself and her approval.

Oh, she said, smiling an engagingly lopsided smile. Is that what you are? Boyd called himself a . . . what was that again? . . . a liberal chauvinist. I suppose all of you are coming up with these halfway definitions these days.

You didn't move very far, teased Tucept, from a liberal chauvinist to a progressive macho.

I've done worse, she said, my first man, Charles, was older than both of you and so set in his ways. At least you're progressive. She became reflective.

Charles was evil. That was when I was young, seventeen, back in the Sixties when I first went to school and got into my militant bag. That man used to talk about me so, I was too everything. I was too cold, too bougie, too yellow, you name it and I was too much of it. He was truly evil. He used to abuse me sexually in front of people.

Abuse her. Sexually? In front of people?

The thought sat there in his mind like it was just minding its own business.

Don't put me on any pedestals, she has told him repeatedly.

He's denied it.

Pedestals strip a woman of all strength and dignity, she's told him.

He's agreed.

Why did you let him do that to you? he asked her. Accusation more than question.

She looks at him, wounded prey, wide eyes searching him.

I don't want to talk about it.

Hours later she volunteered that she had met her father only once. He had come through Atlanta and she went to see him without her mother's permission or knowledge. She had been disappointed. The picture that her mother kept hidden in her bottom drawer was that of a handsome and dapper man. Not this slovenly rundown specimen in a coffeestained T-shirt and dull red eyes. This man who talked the visit into a rut with sob stories of how much he loved her mother and how much he wanted to be with her all these years. She felt nothing but contempt for him because her mother had never spoken of him ever.

When I was four years old, she said, my mother left my father and moved back to Atlanta. She never had another man as far as I know. I didn't know what a relationship was supposed to be like. It was a longtime before I was able to say, well, if this is what it's like then I don't want it.

Well he was glad she wanted him.

I love you, he would tell her just to see that small quirky smile it brought to her face.

I'm in love, he told anybody that would listen.

His momma looked her over judiciously and murmured, She's expensive.

His daddy laughed at him, Don't love her too much, he said.

Oh shoot, said his momma, expensive or not you love her as much as you want to, my momma used to say no fool no fun.

I must admit, said Dan, that the woman fit just right into the crook of your arm.

Her intensity fascinated and warmed him, filled in the gray shadowed areas of his life with bright sharp red, golds, blues and greens, with herbs and spices and wings that he had renounced in the name of discipline. His head is full of dreams of them growing old together, sharing life, good and bad. The summer was a good one, warm and vivid. It was as if he were in a different world, the same old buildings seemed to glow with life, neighbors smiled, the air breathed clean and fresh, his whole world tingled with satisfaction.

It started going bad, he determined when he looked back on it later, during the cooling days of autumn, redorange leaves still clinging feebly to the dead brown tree limbs.

They were supposed to go to this party the Beale Street Repertory Company was giving after the last performance of Levi's *Down on Beale*. She and a couple of others were in the box office and the money was funny. After the play they locked themselves in to get it straight and by the time they came out everybody was long gone, except for Tucept, sitting patiently in the lobby and counting up his progressive man points for being so understanding about her art, her career.

I didn't know you were out here waiting, she said, eyes full on him and, he realized with sudden discomfort, judging him. He had broken some rule.

You should have come in and told me you were out here, she said.

No problem, he said, I knew you were under the gun.

DE MOJO BLUES

She looked fullface at him for long minutes before turning away, Don't ever do that again, she said.

The rest of the night didn't go well at all. He was conscious of her occasional curious gaze. They had their first real fight that night, abrupt and unnecessary. Over nothing.

And he was getting no shows.

She'd say she was coming by and wouldn't show. He should have nipped that shit in the bud immediately, by the time he did complain it had become a habit.

It's because of your roaches, she told him, I'm not comfortable coming by your place because you've got roaches.

Roaches? He looked around. He didn't have roaches.

Realizing that she was drifting away he clutched all the harder.

Stop Tucept, she said peevishly as she removed his stroking hand from her collarbone, You do it all the time, it ruins the specialness of it.

Their summer love grew into an argumentative autumn, especially about his hoodoo studies.

Tucept, she said one brisk September evening, Why do you waste your time with all this mumbo jumbo?

A negligent wave swept his hoodoo paraphernalia, his altar, his fetishes, the chair he was sitting in.

For a moment he didn't answer. His studies had suffered this summer, he realized suddenly. He hadn't been doing his disciplines, his exercises, his reading. He'd been in love.

His answer was sullen, It's going to get me some sayso.

Some what? she questioned, head cocked off to the side.

Some sayso, he said, voice suddenly throbbing with restrained passion, Some people in this world have sayso, most don't. I want to be one of the people with sayso.

He hated being a bit player in this world, a little man without sayso, helplessly watching his people go down because they lacked understanding of the way of things.

Her incredulous expression said that she never knew he took it that seriously.

Oh Tucept, truly you don't really take all this hoodoo stuff that seriously do you.

I do, he said evenly. I am a hoodoo apprentice. He hesitated and then what the fuck, he told her his secret name.

XXX.

She laughed at him, Oh come on, she gurgled, you just can't be serious. Truly now.

He looked at her with hurt, icing eyes. I am, he said, I'm a serious man when I choose to be.

She looked at him, face cocked to the side in wonder as if just seeing him for the first time.

How, she asked, will this give you sayso?

He looked at her judiciously. She had laughed at him. He was no longer willing to expose himself.

It will give me power, he said cautiously.

Power? she said, Why do you need power? Why can't people just live and let live?

Tucept shrugged, It just aint that kind of world, you either have power or you get ate by the powerful.

But you don't even give people a chance.

She sounded like all the rest of blackfolks. Dealing in good faith. Suckers and slaves.

If you give them a chance they will cut your throat, he snarled with sudden anger. It's a cutthroat world baby, may the best predator survive. Expect no mercy and give none. My daddy say that locks are just to keep the honest folks honest, just slow a crook down.

You must be close to your father.

What, he said irritably, has that got to do with what we talking about?

You must be, she said, to have picked up so much of his cynicism.

He snorted cynically. He wished he was as cynical as his daddy. He was more sucker than mean. He took after his momma, supersensitive, feel for everybody, feelings get hurt in a minute.

If by cynicism you mean being for real, then cool, I'ma be for real. Blackmen can't afford to be no other way. We under the gun baby. You run this love thy neighbor bullshit on somebody that aint under the gun. When the whiteboys lay down their arms I'll lay down mine.

That attitude isn't going to help, she said, you should be working for a better world, not just being as big a dog as they are.

Give me a fucking break, he said angrily, It's that humanity shit that got blackfolks on the bottom now, everywhere in the fucking world. We look out for everybody's rights but ours.

Sudden rage made his voice vibrate resonant anger, Don't you understand that we been conquered!

WE BEEN CONQUERED!

He began to pace angrily, Am I the only one who understands this? Am I the only one who cares? We been conquered and enslaved by everybody, the Whites, the Arabs, the Latins, the Asians, goddammit everybody spits on the Blacks. In the four corners of the earth the Blacks are a conquered people. The despised of the earth! And you know why? It aint cause the whitefolks is dogs. They aint dogging us all over the world, it aint on them. It's on us. We just a punk people. We weak. We a weak bullshit people and we deserve to be slaves.

He calmed himself and looked at her earnestly, wanting her to understand him.

I'm a blackmind, he said, My work is holyground. What would you have me do, mouth rhetoric while my people die this slow eloquent death? History would laugh at me.

She laughed at him. You take yourself too seriously, she said, you have delusions of grandeur.

I do not have delusions of grandeur, he said evenly, I have a god complex. And I'm sick and tired of blackfolks crying about how rough life is. So it's dog eat dog, he shrugged, it's time we started dogging it.

Face cocked to the side and blanked out in wonder, she looked at him as if she'd never seen him before. Like he was something that had just peeped out from under a rock and whispered her name. The Antichrist. Without a word she grabbed her coat and got up. It was a moment before he realized she was leaving.

Well we do, he muttered at her back, we got to back up these whitefolks and everybody else on this fucking planet, make em rue the day they ever thought about fucking over the Blacks. They think we gon be their slaves forever. This is war. Total war. And if we don't understand the way of war then we better learn.

ᔓᔓᔓᔓ

THE JUNGLE WAS THICK WITH FOLIAGE, BIRD CALLS BLENDING into the deep quiet. Suddenly the birds were silent. The foliage rustled and Jethro appeared, ears quivering, birddog alert. The pointman. He glided down the narrow path, M16 across his hip. A few seconds later Tucept appeared at the same spot, buried under a rucksack piled high with equipment, a big M60 machine gun at the ready, belts of ammo crisscrossing his torso.

Tucept sweated like a fucking pig. He wiped streams of sweat from his face with the green towel around his neck and watched the jungle and the pointman's back, eyes scanning in ever widening concentric circles, probing the thick green underbrush for movement that didn't feel right, feeling for grass that waved when the wind didn't, for sticks that didn't lie right, vines stretched too taut.

He followed Jethro through the thick grasses and one by one the rest of the men on the patrol followed him.

Jethro turned a corner on the path and Tucept lost sight of him. Using the long barrel of the M60 to force his way through the thick underbrush he hurried until he had him in sight again. Whenever Jethro pulled point Tucept followed him closer than he was supposed to. If Jethro pulled an ambush Tucept wanted to be where he could get to him quick and with the muscle. Charley preferred to let the point walk on by and let the bulk of the unit walk into the killing zone. But if there was an ambush Jethro would pull it. They never got ambushed when Jethro was on point. Tucept fell back into place, absently stroking the warm barrel of the M60. He liked the pig, liked the firepower, liked the muscle.

Jethro stopped and crouched. Behind him the patrol ground to a jerky halt of falling dominoes. Tucept fought back an urge to melt into the brush on the side of the path. He edged up a couple of steps while at the same time shifting closer to the side of the path, his eyes scanning, his finger spasmodically clutching at the trigger of the M60.

Freeze frame. The sun beat down on him and he bared his teeth as the heat drilled at his forehead. He boiled. Sweat ran down his back in a spinal stream that pooled at his waist. He wanted to wipe at it with his towel but he couldn't spare the attention. The pig swung in a slow searching arc as he scanned the brooding jungle for movement.

Tucept didn't like the jungle. The wet ricepaddies, the little checkerboard fields, the mountains, the village compounds, okay. But the jungle was malevolent and foreboding, atavistic, a primal, jealous god. When Tucept moved through the jungle he did so quietly, his soul drawn into a tight unobtrusive ball.

Overhead a westbound jet cleaved the air. Arching his neck, Tucept half followed it. The Freedom Bird, taking some lucky motherfuckers back to the World. A thin silver sliver, a speck in the sun. Back to the World. Wonder what Ruby was doing? It was night back in the realworld. Daydreaming he realized and quickly snapped himself back to this still green world of his. No place to be daydreaming. Sometimes he had to remind himself that this was real, that he was really here, Vietnam, not home, not TV, not Hollywood, Vietfuckingnam. Sun beating on his forehead, flys buzzing him, the hot metal weight of the M60, Jethro's broad olivedrab back, this was his world. Sin Loi. Sorry about that shit GI.

He thought about his first kill, an ambush. He had discovered the Made by Mattel logo on the black plastic handguard of his brand new M16 while he waited, batting flies from his prone body. No shit. Mattel. Just like when he was a kid playing soldier. Then 7 little yellow men walked into the killing zone. Ignoring sweat running down his forehead into his squinting eyes, the sights of his virgin M16 tracked a thinfaced man who slapped at a bug and told the man behind him a joke. Tucept let the joketeller move out of the sights of his M16 and instead sighted the man who laughed. The man died laughing, dancing under the sudden hammer of their rifle fire. A joke by Mattel. Tucept shook the sour memory and concentrated on what he was doing. Daydreaming was a bad habit in a combat zone.

Ahead of him Jethro still crouched motionless. Squinting through sweat Tucept stared at his back. Chooiii man, you see something or don't you?

When he first came incountry he had been scared and amazed at everything he saw, at the people, at the country, at war and death. After awhile the fear and amazement wore off and left a flat carefulness, a decision made, he wasn't going to die in this sad motherfucking war. Jethro decrouched and moved out slowly. Tucept followed him, the long snout of the pig sniffing the jungle. He had been incountry about 4 months now. About 8 months to go. In 240 days and, he checked his watch, 8 hours, Tucept HighJohn was going to get on that fucking Freedom Bird and Tucept HighJohn was going home. Back to the World. Bet on it.

※※※※

NOTHING HE DID WORKED.

He hunted down the roach she had seen and killed it. He killed every roach in the park. Using a C mouthharp he Pied Pipered every roach in South Memphis into the Mississippi River. Still she didn't show up when she said she would.

He tried being blasé, and was appalled when it didn't seem to bother her.

The more he tried to pin her down the more she squirmed.

Finally he put on his cool, his rusty suit of dependable armor, and waited for the inevitable.

※※※※

SIX DUDES, TUCEPT, JETHRO, WELCH, WILLIE D, MIKE, and Prester John, cut around the firebase perimeter on their way to the EM club from their hootch, nicknamed The Ghetto because it was the only all black tent on the base.

Monsoon season soon, he could smell it coming. Tucept kept stopping to stare at the mountains, as always, enthralled by the sight. A thick fog sat on the mountain, fading the surrounding peaks out in shades of green.

Firebase Sin Loi's peak had been stripped by war and baked into a fine dust. The sides of the mountain were scattered with the refuse of war, big metal containers, empty ammo crates, rusted concertina wire, discarded equipment and the shredded remnants of shrubbery. Tents formed a circle punctuated by the long steel snouts of the black artillery pieces the base was set up to guard and support. The firebase itself was a circle of tents inside a thick perimeter built of concertina wire, bunkers and towers. Real photogenic.

It was dark by the time they got to the EM club. Inside the low wood building a long line of Blacks and Bloods stood leaning against one of the walls. The dapline. Jethro, Mike, Willie D, Welch and Prester John started with the first man on the line and dapped their way down, fists slapping the intricate Firebase Sin Loi version of the dap—two fist slaps, the backhand slap, the grasp, the thumb hook, handshake, wrist grip, and the handshake grasp. Thick brass Montagnard bracelets on their wrists clink to the beat.

Tucept walked on past.

A burly brother with a shaved head stood at the front of the line. He called out as Tucept passed by him, Yo brotherme, you gon walk past the dapline without dapping?

Naw man, said Tucept, I don't dap.

The brother frowned and pushed himself off the wall.

He okay, Jethro explained to the angry brother smoothly, He just don't dap, one of those funny dudes, been courtmartialed twice for disobeying the same order, one of those kinds of dudes. But he down, a real brother.

The brother nodded his cueball head reluctantly. A real brother huh, you couldn't prove it by him.

Willie D took a spot at the end of the line. The rest found a table and sat down. Mike went to the food window.

Tucept sat so that he didn't have to face the dapline.

Mike came to the table with an order of fries. Everybody dug in. When that order was gone Mike reached into the side pockets of his jungle fatigues and brought out another order, These, he said, are mine.

Rowdy GIs crowded the little round tables that packed the room. The EM club was it, entertainment, 3.2 beer and cute Vietnamese waitresses in cute shorts. Fun at Firebase Sin Loi, they made the most of it. On stage a loud Filipino band in tight blue jeans, loud striped shirts and dark glasses played an eclectic fare designed to please every enlisted man in the U.S. Army. Otis Redding, the Temptations, Tito Puente, the Stones, Arlo Guthrie, the Beatles, Johnny Cash, etc. Mike and Jethro went to stand on the dapline next to Willie D. Welch kept glancing at Tucept.

At 22 and on his second tour of Nam, Welch was the oldman of The Ghetto. He had a little apartment over in Soul Alley down in Saigon and he didn't stay on the base 2 weeks out of the month. Long, lean, and slick, New York New York and serious about the rituals of Black Vietnam.

Tucept had met Welch his first day incountry. It was Welch who had schooled him and Jethro to their dos and don'ts. Him and Jethro had come incountry at Cam Ranh Bay late evening. They had been issued TA-50 gear and told that orders would be issued in the morning. They followed the other open-mouthed, wide-eyed newbies around the post. Vietfuckingnam. Grizzled-looking GIs in faded grungy fatigues haunted Cam Ranh on leave or waiting to go home. They made fun of the newbies and scared them with horror stories of the bush. Tucept was surprised to find Vietnamese all over the post, tight little stringy people in colored pajama outfits.

Welch had walked up and grinned at them, What's

happening Brothermes? I'm Brother Welch, New York New York. Where you from in the World?

They looked at him blankly.

Where you from in the States?

Memphis, said Tucept.

Mississippi, said Jethro, Taproot Mississippi.

Welch nodded and shook their hands.

You the guys going up to Firebase Sin Loi, right? Sin Loi mean something like "sorry about that shit" in Vietnamese but when you stationed on Firebase Sin Loi you know it really means God's asshole. We'll catch a ride up tomorrow.

He had spent the day taking them around, schooling them.

Anything you want, he winked thick lashes, to make a war comfortable, U.S. dollars, mpc, piaster, reefer, dimes, PX cards, radios, liquor, you name it, you come to me and I will get it for you. Blood rates.

They ended up on the perimeter, Vietnam on the other side of barbed wire, guntowers, bunkers, searchlights and claymore mines. In the distance they heard for the first time the tiny little toy pops of a distant firefight.

Don't worry about it, said Welch, that's way off, what I'm telling you is what's important. This here is the dap, he said, taking their hands and running them step by step first through the elaborate moves of the intricate Sin Loi dap. Then the Namwide short dap.

Bloods here is blackinized, he said. Now you aint gon find this nowhere else in the world, not even New York New York. When you come up on a brother here you give him some dap and ask him where he from in the World. Blacks is Blacks. Blacks, Latinos and Third World is Bloods. Whites is Rabbits 'n Beasts.

They dapped around awkwardly.

When you see a brother at a distance you give him

power, pumping the fist twice in the air like so, said Welch as he pumped his clenched fist twice in the air. Or, he said, twice to the chest like so. Welch hit himself cross his chest twice with his fist.

Beyond the perimeter the little tiny pops of the firefight ebbed.

The point, my brothers, said Welch, is to do your time and get back to the world alive. You owe it to yourself. You gotta stay sharp cause you in a killing zone. Now the brothers here gon watch your back for you. You watch my back, I'll watch yours. That's the trick. You remember that and we will all make it back to the world and the fine foxes no problem. This been tried and true numba one. Bic? You owe it to yourself. Never never never let a brother go down.

Remembering that first day incountry Tucept watched the little Filipino band work out and avoided Welch's probing eyes. He didn't like being defensive about his shit, he knew he had a bad habit of seeing what everybody else was doing and being arbitrarily different. On the dapline Jethro, Willie D and Mike laughed over some joke with some brother they were dapping. Tucept found himself watching the brothers come in and go down the line dapping. Thirty or forty bloods against the wall.

He felt a surge of fraternal affection. He had always assumed that his life had been the norm for blackfolks, that blackfolks everywhere were more or less like him, had lived a life more or less like his. Since he'd been in the army his whole world had opened up. Not only were there blackfolks who had come up different but there were different kinds of whitefolks, and all kinds of other folks, different lands, different peoples, different worlds.

He looked again at the dapline. Fuck it, it was jive, he didn't have to do digital acrobatics to be Black. It had become a big show they put on for the white troops, seeing who could do the most elaborate, most showboat dap. He didn't have to dap to be a brother.

The band, little Filipino lead singer sounding just like a little Sam Cooke, played A Change Is Gonna Come. The bloods on the dapline cheered and gave power, fists hitting twice to the chest and raised to the roof.

$$\text{\textasciitilde}\text{\textasciitilde}\text{\textasciitilde}\text{\textasciitilde}$$

TUCEPT AND SPIJOKO WALKED UP BEALE TO MAIN STREET. The sun was high, the streets filled with shoppers in bright spring colors. The new MidAmerica Mall was open and Main Street was a carless walkway, people thronging the streets and sidewalks. Tucept watched a fine woman in a green jumpsuit. He hadn't seen Lynn in over two weeks.

Spijoko cleared his throat.

Tucept didn't respond.

Apprentice HighJohn.

Oh, he said, What? You said something?

Attention Mr. HighJohn, said Spijoko, today's lesson is coming.

He nodded his head at a thickset black man approaching them. The brother was unshaven with an unsteady gait and soiled clothes.

Tucept frowned. This dude was his lesson? What could he learn from this? He was about to question the statement when the man stumbled against Spijoko and turned on him redeyed angry, Watch where you going old fartfaced motherfucker.

Tucept started to jump bad, Say man . . .

In his head he heard Spijoko's amused objection, *Never wrestle in the mud with a pig, you just get dirty and the pig enjoys it.*

Excuse me brother, said Spijoko with a nod of polite

deference, I wasn't paying attention to where I was going.

The man tried unsuccessfully to find fault in word or tone.

Well be more careful in the future oldman. What you doing still hanging around taking up space anyway? Old motherfucker like you should have been dead.

He walked on past and into a corner liquor store.

Tucept looked sour.

Spijoko smiled, You wanted me to accept his challenge HighJohn? To fight and argue with him. Why? He is of no consequence to my game. If you wanna be a man of power you must learn the proper use of humility. To fight a factor is to shed power. To let him upset me is demeaning. He is only a factor and for the moment serves me best as a tool of instruction.

Spijoko looked at him expectantly and Tucept realized that he had missed something.

I missed something, he said.

Spiritwork Apprentice HighJohn, sighed Spijoko, Are you a spirit doctor or aint you? You did take a reading didn't you? I assume you were listening yesterday when I showed you the tech and asked you to practice it. I hope I aint wasting my time with you boy. Please Apprentice HighJohn, get in the habit of automatically taking a reading on anybody you meet. It will make your life and your chosen profession much easier.

Spijoko put his pipe in his mouth with a tight snap of his lips.

The man walked out of the liquor store and toward them stuffing a packaged bottle in his back pocket. Smarting from his chastisement and embarrassed at forgetting such a recently learned SOP, Tucept waited until the man was right up on him before shifting into his spirit vision, a sudden shifting of eye and mind that stripped the man of his fleshy envelope and bared his soul. Tucept's tech was clumsy and it was a moment before he clicked and the man's soul was exposed. Tucept almost gagged. He shifted out immediately, a foul taste in his mind.

Mr. HighJohn, it ill becomes a spirit doctor to be afraid of a sick spirit. A reading please. When you get the time, of course.

Tucept settled himself and shifted back into spiritvision. The man's soul was a garbage heap. Degraded, putrid, festering. Tucept felt like his mind was being fondled by a leper. He relaxed himself and resisted the urge to withdraw. The man's soul felt his perusal and stared back, malignant and challenging. Tucept declined battle.

Feed him, said Spijoko.

Who me?

Quickly Apprentice HighJohn, before the moment of opportunity passes.

Tucept cautiously reached out his will and touched the man, slowly tuning himself to the man's rhythm. He moved cautiously until he had an idea of what kind of treatment the soul needed. Once he grasped the man's soul he began to pour mojo, feeding the ailing soul in small regenerative doses, awakening him, planting a consciousness of self and a determination that life had to be more than this. He was a disgrace, to himself and his people. A small frown creased the man's face.

It went rather easy, thought Tucept. He felt Spijoko's approval.

They walked past the man now frowning uncertainly at the uncapped bottle in his hand.

Very well done, beamed Spijoko proudly, very well done, there's some promise in your feed tech, strong, steady, precise, real promise.

Tucept tried not to grin too hard.

Spijoko pointed at a line of kids, mostly young and black, waiting to see a movie at the ornate Malco The-

atre on the corner of Beale and Main. The movie line
there, he said, a reading please.

Tucept shifted into spiritvision with more confidence
and less power shed this time. Even though he was
braced and ready for it, the line of people become suddenly a line of spirits brought a surprised grunt from
him. So many different kinds, individuals and personali-
ties even, aint that something? He frowned, most all of
them ailed, lackluster, ill, tattered, some stunted and
stilted, cramped into low horizons. Some were half alert,
staring sluggishly back at him. Most were dead, totally
asleep. Tucept frowned, thoroughly shocked. Without
even realizing it he guessed he had always thought that
souls would be Disneyland sets, euphoric gardens with
bright butterflies, singing bluebirds and floating quarter-
notes.

Very few advanced spirits in this world, said Spijoko,
Just aint that kind of world. Be thankful most folks is
just cramped and not out-and-out sick. Spiritual eleva-
tion, now that take a special effort beyond most.

As Spijoko spoke Tucept stared at his weathered
face, tempted to view his soul and knowing that Spijoko
knew it, waiting for Tucept to make his move. Tucept
turned away.

Perhaps later, murmured Spijoko, Possibly these two
will be more instructive anyway.

He pointed at a classy-looking white couple in an
executive mode, a crisp blue pinstripe 3-piece and silky
designer's drapings, pampered and well groomed, obviously rolling in dough.

Tucept looked. More garbage. More sickness. More
pain.

Just so's you don't confuse money and position with
a well soul, said Spijoko with a short laugh. Let's walk a
bit. This way.

Tucept knew he was expected to stay on spiritvision.

Before he had walked a block he was demoralized. So many black spirits crippled and cramped if not out-and-out dead. Tucept began to hurt for them, his eyes full and trying to blink back the tears that threatened to fall from them. But the longer he walked the more he saw, the more he hurt. Finally he could stand it no longer.

We are a broken people, he whispered. Tears began to stream silently down his face. He wasn't really aware of them, like they belonged to somebody else's face.

Spijoko said nothing. He led Tucept off Main toward the river. Pain drove tears from his eyes. How far have we fallen as a people? How much further can we fall and still exist as a people?

It wasn't until they reached the rough cobblestones of the riverbank that Tucept's tears cried themselves out and Spijoko spoke.

As hoodoo, you are tribal shaman, the tribe's spirit is your responsibility, said Spijoko. We have suffered much during the long years of our defeat and enslavement, Spijoko stared across the darkness, As you can see there is much work to do.

But what can we do?

Well for the moment Apprentice HighJohn, I suggest you be a little more diligent with your exercises and disciplines. And practice your spiritwork regular boy, you should be able to read, feed, take or destroy a soul with a hoodoo glance.

Spijoko walked. Tucept sat on the river's cobble-stoned edge and the river washed away his pain.

CHAPTER 5

〰〰〰

TUCEPT STEPPED AROUND A SUSPICIOUS-LOOKING VINE without taking his eyes off Jethro's back. Letting the pig hang from his neckstrap, he wiped sweat from his brow with the green towel around his neck and cursed the sun, the fucking heat, the fucking war. Number ten fucking thou. Seemed like he had been on patrol forever. Couldn't have been that long HighJohn, you got 205 days left. Jethro stopped and crouched. Tucept was suddenly alert, radar flaring out. Still crouched, Jethro waved him up. A tunnel. They called up Kicks. Second Lieutenant Andrew Kicks, a big narrowfaced man, Kansas fed, fresh out of ROTC and OCS and eager to make captain. Any old war would do, might as well practice on the gooks he told them when he had been drinking and felt democratic. Army through and through. Airborne ranger. Liked nothing better than to engage Charley. A bodycount freak. Far as his troops, black and white, were concerned, the war was over. Mr. Nixon and Mr. Kissinger said so. The troops were being pulled out, the war was being Vietnamized and nobody wanted to be the last asshole to die in Vietnam. Kicks came up grinning and squatted over the tunnel lip, Get John up here, he said.

Prester John, one of the brothers from The Ghetto, worked his way up the line to them. He nodded at Jethro and Tucept and without a word he took off his shirt and handed it to Jethro. Muscles roping his wiry chest, he squatted at the lip of the tunnel and tied a thin rope around his waist. If he died in the ground he wanted to make sure somebody retrieved the body. Tucept picked up the end of it. Prester John snapped his flashlight on and wiggled on into the tunnel. Just like that.

Tucept let his breath out. He wouldn't think of going down a tunnel what with snakes and bugs and crawling wiggling things. Bare skin pressed against a clammy dampdirt wall. Just thinking about it prickled his back with goosebumps. He noticed Jethro was uneasy, scanning the jungle. Suddenly Jethro's M16 was up and blasting. AKs answered him. GIs screamed and went down.

Tucept, Jethro, Kicks and the radio man dropped into the underbrush near the tunnel and returned fire. The incoming was too heavy for them to do anything with. Kicks yelled that he was calling in an airstrike. He motioned the patrol to fall back and reached for the PRC-25's horn.

Airstrike, Tucept thought wildly, Prester John would be buried in the fucking ground. Even as he thought it Jethro put a round into the radio, exploding it in a spray of metal, wires and flashing sparks. Lt. Kicks jerked his hand back and turned on Jethro furiously, his M16 swinging around with him. Still on the ground, Tucept put the nose of the pig on him. Mike and Welch scrambled over the ground toward them.

Tucept only heard snatches of Jethro's yelled explanation under the *braabarraabappp* of the firefight.

Sorry Sarge . . . *brabpapppapbab* . . . didn't see . . . *rabbabappbap* . . . was aiming at somet . . . *barrraappp* . . . missed . . .

Kicks looked at him hard, face muscles working. Tucept's focus narrowed down to Jethro and Kicks, to the nose of the pig centered on Kicks's guts, to the faintest trigger finger twitch on Kicks's M16. The firefight raged around their little frozen tableau, an oasis in chaos, every moment sharp and clear to Tucept's wired-up senses.

Welch lowcrawled up beside him.

Got to get Prester John out of that fucking tunnel, he yelled.

Kicks held the 16 on Jethro for a furious moment before letting the barrel turn back to the battle.

Break it goddammit, he yelled, break the fucking thing. He let a barrage of M16 fire loose in the direction of the ambush.

Tucept pulled the M60 around and laid down a wall of firepower so fierce the barrel of the M60 overheated and burst open in his hands. They broke the ambush and the silences came. Reverberations of the firefight rang in Tucept's ears and clipped-up leaves still rained from the trees around him. He anxiously watched the tunnel lip, waiting for PJ to pop up. It was a minute before they felt it safe enough to check it out.

Tucept scrambled over to the tunnel, Come on sucker, what you doing down there? He took up the rope lying loose by the lip and started pulling on it. It wouldn't give. His heart caught in his mouth in the way it hadn't done since his early days incountry before he learned to wrap it in thick layers of callus.

Well pull it dammit, said Mike, tense and on edge, catching up the slack in the rope.

I am pulling motherfucker, grated Tucept.

The rope gave. Almost smiling Tucept pulled harder. The rope started giving on its own and he grinned stupidly.

Prester John popped out of the tunnel, his brown body covered with streaks of muddy sweat and the waist of his fatigues stained bloody. He took the knife from his waistband and drew broad bloody lines in the longgrasses next to the tunnel.

You alright John? asked Kicks

Prester John nodded, wiped himself with Tucept's towel and put his shirt on. Told what happened, he dapped Jethro murmuring softly, Good looking out.

Kicks looked at Jethro for a long moment, narrow sun-crinkled eyes narrowed, Okay Tree, back on point.

I'll take it, said Welch.

I said Tree.

Long pause. The jungle held its breath.

Tucept broke the silence, Jethro been on point most of the week, been on point all day.

And he's on now.

Jethro moved out.

Tucept gritted his teeth, braced the pig and followed him, close on his back.

Spread out HighJohn, yelled Kicks.

Tucept ignored him. Tucept rode the pointman's back.

*SS*SS*

AS USUAL MIKE CAME INTO THE OFFICE 30 MINUTES EARLY. He looked at his watch more out of habit than concern. Twenty minutes for a cup of milk, toast with butter and two apple jellys and he was at his desk working at 10 till. When he finished charting the options he was satisfied that there were no holes to fall into. He had them typed and went to McLafferty's office. Tiffany sat at her desk working on the office budget. He leaned over and indicated Mac's office with his head, What the weather like today Tif? he asked.

She smiled, swept long unruly black hair out of her eyes and gave him a thumbs up.

Good. He knocked and entered.

Green carnation in his lapel, McLafferty was on the phone when Mike walked in. He sat down across from the desk and waited. St. Patrick's Day. Mac was a big bear of an unreconstructed Irishman whose suits hung squarely from his clothesrack shoulders. The office never knew what kind of mood he would be in. Either way it was extreme, blue jokes or blue fury floating from his corner office to set the tone for the whole floor.

McLafferty got off the phone and looked at him mischieviously, How you doing Mike, what's French birth control?

Mike thought about it a moment, I don't remember.

A little guillotine for the balls.

He made a chopping motion and laughed aloud. Mike knew that outside the whole office was relaxing, Mac was in a good mood. Mike laughed with him. Gearson came in and was treated to the French riddle. Mike kept his smile on. Gearson was one of the ones who looked straight through him from his first day on. In the 2 years since they had said barely 10 words that weren't job related. Fine with Mike. One less ass to kiss. Mike liked him. They understood each other.

Mac got serious and Mike pulled out his papers. He made a good presentation, moving through and finishing crisply. In conclusion he suggested Alternative 3.

He passed the backup material across the desk and sat back while Mac and Gearson went through them, noting when and where McLafferty smiled, frowned or nodded his head in approval.

By the time he left the meeting he was tired, a full day at 11:30. Tiffany's cocked eyebrow got a thumbs up that he didn't really feel. In his office stacks of paper lay in apparently haphazard piles. He dug through a pile looking for some material he wanted to check.

Where are these motherfuckers, he muttered aloud.

From their desks outside his office, Vlyma Tiger and Snessa laughed.

Mike looked up, That loud huh?

More than loud, laughed Vlyma.

Tiffany peered into his office, Mr. McLafferty wants to know if you can have lunch with him and Mr. Samson at twelve.

Mike looked at all the paperwork he had to get out today. But Samson was Mac's boss's boss. Mac was just looking out for him. Working for McLafferty had been an invaluable experience, every day Mike learned new tricks of the trade. He liked the big Irishman. Ireland for the Irish.

Tiffany smiled at his expression, I'll tell him more than pleased, right?

Right.

Taking his suit coat from his rack he slipped into both it and his sociable personality. He took two quick puffs off his cigarette, put it out in the ashtray and went to the hallway to wait for Mac.

At it again Mike? asked Vlyma.

I'm always at it.

Mike left the office on time that evening, piles of papers undone on his desktop. He was picking up Jean after work and decided against taking anything home tonight. Tonight he would leave the office at the office. He easily picked her lean graceful figure out of the seething mob that erupted from the federal buildings at the end of the workday. She slid into the car with a flash of long brown thigh and kissed him, Mike, she said with a smile, how are you?

Don't ask, he muttered.

I won't, she said, thanks for warning me.

I feel like a drink, said Mike, pulling off into the stream of cars, Okay?

Same place as always?

No, I need a break from the Anglos.

Hard day at the office huh?

Not really.

His tone said it had been and that he didn't want to talk about it. She let it go.

At the bar he drank his first kir down almost immediately and ordered another while bitching that the first one wasn't sweet enough.

It has been a rough day hasn't it, she said, touching his arm.

Every day is a rough day.

Maybe it's time to move to another firm.

Quit Acme? he snorted into his kir and, draining it, ordered another. Baby if I got to work on Massa's plantation, I'm gon work at the best.

He drained the second drink as quickly as he had the first.

They got us by the balls baby.

Her plucked eyebrow raised.

Who us?

Blackmen, blackwomen, blackpeople. They got us by the balls.

Who they?

The whiteboys. Acme. Chase Manhattan. The IMF. My landlord. Crackers. The White House. They got us by the balls baby, by the black balls. Eenie meenie minie mo, catch a nigger by his toe, if he hollers let him go.

Mike, she sighed, no war stories today okay.

War stories? Who me? I got no complaints baby, no more than any other junior executive on the make. I'm just talking. Hell I'm Mac's fairhaired boy you know, being groomed for a nice supporting role in the ongoing saga of Western Civilization. All I have to do is constantly prove that I'm one of the gang. That my skin may be black, or yellow as the case may be, but inside I'm as white as ole Gearson here. The price of admission is my black heart on a platter.

With the imperial manner and tone of the British raj, he motioned the bartender over, Say there Gunga Din.

The brother came over frowning, Whatcha say man, you talking to me?

Water man, water, bellowed Mike, Water Gunga Din, damn you, your hide may be black but inside you're as yellow as I am.

Mike, Jean chastised him under her breath.

The bartender looked dubious but came back with a glass of water. He slapped it down to the bar as if to say, okay, that's it with this Gunga Din shit.

Mike didn't touch the water, his elation was gone and his face had soured. Aw hell, he said, I'm leaving. I'll drop you off if you want.

He slid out of the bench and threw some money down on the bar next to the water. She put an extra 5 down for the bartender and they left.

๑๑๑๑

SPEC 4 HIGHJOHN, YOU WERE THERE WHEN THE INCIDENT happened with Private First Class John and the tunnel.

Tucept nodded. He watched a Freedom Bird outside the window of the hot little courthouse. Tucept wondered if the GIs going home on the bird were watching out of the little porthole windows, sitting back in air-conditioned cushioned seats and crisp khakis, being served by roundeye hostesses talking about coffee, tea or me. Wonder if they were looking down at us fools still down here on the ground.

Lt. Lawrence nodded, stepped back and smoothed back the hairs on the top of his head. What happened? he asked.

We got ambushed and Kicks wanted to pull back.

You objected.

No I didn't.

Weren't there some unusual circumstances about this ambush?

Well, uh, Prester John was still in the tunnel. The lieutenant wanted to call air and arty on him while he was still in the tunnel, he would have been buried alive. But Jethro accidentally shot the radio.

Jethro accidentally shot the radio?

Yessir, it was an accident.

Pretty difficult to accidentally shoot a radio isn't it.

Not really, said Tucept, it's a pretty big target, Charley does it all the time. And you got this long antenna waving over your head you see, a damn good target, even by accident. And even then Kicks wasn't on the radio. Dubcheck was and he didn't get a scratch.

Then you are saying that there was at no time any threat to Lieutenant Kicks?

Yessir, or rather nosir, none at all.

$$\text{\textcurrency}\text{\textcurrency}\text{\textcurrency}\text{\textcurrency}$$

I WANT MY MULE!

Willie was raking the book when a bonethin brother with a hollowedout face, a scraggly goatee and a Big Red 1 patch on his raggedy fieldjacket started yelling at a caseworker.

I want my fucking money, he yelled, you owe me dammit and I want my money, I went to the fucking war, I want my money.

The bloods on the 2nd floor waiting room turned toward the commotion. 90 Myrtle was the New York

City Welfare and Social Services office for Vietnam veterans. Willie had been coming down here for two years now, every other week, playing cards regular with three cronies, Bailey, Roscoe and Jeremiah, while they waited to see a caseworker and sign for their biweekly welfare check. Veting it. As were the majority of the mostly black and Hispanic men in the waiting room, they were practically in uniform. Between the 4 of them they were dressed in 2 fieldjackets, 2 pair of jungle boots, 2 boonie hats, 1 fatigue hat, 2 shirts and Willie's army issue olivedrab underwear.

Willie threw a jack of spades to the table and leaned the chair back on its hindlegs to look over at the raging brother.

You owe me, gimme my forty fucking acres!

The room of vets yelled encouragement, Damn right blood, make em give up that mule too.

A couple of brothers in blue security uniforms walked into the room and over to the hollowfaced brother. They talked to him in low intense whispers.

He loudtalked them, Yessir boss, yessir, I'se gon be good, just want my acres, just want my mules.

Caseworkers peeped out from their cubicles. The brother walked around the room, forcing the guards to follow him. Suddenly snatching his shirt open to show a throbbing gouge carved out of his chest, he waved a Purple Heart medal over his head. I want my money, he yelled, I did my time, I paid my dues, you owe me.

The joking and the yells of encouragement dwindled and died as the bloods realized that the brother wasn't on top of it. All of them had put on the Vietvet Freakout Show once or twice to break that check loose. When the bills were due and the digit late. They had expected a good performance. But it was becoming obvious that the brother's demons had him. The room grew quiet. A Latino brother walked up to him, boonie hat sitting on the back of a huge fro. Come on bro, he said in liquid sibilant plea, The screws, they gon bust you bro.

Pacififuckincation!

The brother slapped at the wall, each pistol slap accenting the syllables of the long word, *pa ci fi fuck in ca tion,* that's all this shit is, keep the niggers happy, pacify their black ass, just like they tried to do the gooks. Pacififuckincation. Well gimme the fucking mule. Pacify me.

Willie half rose out of his seat to try to calm the brother down. Suddenly the guards grabbed the brother and hustled him to the stairs, his arm twisted behind his back, speechless with the suddenness of the move.

The room of vets surged after them. Willie was the first one through the door and down the stairs, coming out of the stairwell on the first floor just as the guards hustled the chestgouged brother into the guardroom.

Behind him, the crowd of vets boiled out of the stairwell and at the guardroom door in a river of anger. At the heavy door, Willie reached out to grab the doorknob and Bailey's foot slammed against his wrist. Willie jerked his throbbing wrist back and Bailey kicked the door. It held. He drew back for another kick when the door was suddenly flung open and a big burly brother in a blue uniform came rushing out, dark face flushed with anger, nightstick flailing and frothing motherfuckers.

Okay mothafuckas, he frothed, who kicked the mothafuckin door, huh, bad mothafuckas, kick this mothafuckas.

Willie threw up a elbow and caught the nightstick going for his head. He grabbed his suddenly numbed arm and fell back with the others, the momentum of their anger broken.

The other guards pulled the burly, still frothing guard back.

An older brother, Lt.'s bars heavy on his stooped

shoulders, came out of the guardroom and tried to calm things down.

What did yall do to the brother? Willie called out, What did you do to him?

Nothing, nothing, said the Lt. soothingly, already tired.

The crowd muttered angrily.

Open the door, he told the guard standing in front of it.

The guards opened the door. The brother sat in the middle of a bare concrete floor. Crying. The crowd behind Willie surged forward in a reflex action.

What did you do to him, why is he crying? cried out Willie, tears threatening his own eyes.

The Lt. looked hurt, We didn't do anything to him, he said, I swear, ask him. Ask him, he repeated, sad eyes asking them to understand that he was just another brother with a family, kids and a job to do.

Willie approached the man sitting on the floor as cautiously as he would have approached a bomb, You alright man?

The brother nodded that he was.

The other guards were working the crowd now, The brother is okay, they said, Now why don't all of you go on back upstairs, they'll be calling your names soon and if you miss your check you'll have to wait until tomorrow. Almost closing time, better go back upstairs now.

The crowd started dispersing. Willie, Roscoe, Jeremiah and Bailey were soon the only ones left, still begging the sadfaced Lt. to let the hollowfaced brother go.

He's cool man, he aint gon hurt nobody, see, said Willie, Can't you just let him go, he aint gon bother nobody, Willie looked over at him, Will you brother, you cool right?

What if he got family? said Bailey, a family man himself with a wife and two kids in a little apartment in Queens.

Bailey had the Lt.'s sleeve. The Lt. wanted to pull away but didn't.

He just came up here to get a check, said Bailey. And probably got to feed his family or something and if you send him to jail he got to go through that whole thing and it will be really fucked up.

Can't do anything, the Lt. said wearily, you have to speak to the arresting officer.

He pointed out the big burly guard, glaring both at them and at the brother sitting on the bare floor of the guardroom.

Willie, arm throbbing where the guard had hit it with the nightstick, wrist throbbing where he had been kicked, didn't want to say shit to the big motherfucker, but he looked again at the hollowfaced brother, shirt still open and the purple gouge on his black chest still throbbing. They begged the big burly motherfucker to please let the brother go.

Willie noticed a *Daily News* somebody had left. NYC patrolman Tornsey had been acquitted of blowing open the head of a 13-year-old black boy who had walked up to him and asked him a question in front of a multitude of witnesses. Temporary epilepsy.

By the time the police arrived at the center, he had a attitude. Nine of them. Alert, hands on guns, a disturbance at the Vietvet center could mean anything.

They continued to beg. The ranking police officer watched them with a bored, almost amused, expression. Willie looked at the faces of the other cops, irritability, resentment, boredom, amusement. They bothered him and he wondered why. Suddenly he saw himself in Nam. Keeping the natives in line. The same colonial arrogance the cops were using on them.

A curiously guilty anger went through him and focused itself on the soldier. He corrected himself, policeman. In Nam, they had been the soldiers. Caesar's legions in blackface. Colonial troops patrolling Vietnamese villages and Harlem streets, keeping the peace in the name of Western Civilization. Willie remembered the sense of power, the too easy growth of emotional callousness on soldiers who control a subject people and play god, arbiter of life and death. He remembered the time Tucept slapped the water buffalo and the Viet family that had backed up from them bowing and praying thanks like they had been gods.

The cops took the hollowfaced brother away, quiet now, scared, broken.

By the time Willie, Roscoe, Jeremiah and Bailey went back upstairs their names had been called and they had missed their checks. They would have to come back tomorrow. They picked up their papers and left. They walked slowly to the subway in a wind coming out of downtown Brooklyn and made sure that everybody had enough change to get back in the morning.

Roscoe said what they were all thinking.

When we were in the war we could've help that brother, he paused, somehow.

When I came back from the war, said Willie D, zipping up the liner of his fieldjacket and pulling his hood up against the hawk, the Freedom Bird that we came back on stopped in Hong Kong. The pilot said that six people had to be bumped so that a general and his family could go home. Now we had just spent a year in Nam. Everybody on that bird was scared shitless that he was about to get bumped off the fucking Freedom Bird so some shithead general could go home. Wasn't that many bloods on the plane but they bumped four bloods out of six. The rest of us didn't say shit, just glad it wasn't us. And we had just left Nam where we didn't let a brother go down for nothing.

Back to the World, said Roscoe bitterly.

Sin Loi, said Jeremiah.

At the subway they stopped and stalled before going into the ground. They had spent a lot of unnecessary time here at the center these last few years, Willie had enjoyed sitting around with all the brothers, feeling that sense of camaraderie and strength that he had felt in the Nam, talking that Vietvet talk, dressed in old leftover army issue and trading old leftover warstories, junkies skinpopping a memory. But they hadn't been able to help the brother. They hadn't had the heart or the muscle. It wasn't Nam, it was New York and it was 1975 already. He wouldn't be back at the center tomorrow, he was never coming back here if he could help it. They shook, almost a dap, and Willie went down into the dark maw of the subway.

TUCEPT AND LYNN WERE SITTING ON HIS TOP PORCH. ACROSS the river the sun went down in Arkansas.

Lynn sighed and turned to him, Tucept, she said, I've been wanting to speak to you about us.

He nodded from a mask of indifference. He'd expected this and had armored himself in cool.

I don't think, she said, that we should spend so much time together.

Tucept shrugged, Okay.

She was relieved that he was taking it so well, yet curious, a little disappointed.

I didn't know if your kind of chauvinism could take it.

Macho, he said testily, Not chauvinist, macho. Progressive macho.

He could see she was more amused than enlightened by the distinction.

And just what, he asked, does taking it entail?

Not much, she said, not any big changes, maybe not even in the time we spend together, basically just a change in attitude.

He wanted her. While she talked he wanted to let his flame lick her, to singe her nerve endings with his passion. He wanted to get next to her but all he'd been able to do was flutter around the edges. His flat face gave nothing.

I don't want to be anybody's woman, she said, somewhat uneasy at his apparent lack of response. I just got out of a stifling relationship with Boyd and I want to be myself. It's always been all or nothing with men for me and I've got to change that. And all the other old habits that don't serve me anymore. It's just too strong Tucept, I need some space. I want to see if I can do some things, be sufficient unto myself and sometimes things you do fuck with that. Truly. You understand?

Big smooth round thighs flashed from under her housecoat, begging to be stroked. But not by him. What could he say? He couldn't argue with such a smooth rap. He decided he didn't like her anyway. She obviously lacked taste. She spoke with a foolish drama that used to fascinate him. Pretentious bitch.

If that's the way it is, he said, shrugging, it's cool with me.

She laughed with relief and smiled that lopsided smile he hadn't seen in so long.

I didn't know, she said, if your kind of, uh, what kind of chauvinism was that again?

Macho, he said, jaws clenched tight and talking through his lips, Progressive macho.

I'ma be cool, he told Caldonia later the same night. Sensitive is no good when it comes to taking a punch.

They sat on the same steps, full moon a dull gold haze in the night sky. Tucept slumped dejectedly on the top step.

Caldonia was tickled, It wasn't that hard a punch, she said.

It was hard enough, he said, pouting like a little kid, I

was going to try to play you women for a bunch of punks but you force me to respect you, I'ma play you as hard as I play a man.

Bitter bitter bitter, said Caldonia.

He started to deny it and shrugged, Yall survived bitter, I will too. At least I didn't blow up her car.

Tell me this, said Caldonia, Did you enjoy it? Did she enrich your life? That's my criteria for everything, what does this do for my life. I seek the gold dear brother, I shall live every moment of my life to the max. And for a minute there, take my word for it, you had it, you were enjoying life.

He shrugged, unwilling to admit it, All I'm saying, he protested, is that I'ma be cool. What am I going to do Caldonia? I just love bad bitches. Bitches with balls. Or on wheels. Whatever. Those sharpedged women that be going somewhere. I just love them. Women with character. But if I wanna keep one I have to treat her with a certain passionate indifference. They won't take a hardman and can't stand a softone. There's a balance there that makes for mastery in the art of queens. And I'ma walk the line. From now on I'm the boss. I'm the king.

Oh bitter bitter bitter, Caldonia sang at him, I thought your hoodoo studies taught you better balance than that. What happened to Equanimity? Unassailability? Ultimate cool?

She was playing with him, running his own rhetoric back at him. No defense. He sulked and changed the subject.

How's business?

She and a friend had opened a shop down on Beale together.

She shrugged, Getting the hang of it.

Bright yellow headlights cut through the darkness and

raked the house. A car pulled up out front and honked its horn.

My date, said Caldonia, getting up and brushing her skirt wrinkles out.

So what did you do, about bitter I mean.

I am Caldonia.

And? he asked.

That's it.

She pecked his cheek and started down the stairs, Remember what Momma always say, no fool, no fun. She ran down the steps with the loud wild laugh that used to bother him so. He didn't know why, it sounded like fun.

Tucept stayed on the top of the stairs, listening to crickets singing chorus to wind whispered trees and wallowing in 2 o'clock in the morning blues. He put the collected works of Randy Crawford on the box and blues draped the night woods and the bright hole of a moon.

Overhead thick gray clouds slowly covered the full moon and the pearlgrayblack sky collaged with majestic dignity. It was so pretty. He stared, awed and pleased that he had seen and experienced such a thing. It would have been nice to have shared it with a woman though, to be able to point it out and say, wow, look at that. A memory to share in old age. The selfpity that he had been fighting all night stole over him. He watched it come, unable to resist its embrace.

He decided that he would go for a walk, he felt a blue mood coming on.

The black flathead tom loping alongside him, he went walking, hurting and fighting not to slide off into the pain, conscious of its allure, even pain is emotion, even pain would thrive in the small barren spaces in him crying out for emotional stimulation. If hurting is progressive fuck progressive. Vulnerability stinks. He was going back to cool.

He crossed the expressway and walked up Person Avenue. It was quiet and still this time of night, him and the black cat the only ones on the street. He walked at an even aimless pace, his stiff dejected figure rhythmically lit by streetlights pacing the darkness.

The houses on the street were quiet, the windows dark. Here and there the muted light of a lit window, little squares of domestic warmth. In one yard a tricycle lay on its side near the sidewalk. He righted it, moved it further into the yard.

He saw himself old and alone, a tired bitter oldman about whom no one really cared or knew well enough to know how to care. He cursed his softness, his need for love and affection and companionship, for someone to know and be known by. The Game demanded the slavery of emotion, if you can't rule your own needs, he told himself viciously, then he didn't need to play. Master yourself before you would master others.

He thought about how much he was into women. His need for love and companionship drove him more than any other. Hell he wouldn't get out of bed in the morning if it wasn't for the women. For all practical purposes he was a kid riding a bicycle with no hands and yelling at the little girls to look at me. Grow up HighJohn. I am a man. And by the gods I will be driven by other than the love of women. He could spend his time chasing women or getting his work done. Let the work chase the women. My heart is closed.

Spijoko was suddenly walking beside him, dressed warmly in thick wool pants and a worn tweed jacket, pipe going in short quick puffs. Tucept was in no mood for no philosophical bullshit, he didn't want to hear about extracting strength from the blues, or nothing. He just wanted to hurt, by himself.

Go away, he said.

Spijoko, as usual, was amused. One of his favorite and most effective modes. All this drama, he said, is really unbecoming a hoodooman, even an apprentice.

You don't know nothing, Tucept's voice was bitter, You don't know nothing about how I felt. I wanted her, he mumbled.

They walked in silence.

Spijoko cleared his throat, I am more than what you have seen of me HighJohn. Spijoko's voice was low and sincere in the darkness. I too am a man, I have lost, many times. He paused. I too have suffered HighJohn.

Tucept looked at him. Spijoko momentarily removed his mask and was open to Tucept. Tucept fingered the callused scars of an oldman's life.

I'm sorry, he mumbled.

Nothing, shrugged Spijoko, Your timing was off HighJohn, that's all. Patience.

He put his arm around the younger man's shoulder, A few more pithy words if I may, he said, and I will leave you to enjoy your drama. Youngmen seem to require occasional excess.

He removed his arm from Tucept's shoulder. Understand this if nothing else Apprentice HighJohn. It cost a man to bid for power. Always will. Don't do to cry when it come time to pay your debts. You wanna be a great hoodoo you gotta be a no-nature man.

Tucept shrugged, A study in cool. My eyes are open, he said, My heart is closed.

Spijoko almost laughed at the solemnity of his pronouncement, I wouldn't worry about that, he said, a young man's heart is notoriously easy to reopen.

On the corner of Swift and Person they waited for a car to pass. The flathead tom rubbed his arched back against Spijoko's leg.

But perhaps while it is closed, you can get a little

more work done, eh? Your studies have suffered some while you paid homage to your passions.

He went down Swift. Tucept and the flathead tom went down Person and disappeared into the leafy darkness of the woods. Back at his place he went to his desk and worked. Hungrily.

ഗ്ഗ

ON FIREBASE SIN LOI, THE LATRINE CONSISTED OF HOLES dug into the ground with wood stools placed over them. The accumulated shit and piss was burnt daily. Shitburning detail. Damn near punishment duty. Kicks had Tucept and Jethro burning shit Monday and again on Friday.

Jethro poured more kerosene in the last shithole and Tucept lit it. They stepped back quickly from the thick column of acrid smoke that rose into the air smelling of burnt shit and kerosene. Tucept frowned, nose wrinkling as the smoke thickened. He stepped back further, using a long pole to work the shit around so that it would burn right. That fucking Kicks, Jethro muttered foully through an olivedrab handkerchief on his face, Fucking lifer, fucking shit, fuck this, fuck it. Jethro threw his pole down and walked off angrily, I aint burning no more shit.

Tucept stopped stirring and looked at the blackened bubbling pool of burning shit and sniffed the foul smoke, his eyes watering from the stench.

I'm with you man, fuck it.

Leaving his pole sticking up in the smoking shithole, he trotted after Jethro until he caught up with him.

Fuck it man, Jethro muttered as they walked back to The Ghetto. I aint burning no more shit.

That was fine with Tucept, Me neither man.

Yeah man, fuck it and fuck Kicks, he gon have to

find somebody else to play with, I aint in the mood no more.

Fucking lifer, agreed Tucept, working himself into a righteous anger. Anything was better than burning shit.

They got to The Ghetto and stomped in still mad.

Whooee, choooii, gasped Welch as he tumbled off the side of the bed holding his nose, What is that?

Fuck you medin, said Jethro stripping off his shirt and fanning it at the hysterical Welch.

Death be kind, gurgled Prester John.

Tucept stripped off his fatigues, rolled them up in a ball and took them to the shower stall with him. Jethro walked around fanning his shirt at everybody in the place, including a new brother that Tucept hadn't seen before, heavyset brother, face bright and clean, dressed in shiny new fatigues without the look of ground-in grunge that the others had after half a year in the boonies.

After showering Tucept and Jethro both felt better. Human again. Kicks would burn em for walking off the shitburning detail but fuck him. Kicks had been leaning on them ever since he and Jethro threw down on each other. They always got the dangerous assignments like walking point and all the shit details, like burning shit. They had been putting up with his shit for a month now. Fuck him. Tucept was almost a 2-digit midget. One hundred ninety-eight days.

Back in the hootch Welch was running the new brother through his dos and don'ts. A big widefaced brother, Jackel, PFC, just transferred from Germany. The brother had all the latest jams from the States, Temptations, Gladys Knight, Isaac Hayes, everybody.

Welch was running him through the dap when Mike and Willie D walked in grinning.

Guess who just got transferred? said Willie D.

They frowned but Mike and Willie D were grinning.

Transferred? Welch echoed hollowly, Transferred where? Who?

The orderly room, Mike, chortled Willie D.

Alright!

Git down!

Number one!

Choooiii!

The canvas walls of The Ghetto practically vibrated with their shouts and congratulations.

They just told me, said Mike, sitting on his bunk and crossing his legs cockily, I start day after tomorrow. My MOS is clerk, he shrugged. When I got here they stuck me in the boonies, but my MOS is clerk.

Jethro reached under his cot, This call for my personal stock, he said, bringing out a plastic jug of the watermelon wine he brewed from little scrub melons he brought from mamasan. Not really ripe yet, he said, tearing off the tape he used to seal the cork, But what the hell. He filled everybody's canteen cup and proposed a toast, To Mike, lucky son of a bitch got transferred out of the fields to the big house with his balls intact. May he make a damned good house nigger.

They toasted, cheered and drank. A clerk slot was too sweet, automatic promotion to spec 4, work in the office with an overhead fan and a personal one, clean fatigues, a radio, a nine-to-five and no more boonies, no more pungi sticks, no jungle rot and no whining bullets, no more guard duty. Mike had it good. They were all jealous as hell but if somebody had to get it, it might as well be Mike. Even the new brother was caught up in their enthusiasm.

They broke out herb and Willie D and Welch popped a couple of dimes. The canteen cups were filled and toasted until both the jugs were empty. Then, thoroughly drunk, they stumbled through the evening to the EM club.

DE QUEST

At the EM club Tucept hesitated at the door, the cueball headed brother was at the front of the dapline. His look questioned. Tucept walked on past him and to a table. Everybody else went down the dapline, even Jackel, who, Tucept noted, dapped right smooth for somebody who just came incountry. He felt selfconscious sitting at the table by himself while everybody else was dapping and went to the food window to order a hamburger and fries. By the time he got back to the table the rest of the fellas were there. Willie D stayed on the dapline.

Another Filipino band was playing. They hadn't been there long when Red, a down, potsmoking white dude from their company, came into the club and waved at them. Prester John started to invite him over and Jethro snatched his hand down to the table.

What you do that for man?

Don't want him over here, said Jethro.

Red's alright, said Welch, he's cool.

I didn't say he wasn't cool, said Jethro, I just said I don't want him over here. I know he's cool, I like Red too, but I don't have to socialize with him do I? Yall folks up north have been living up on these whitefolks so long yall done forgot what's real and what aint. Down home in the Delta we got a understanding with our whitefolks. We'll work with em, we'll cut a deal with em, we'll shuffle and grin in they face if we have to . . . His face and tone soured . . . But we aint friends with em.

He snorted his contempt for the idea, looked around the table like he wanted somebody to challenge him on it and sat back muttering, They got to be taught a lot more respect first. Till then it's war.

Will somebody tell this Arkansas farmer that this is the twentieth century? said Prester John, laughing easily, urbane and cosmopolitan, a jaded Californian and proud of it.

That might be so, said Jethro, but war is war. We know that down on the Delta, aint that right Tennessee?

Tucept grunted noncommittally.

Yall the ones behind, said Jethro, not me. Yall ever hear the old Delta story about the brother got captured by a bunch of crackers down in Mississippi. They dug a pit, right, and buried the brother up to his neck, then they sicced these three bulldogs on him. First bulldog charged, snarling and growling. The brother weaved and ducked his head so fierce that the bulldog missed him. The second bulldog charged and it missed. As the third bulldog was going by the brother grabbed the bulldog's hind leg in his teeth and held on to it. One of the crackers ran over, kicked the brother in his head and said, Fight fair nigger.

They laughed. Sort of.

Jethro got up and walked over to the dapline to stand beside Willie D.

He left a silence behind him but it didn't last long, they were already drunk. They drank more 3.2 beer and told the new brother horror stories about the bush. On stage the Filipino band started La Bamba'ing. A bottle flew from the audience to smash against the wall behind them. The band stopped. A drunken Western drawl yelled that it didn't want to hear that shit, it wanted to hear some real music. Real quick the Hispanics were up and yelling. La Bamba! La Bamba! A pushing swirl began around the stage and the fight was on. Big Keone, biggest Hawaiian bastard you ever saw, started throwing folks across the room. The dapline erupted off the wall and Tucept waded into the fight, grappling with a big white dude from the table next to them. Oblivious to the yelling chaos around them, they strived mightily and unsuccessfully to throw each other, fatigue jackets bunched up around their shoulders. *Threeewwwthrewwww*. The MPs. Everybody broke. Tucept and the big dude looked at each other, let go and backed up until convinced of the other's sincere change of heart. The fellas from The Ghetto whipped through the kitchen and out the back door, through the mud out back and across the field to safety. Behind them they heard MP jeeps screeching up, whistles going. Once out of range they stopped and looked back at all the commotion, laughing and clowning, still wired up.

Anybody see the new guy? said Jethro, fingering a bruised jaw.

Jackel? I didn't see him once the fight started.

I told him to follow us. But you know how it is after your first firefight. You be shook up.

They cracked up.

They gonna close down the EM club again, said Prester John nursing a swollen lip, hey that Keone is a one big crazy motherfucker. Beaucoup dinkidou. I'm glad we on the same side.

They laughed and dapped and found their way back to The Ghetto, where they convinced Jethro to pull out another jug of watermelon wine. They sat on top of the sandbagged bunker and watched helicopters fire tracer rounds into the jungle outside the perimeter, smoking, drinking and tripping off thin fiery tracers streaking real pretty cross the night sky.

A RICEPADDY. ON THE OTHER SIDE SAT A VIETNAMESE village. Jethro stopped to check it before crossing the paddy. Tucept wiped his neck with his towel. One hundred eighty days, he marked off the day on his mental calendar. Halfway, be on the downstroke tomorrow. It had been a long day and a long patrol and he would be glad when they stood down for the night. They must have humped every mountain in Vietnam. Today. He shifted the rucksack on his back to distribute the weight better and wondered how far Kicks intended on pushing them.

Jethro eased into the muddy water of the ricepaddy, a shallow lake patchworked with tall strands of rice and crisscrossed with mud dikes. Behind him Tucept worked his way to the grassy bank and stopped, nose and ears twitching like a dog.

Wading cautiously and head weaving, Jethro was about a quarter of the way across when Tucept stepped in. He frowned as he felt the clammy water work its way into his boots, his pants. He held the pig up, keeping one eye out for Charley and the other one out for snakes. One by one the rest of the patrol eased into the water behind him.

Ahead of him Jethro suddenly stopped. He turned and started wading back, casually, real cool, as if he just wanted to speak to Tucept for a minute.

Tucept's world stopped. The sun in the sky, the stagnant water, all froze into immobility, his sense of being so enhanced that he was suddenly aware of thousands of tiny little bugs that filled the air around him and he wondered how he could breath without choking. Jethro waded up to him.

Ambush he saw by Jethro's expression, his attempt to look casual. Risking a quick glance behind him, he saw that the rest of the patrol had stopped too. The 8 guys in the paddy were already backing up, the rest were still on the bank. Tucept stood there in the middle of the fucking paddy, if he turned around the ambush would be sprung and he wanted to let Jethro get as close to the bank as possible.

What's up man? Tucept asked when Jethro got close enough on him, still moving slow and steady.

It aint right homeboy, said Jethro, I don't see it but I don't like it. Work back easylike.

DE QUEST

Tucept and Jethro backed up easylike. No good.

Raaatttaaaatttaatttaoooooowwww. The sky opened and AKs rained chances, here, you, you and you, you die—you and you, you live. The breaks. *Raaatttaaaatttaatttaoooooowwww*. Tucept and Jethro started boogying it, splashing water and mud as they tore back through the paddy to the bank. Jethro John Wayned it, firing his M16 under his arm as he ran. Tucept just ran, trying to get out of the fucking water with the heavy fucking pig weighing him fucking down. Bullets whipped past him, slapping little geysers of water around his pumping legs, tugging at his fatigues. He almost tripped over a dead man, pukepink brains leaking into the muddy brown water, and knocked the body aside as he barreled past, wondering as he did how did death feel, was it a blinding hurt, an explosion or was it just poof, Dead? Shiiiiitttt! He grabbed his boonie hat with one hand and clutching the pig to his chest with the other he ducked down low to the water and ran like hell. Boy so low to the water look like he swimming, yelling and dodging forever until finally, oh god finally, he made the bank, threw himself into the brush and commence to crawling. He and Jethro scrambled away from the paddy and lay in the grass catching their breath. He heard Jethro laughing. Laughing he thinks, what's so fucking funny, even as he started laughing himself.

Jethro showed him his sleeve, a tear spurting dark red blood. I'm wounded, laughed Jethro, lying on his back, holding up his arm and looking at it happily, I'm wounded Tennessee, got my black ass a ticket to Japan. Back to the World.

Tucept turned the pig across the ricepaddy. Jethro just lay there laughing about his wound. Kicks called in artillery on the village. Incoming rounds ripped through the sky and took names, a furious laserlight show. The firing stopped. They called off the artillery and called in

159

the medevacs. Bodycount 1–0, the home team. Two wounded, 1 not seriously, dammit. A medic slapped a bandage on the flesh wound of a sullen Jethro and Tucept laughed at his attitude.

They skirted the ruins of the village the artillery had converted into steaming moaning rubble. The unit was pissed. Having lost a man to an unseen enemy, again, they were spoiling for a real fight. To put some points on the board for the visiting team. They walked past the village slowly, looking for something to fuck with.

Jethro crouched, Tucept followed suit, the snout of the pig arcing. Jethro came out of his crouch. A family of Vietnamese came into sight, Jethro's ambush. The pig relaxed, hanging limp in Tucept's hand. Two old men, three women and a little boy walked behind a big gauntribbed water buffalo loaded with bundles. Heads carefully down, they filed slowly past the watching American soldiers.

La dai, called Kicks, La dai.

The Vietnamese stopped and stood trembling with fear.

La dai, Kicks called again

They stood rooted to the spot. The Americans walked over and surrounded them. Menacing.

One of the oldmen started jabbering, U.S. number one, VC number ten thou . . .

The American faces were hard, tension gathered, a war crime waiting on a catalyst. Suddenly one of the oldmen looked up and into Tucept's eyes.

Tucept blinked and stepped back, M60 coming up in reflex before he caught himself. A look both plea and accusation. Tucept stared back angrily but the oldman, a veteran survivor, dropped his head, eclipsing it with the gold brim of his conical straw hat.

Tucept replaced his own survivor's mask, a 19-year-old grown old too soon. But the oldman had already gotten through, had looked into the eyes of a grandson of slaves and asked *why?*

Angrily Tucept slapped the rough hide of the gaunt water buffalo. The animal protested with a hollow grunt and started off jerkily. The Viets waited to see if the Americans objected and shaking their heads as if in prayers of thanksgiving to benevolent but capricious gods they backed off. Finally they turned and followed the water buffalo. The Americans watched them go with cold eyes. Jethro moved out. Tucept braced the pig and followed him. He turned before they were out of sight and saw the oldman look over his shoulder at him.

Dink motherfucker.

MORTAR ATTACK. INCOMING ROUNDS SCREAMED IN AND gouged plugs from the earth and flesh of Firebase Sin Loi. The post siren banshee wailed. The seven of them broke wildly from The Ghetto, dived into the long sand-bagged bunker sitting outside their tent and clustered together near the dark center. At the two open ends of the long bunker fiery chaos danced. A rain of incoming rounds threw violent clumps of earth into the air and sliced them with metal shards. The bunker shook with thundering impacts of earth and war. The siren's wail peaked and ebbed, cutting through the incoming rage. The firebase's artillery went off in soundwaves of fury and the earth thundered and moaned.

Tucept sat against the sandbagged wall in the middle of the bunker, head tucked deep into the neck of his jungle fatigues and the green towel around his neck. His head jerked up every time an incoming mortar round shook the bunker, raining sand on him and the rest of the bloods crouched in its belly. A scared rat leaped from nowhere to his neck, its hard little feet beating a tiny tattoo pattern across his shoulder down his chest and leg. It was gone before he realized what it was.

I don't want to die!

I don't want to die! screamed Prester John as he scrambled for the door.

Willie D grabbed him, they tussled.

I'm not going to die here! screamed Prester John, his body lashing out at Willie D with all its wiry strength, I can't wait to die in this hole, I don't wanna die.

Shocked, the other brothers just watched Willie D wrestle with the frantic Prester John, veins and muscles etching his skin as he strained to get out of the bunker into the death outside. Suddenly he broke free and they sprang into motion, throwing themselves on him. All seven of them tussled wildly in the dark bunker, Prester John sobbing.

I don't want to die.

I don't want to die.

His panic was contagious and fear ran through the tight little space and tussling men like an electric current. Their voices worked him over with a desperately soft passion, Come on man please, gon be cool medin, relax man, aint no tunnel PJ, just a bunker, we here with you man.

Prester John thrashed immobile under them.

I don't want to die.

I don't want to die.

THE OVERHEAD FAN *WHOPP*ED *WHOPP*ED SLOWLY THROUGH the incense and smoke-filled air. Tucept passed the opium bowl and lay back on a gaudy satin throw pillow, one of many strewn about the little room. Outside the wood-framed window of Welch's little apartment, Saigon's sun was going down and the brothers who had made the street called Soul Alley theirs came out for the night. Welch, Willie D, Tucept, and Jethro had been there most of the weekend. They had to be back on the base by tomorrow morning so this was their last blast before checking back in. Tucept had been barhopping all last night and still felt like he was on a dingy little cloud.

Welch's babysan brought more herb from the backroom and left it on a low table. Oop. Cambodian woman. Looked just like a sister. She claimed she was one and they took her word for it. Sleek as she wanted to be, wore a Western jean skirt under her blue silk ao dai top. They watched her enviously as she went out of the room. Willie D emptied the waterbowl and filled it with more herb, laced it liberally with opium. He started the reel-to-reel Coltrane tape over and the music came muted from hidden speakers.

Welch and a little Vietnamese man came from the back. Welch started to introduce him but the little man held up a restraining finger. Welch nodded and saw him to the door.

When Welch returned, he brought out a bottle of Remy.

A toast fellows, he said, to a very lucrative evening. I just closed a deal that's going to put me on the big board.

He was pouring when they heard the whistles and the shouts, *MPs on the Alley.*

Welch was on his way to the window when the door burst in and MPs flooded the room. They just barely had their wits about them. Busted, was all Tucept could think, pipe in hand, fucking busted. The MPs lined them up and went straight to the space behind Oop's Buddhist altar where Welch kept his stash of PX cards and black market records. Welch's eyes narrowed suspiciously as the MPs gathered his goods before handcuffing and marching them off. Welch told Oop he would be back, not to worry. Outside Blacks were pouring out of the bars and rooms around them. Eight jeeploads of MPs menaced them with M16s and jeepmounted M6os. When the MPs came to Soul Alley they came in force.

Take it easy bloods, aint no big thing, said Welch to the milling brothers, most of whom were AWOLS anyway and shouldn't be nowhere near an MP.

They hustled them into 2 jeeps, took them down Highway 1 to Long Binh and stuck them in Long Binh Jail until somebody from Sin Loi could come to get them. Willie D refused to go in a cell and was taken away. A man in the cell with Tucept said the MPs were going to put him in a conex. He'll be a model prisoner tomorrow.

The next morning Tucept was called out of the cell. The fellas looked at him quizzically. His shrug said he didn't know nothing from nothing. The guards took him to the adminstration room where two spec 4s waited with the officer of the day.

The Lt. pointed at the two spec 4s, young, boyish, longhaired dudes.

You go with them HighJohn, they want to ask you some questions.

They looked curiously similiar, both had the clean-scrubbed starched look the army likes, open, boyish, All-American faces. Greek lettermen of his State University days.

He nodded and they nodded in return. He followed them outside and got in the back of their jeep, checking the dusty bumper insignia before climbing in. 525 Military Intelligence.

Tucept frowned. What would Military Intelligence want with him? They had been AWOL sure, he had done a few black market money transactions but that would be CID. Not Military Intelligence. Why just him? He wondered what the fellas thought about him being singled out. The way they had gone straight for Welch's stash made it look like somebody had put the mouth on them.

The driver turned around and offered his hand, James, he said, pleased to meet you. This is Charles.

Tucept shook.

Tucept decided not to panic until he had a better idea of what was going on. He put his questions out of his mind. When they asked theirs, he would ask his. On the way out of LBJ he saw two MPs putting a black soldier in a big green metal container used for hauling heavy machinery. And, he thought sourly, taming unruly Negroes. Sitting out under the Viet sun made the green metal glimmer with little heat waves rising from it. Tiny little holes were cut for air. He frowned, his head swiveling as they drove past. Willie D had to be burning up in there. Motherfuckers.

They drove through Long Binh quickly, past whitewashed blocklong prison walls topped with glass and barbed wire and stenciled with periodic signs: Do Not Walk On This Side Of Street.

They pulled up in front of a hootch on the other side of the base, a little sign out in front: 525 MID.

Inside the place looked like a stateside office, divided into rooms and with a water fountain even. In one of the rooms the two spec 4s sat, one behind the desk, the other on a corner of it. Books lined the wall behind them.

Ice tea? asked James, too-long and unarmy hair falling off to the side of his forehead.

Tucept shook his head.

Maybe some juice? said Charles, We don't have anything stronger.

At least we aren't allowed to give it out, said James.

They exchanged conspiratorial smiles with Tucept.

They talked about the weather, about the firebase, being in the army, in Vietnam, how long did he have left to do? James did most of the talking, Charles adding a point of clarification or question now and then.

Charles acted as if he didn't like him, barking his questions and scowling, and Tucept wondered if he was getting the classic goodguy/badguy routine. Suspicion closed down on him like a shade.

While they talked, he scanned the room for clues to the game. The books on the shelves were contemporary, politics and liberal arts dominating, quite a few black consciousness books. Tucept drooled, he hadn't seen such an extensive collection of books since he got to Nam.

I hope you don't mind man, said James, but we have to ask you some questions.

I don't mind, Tucept said unconvincingly, What's this all about though?

Nothing much, just routine security checks.

What do you think of the war? James asked him casually.

Tucept shrugged. Not very much.

He smiled and got nothing in return. He tried to keep his face open and relaxed, but his eyes squinted on him. Somewhere somebody obviously had him on file. But why, his little light '60s stuff? The dean's office, sit-ins, marches, the picket-lines his mother took him and Caldonia on as children, voter registration in Mississippi.

They waited for him to continue.

Tucept shrugged mentally and ran a song and dance of what he figured they wanted to hear, the war was not a fun one, if we here and dying then we should at least be trying to win, we ought to leave or play to win, he's ready to leave, immediately, mom, apple pie, integration, nonviolence, blacks and whites all Americans all together. And so forth along that line. A soothing string of rhetoric that indicated that he had not one original thought in his head.

What do you think of Malcolm X, black power, the Panthers?

He decided to take a stand of sorts. What can they do, send me to Vietnam?

DE QUEST

Blackfolks got a right to live, he said evenly.

This led to a spirited conversation on civil rights and black power. They were surprisingly knowledgeable.

Oh, said Charles, by the way, you know anything about a black deserter up north called the Candy Marine?

The brother who worked with the Cong? Tucept had always figured the Candy Marine was more myth than reality. Not that he had anything against myth.

Tucept shook his head, No more than anybody else.

Back in the jeep on the way back to LBJ, Tucept's mind was full of unanswered questions. He wished he had a more facile tongue that could've questioned them as they questioned him.

The wind tossed Charles and James's too-long hair. No sense in him being upset with them, they hadn't really done anything to him. Wonder what they would say in their reports. Had he cooled them out? Why was he on file? He shrugged and put it out of his mind. What can they do to me, he thought again, send me to Vietnam?

Tucept laughed.

What? yelled James from the driver's seat.

I didn't say anything, Tucept yelled into the wind.

What? yelled James.

I said, yelled Tucept, leaning up into James's ear, What can they do to me, send me to Vietnam?

James turned around to look at him. Just the hint of a smile crossed his face.

He was alright, thought Tucept. Tucept would have liked him, both of them. Under different circumstances. A '60s marching cadence slid through his head.

Before I'll be a slave I'll be buried in my grave
There will be no more whitefolks over me

They could never really be cool. In the front seat, James turned back around. Mine enemy.

〽〽〽〽

Tucept was hunched over the keyboard, eyes glued
to the screen of his computer when he heard a car
pull up outside. He stretched and went to the window.
His father's blueblack caddy. Dr. HighJohn got out and
stood in the road, looking up at the old house. He took
off his hat and wiped the sleeve of his jacket across his
broad forehead before starting up the steps.

What's up, Tucept wondered as he turned the system
down and went to the door. His father had never been
by the house. Questions on his face, he was at the top of
the stairs when Dr. HighJohn got there. Hey Dad, what's
up, anything wrong?

Just these steps, gasped Dr. HighJohn. Tucept held
the door open and he came in, How many of those
mollydodgers are there?

They shook, Dr. HighJohn touching his son on his
shoulder, Your mother told me about those stairs but I
didn't know that there were that many.

He sat in Tucept's chair, idly running his big blunt
hands down the armrest. He looked over the cramped
front room.

Kinda incoherent huh? said Tucept selfconsciously.

Probably, said Dr. HighJohn noncommittally.

You want something to drink? I got some nice herb
tea. Personal blend.

His father shook his head, I prefer Tetley or something.

They talked for awhile, the woods, the house, school,
bridge, business, the weather.

How have your studies been coming?

Tucept didn't know which studies he was talking about.

Ah, hoodoo? said Dr. HighJohn.

Fine, said Tucept, pleasantly surprised. He didn't know
that his father took his shit too seriously. He thought of

himself as a doctor too, following in the oldman's footsteps.

Pleased with his interest, Tucept told him all about his latest spiritwork, and about his mythwork. Mythwork excited him, I've been learning how to seed myths these days Daddy, they're a real delicate conjuration but they carry big power. Big mojo. My instructor says that I've got the knack, that I'll make a classic Delta mythmaker.

They talked about the family, everybody was fine. After awhile it became apparent to Tucept that his father was working his way around to something.

The sun had moved in the sky and the shadows from one side of the room to the other when Dr. HighJohn cleared his throat.

Uh Tucept, he said, uh, well, I've always thought that a pampered child is one that will be weak in the world. So I've always believe in laissez-faire with children, with you and Caldonia.

He paused and looked away. Tucept had never seen his father tonguetied before. Almost frightening.

And, Dr. HighJohn continued, I think sometimes that maybe I was a little too distant when you and Caldonia were growing up.

Tucept kept his face flat and noncommittal but conflicting emotions charged through him. His father's distance had hurt him as a child. They had never spent time together when Tucept was growing up, never went fishing or to ballgames or even PTA, never talked or did things like other folks did with their fathers. A lot of things that Tucept had to pay big to learn he always figured his father could have helped him with. But Daddy was always working. The only time Tucept existed was when he fucked up and the holy terror was unleashed on him. Dr. HighJohn had treated his kids with the same dictatorial brevity he practiced with his patients. Lifebringer. Deathdefier. He was used to playing god. A vague resentment surfaced in Tucept as he listened blankfaced to his father's hesitant, embarrassed words.

Dr. HighJohn cleared his throat and went on, Well I did what I thought was best at the time, what I thought was right then, but I guess I had some funny ideas of what being a man was.

Behind Tucept's blanked face the conflicting emotions collided like scrimmaging football teams, love resentment embarrassment affection pride.

And for sometime now, uh, Dr. HighJohn looked out of the window, at the sky, the room, I've uh wanted to apologize to you, for the time I made you wear that dress.

An almost forgotten memory suddenly sharp. Tucept remembered a little boy about 9 years old standing in the backyard in one of Caldonia's dresses, a flowered print with a sash that hung loose. He remembered the backyard wavy through crying eyes and his father's angry stinging voice, Aint no boy of mine going to be crying every time some little thing happens to him. You'll wear that dress until you're broken of it.

I had, Dr. HighJohn went on determinedly, some funny ideas of what being a man was about and I guess I tried to put them on you. I thought men didn't cry.

He looked away and added, Shit, I cry myself sometimes.

Tucept liked who he was and how he conducted himself in the world. Listening to his father stumble through his apology he realized how much he was like his father, how much he owed him for what he was, even the mask of cool he now clutched so determinedly to his face. Now that he has learned to wear his own manmask he sees the man beneath his father's mask and he knows how much effort it cost him to make his apology.

Tucept's face cracked into a smile and tears rolled down his cheeks, It's alright Daddy, he said, I still cry when folks aint looking.

〰〰〰〰

TUCEPT SAT MOTIONLESS IN HIS CHAIR, HANDLING THE BONES in his left hand, eyes focused elsewhere.

THE BIG PASSENGER BOAT TURNS THE BEND AND THE OLD-city looms up on the bluff. Excited passengers crowd to the rail but I stand apart as befits my calling. In spite of my studied disdain I feel a warm tingle of excitement. It's been a longtime since I've been home. Even from here I can see that the Oldcity continues to sprawl unchecked, an overgrown rivertown. Home.

The boat docks and I and the other passengers go ashore. Beggars converge on us, hands outstretched, begging for coin. Cursed zombies. Most of them are Blacks and broken. They cluster around us and my face sours, for my people's weakness is ever a sore in my eyes. I gather my poncho about me and walk through the throng quickly. Not wanting to be noticed, I drape myself in a spell of invisibility. Seen but not seen.

It is good to be home again. I pass trees that are old friends and places where the sweet and sour memories of my youth mingled. I find myself dallying, breathing deeply of the river-tainted air, nodding at dusky families out on shopping strolls, savoring the smiles and laughter of the folk. It is always good to walk amongst the folk on festive occasions, when the spirit of us is strong and happy. The Oldcity and the mudrich delta land that it guards is one of our strongholds. We are plentiful here. Here we are strong.

At an openair vegetable market bright with ripe colored fruits, four earthtoned women in light spring dresses catch my eye and my fancy. Fingering a ripe melon, I linger close enough to catch their scented fragrance and listen to the melody of their words. They, of course, do

not notice me. Cloaked still in my spell I am perceived
only as a wimp of no interest. Except by one who stares
frankly. A tall deep honeybrown woman, long and lean
and fierce, with bold eyes and a wild forest of hair. She
obviously knows me for what I am. I look with truesight
and see ochawitch. Sensible order Ocha. Coed. Our
eyes meet and speak greeting.

A man bumps me. Another zombie. I recoil from the
deadness of his soul. He turns on me, I pass. He walks
off, muttering niggers aint shit.

Again my face sours. The zombie have long been with
us. Souldead casualties of our long years of defeat. But
now they sprout like weeds, evidence of our genocide. It
is the reason I am here. The Masters of the Order have
read the signs and consulted the Great Book of Hoodoo.
Runners such as myself have been sent to all the Tribes
of the Black World. The Time of Gathering is upon us.
And I, Tucept HighJohn of clan HighJohn have brought
the summons to the Delta. I have brought the Call. In
the morning I am to speak before the Tribe's Council of
Elders. Oldcity is the seat of the Delta Tribe. My Home.
That is why I, though still only an apprentice, was
chosen by the Masters of the Order Ascension to deliver
the Call to the Delta Council of Elders.

I hurry. My place is on the outskirts of town and it
will be dark soon. I have almost left the market district
when I see the enemy. Soul snatchers seeking victims.
Eight strong. With slitted eyes I watch them move with
impunity among my people. My liberal humanist honor-
able slave people. We are not an arrogant people and so
we make comfortable victims. Glancing around quickly I
see none of the warrior clans. Our thin black line of
defense is very thin. So few warriors. Most of us are
slaves, asleep to the ways of the world and pawns to the
strongest game to come along. We are a weak people.

I draw my hood up and follow inconspicuously. It is

not good game. A mission should never be jeopardized for the sake of a few damned souls. But the zombies have angered me. This is my Tribe and I am of the Hoodoo Brotherhood, I do not suffer losses to the enemies of my people lightly.

Outnumbered and still only an apprentice, I cannot jeopardize my mission with a frontal toe-to-toe assault that I would surely lose. I cannot tell if there are any trained wills among them without engaging them in battle. I beam a call for assistance and follow their apparently aimless market shopping, hoping to get aid before they select victims.

A group of young Blacks approach, young and sturdy, with vital spirits alive still. I feel the enemy's quick surge of excitement and know that they are going to snatch. I compose myself and feed the youths what power I can. When the enemy tries to snatch, they find alert powerful wills. I brace myself for the counterassault and easily swallow the force they throw at me. There is no trained will among them. That is a relief, even I get a break once in awhile. My guardian spirits are finally on the job. They throw power. I swallow. Unable to crack my defenses but aware now that I am only an apprentice they renew their attack on the youths. As fast as they drain lifeforce I pour it in. The effort eats up my power in great gulps and I plant my feet, drawing power from the earth, solid implacable earthforce power. They turn on me, a wall of will smashing into my head. I reel in pain as the protective layers of my psyche are stripped away to expose my crippling vulnerabilities, my doubts, my fears, and anxieties. They strip me of my power. Foundering, I step back inside myself, consciousness expanding in encompassing waves of force to swallow the assault, *I am HighJohn, I refuse to fall, I am HighJohn, I am the rock.*

Sweating and trembling with the strain, I chant my

litany of power. Suddenly the pressure eases. Another's will feeds the souls, my power is freed. Without taking time to question I strike viciously at the offbalanced enemy. I call up Diaumbe, front and center. Diaumbe rages and I make the kill, reaching out and taking them hard. The other sorcerer takes 2, cleanly, without venom and powershed. The 6 I take I hurt, with more enjoyment than becomes a hoodooman, even an apprentice. All the anger and frustration that I feel for my people's weakness in slavery is poured into them like slashing knives. I smash their wills and make them toys.

Afterward I turn to thank he who had assisted me. Excuse me. I stand corrected. She. The witchwoman tends to the wounds of the souls we have saved. I beam thanks and as our minds touch a thrill runs through my veins. Oh the flesh. Desire nature got down and dirty with me, one of the reasons I'm still an apprentice. I step back far enough inside myself to regain observational perspective. She tends the souls efficiently, mending and healing. In addition to being a warrior clan, the Order of Ocha is good at healing. The talents of my Order lie elsewhere.

Again I hurry home through the folk but this time I don't see the old memories, the families and couples and children, the smiles and laughter of my people. I am in my warhead and I take no pleasure from the meager amenities that my people have managed to extract from this slave's existence.

A beggar approaches me, hand outstretched. I look on him with contempt. Is it any wonder we die as a people, driven by our enemies until our backs are against the Great Wall of Destiny? Moj curse us for our weakness. My anger is whitehot and it is all I can do to refrain from spitting curses on his generations to the third power. That I cannot do, he is a zombie, not a renegade, not an enemy of the folk. Though weak he is still Firstborn.

A coin brother? he begs.

Stand Firstborn, I beam fiercely. Where is your dignity? We who were once a mighty people shall be again so! Be worthy of your legacy!

The man in him flickers but the will is dead. A broken man. I withdraw, feeling vaguely soiled.

A coin brother?

I am not your brother, I mutter and hurry on, sunk deep in the folds of my poncho and dark brooding thoughts of a weak people.

We break so easily.

CHAPTER 6

A DISTURBED TUCEPT WALKED DOWN BEALE WITH A determined stride. He passed construction men working on the facades of new buildings, modern brick modules. Urban renewal had finally gotten around to rebuilding Beale but not like before. A new gentrified look designed to lure tourists. He understood the need for any and everything to be commercially viable and pay its own way but it just wasn't the downhome gutbucket Beale that he remembered. He didn't like it.

Spijoko sat on a bench in Handy Park.

Tucept sat next to him.

I have had another vision, he said.

Spijoko's thick gray eyebrow questioned him, Like the one that sent you to me? he asked.

Tucept frowned. The survivor's vision was what he had finally named it. He'd thought of it often, trying to probe secrets he knew it held for him.

No, he said, nothing like that first one. That one was

like a splitsecond photograph. This one was more like a film, some vivid daydream but more somehow. More detailed and complete, almost real.

Tell me of it, said Spijoko.

Tucept told him of his mission to Oldcity, of the Call he brought.

What Call? Spijoko interrupted his account.

I don't know, said Tucept, Only that it is important to me.

Go on, said Spijoko, alert and attentive.

Tucept finished the tale with as much detail as he could remember, which was considerable.

Spijoko was looking at him queerly, eyes bright and boring deeply in an eyelock that Tucept was unable to break.

Repeat it please, asked Spijoko.

He did.

This time Spijoko listened without comment, frowning deeply by the time Tucept finished.

Come, said Spijoko, walk with me.

They walked past the construction workers. Tucept's frown was eloquent and Spijoko noted it.

Old Beale just keeping up with the times, he said, that's all. Just like the blues, it adjusts to its time and circumstance. As we have done and continue to do. Taking the hump with style is the genius of our survival. Not only do we adapt, we finesse.

They crossed Main and followed Beale under the viaduct to the riverfront. They walked in silence. Spijoko was obviously in deep thought and Tucept didn't want to disturb it. They sat on the grassy slope of the bluff high above the river and Tucept watched houseboats tied up to the bank roll fluidly to the river's rhythms.

Finally Spijoko spoke.

Soon, it appears Apprentice HighJohn, you will be apprentice no more, you will be master.

He paused and his voice became a lecture, As a master hoodoo, he said, you are the tribal shaman, responsible for the survival and destiny of the Tribe. You cast your futuresight as far as possible into the future of the Tribe, determine the Tribe's needs and mold the Tribe's spirit to meet the challenges of survival.

As he spoke Spijoko's gnarled bark hands molded the air as if he worked with the clay of the Tribe's spirit in his hands.

How you do that, he said, is conjurer's game.

Tucept looked confused.

Longgame on the Board of Destiny boy, said Spijoko with a laugh of pleasure, Master Game. Now each master play a different game, according to the master's position on the board, to his resources, powers, strengths, weaknesses, temperament, everything counts when you running game. The mix of factors must be constantly orchestrated into the desired configurations. Each master walks a different path. There is one Way but many paths.

You with me?

Tucept nodded tentatively.

Spijoko looked at him fullface. Your visions, Apprentice HighJohn, are the spotlights on your path. They show you your way.

Oh, thought Tucept, starting to understand connections, patterns, implications.

Already your game begins to shape itself. Much sooner than I would have thought. You carry much power boy.

Spijoko became pensive, the Call? The Call? A interesting board, he murmured absently, very intricate, much possibility in it.

Spijoko looked thoughtful, There have been moments, have there not, he asked Tucept, when you have felt yourself, if only for a minute, one with the power, moments when you have felt truly alive?

Tucept looked confused.

Surges of power, clarified Spijoko, sensations of strength and clarity, when you have felt yourself a force in the world.

Those, Tucept realized. Those strange thrilling surges he had occasionally experienced. Shukim's meeting. The survivor's vision. Other times.

I know them, he said.

Those are the moments, said Spijoko, when you are firmly on the path. When you are so precisely positioned on the Board of Destiny and your Game so strong that your every move bends reality to your will and shapes the destiny of the world. That's when you have centered yourself on the balance point of reality and illusion. When your Game is the longest and most powerful one in existence, swallowing all others. When you are the power. De mojo.

What does this Call have to do with it?

Spijoko hesitated, It aint for me to speak on, he said finally.

Why not?

Aint my Game, said Spijoko, face closed, And it has not formed itself sufficiently for me to interfere. Patience HighJohn, your Game shapes itself quickly enough. It will make itself known to you in due time. This I can tell you, the length of a sorcerer's game is the measure of his power. Your Game is a long one, one of the longest I ever seen.

Spijoko sighed almost apologetically as he cleared away a work area. Today I will teach you to mount the Board of Destiny. Enjoy your remaining days Apprentice HighJohn. Soon your life will no longer belong to you. Already you belong to the Tribe. Already you are in the hands of the power.

*   *   *

Tucept sat in storm. Rain whispered through the trees to splatter against his thick torso and run rivulets from his plastered wooly hair and into the tangle of his beard. He held his face up and washed it, feeling the blues walking and tension releasing him from its jealous possessive grip. Taking the soul of the Tribe in his Hands he bonded himself to it until he had a firm grip on it and then let the Board of Destiny unfold itself in his mind, a great fanning out of the future, its linked random possibilities stretching out into infinity. His futuresight leaped out, noting the points of power, the forked moments where the decision of the moment brought the race's generations closer to survival and prosperity or decline and genocide. Those moments when fate could be orchestrated by the hoodoo will. His. He studied the board with daemonic concentration.

A break in the dark clouds overhead suddenly showered him with a soft beam of sunlight. Sparkling raindrops fell through the sun's spotlight and he felt the warmth of the beam and glowed, soaking up power. The small circle of light evaporated as the fast dark clouds closed up and left him pondering longgame on the Board of Destiny.

On Riverside Drive, an oldwoman rocked and puffed on her first husband's favorite pipe. He had been a good man, the best of many she had loved. Shame he aint here to see these days finally come. When the sun peeped momentarily bright through the dark clouds she took the pipe from her mouth and spit into the beam. She knew a sign when she saw one.

Tucept sat on a treestump before a half circle of neighborhood kids. In the center of the half circle Jabbo and the little gingerheaded boy sat bracketed by two little chocolate twingirls in dual pigtails. They and all the other kids in the half circle listened intently, big eyes riveted on Tucept's hands weaving pictures as he spoke.

. . . and, said Tucept, all over the earth were only monkey tribes who walked on four feet. And all were satisfied with the way of monkey but Moj. Moj was shaman of a monkey tribe in the heart of Africa. Moj the monkey shaman was a monkey with vision.

This is a dead end, said Moj to the tribespeople one day, Our tribe will die, our generations will wither. If we are to survive we must be more than monkey. We must stand.

It is not allowed, laughed the other monkeys, to be more than monkey. Our legs are not made to stand. O Moj the Dreamer, we are what we are. As the gods have made us.

But Moj was Shaman, the Tribe's destiny was his responsibility.

I am Moj, he thought one day, I who do what must be done. I will not be denied.

And Moj stood.

The other monkeys crawled and whimpered in fear.

Look they said, Moj the Fool stands on two legs.

They fearfully waited for divine retribution and their enemy's blows to bring Moj down. But still Moj stood and the other monkeys saw that Moj was strong. And so the Tribes of Moj stood and ascended monkey. They conquered and spread across the face of the earth.

Tucept's hands stilled and his words carried cleanly around the half circle:

Where others must crawl and whimper the Firstborn stand, unafraid.

That is all.

MIKE FELT A LONG DAY ACCUMULATING IN THE BACK OF his eyebrows and rubbed them. At the podium in the front of the spacious ballroom the judge was talking about the good old days when he was just a lawyer. Like most of you here, he said.

The table full of chattering guests irritated him. He was only two tables from the judge and his table was full of dignitaries. He would have liked to add a couple of them to his network but he didn't feel like making the effort to cultivate them just now. His idle eye roamed the room, alighting periodically on an attractive woman or an interesting man. At the judge's table he noticed a stunning darkbrown woman with an expressive face that elegantly spoke as he watched her. A little pillbox hat sat jauntily to the side of curly redhair. He watched her for awhile but was unable to get her attention and lost interest. His eye continued to scan the room and he noticed Thembu smirking at him. A wide broadfaced brother with the ANC mission, Thembu had obviously noted his attempted eye contact. They exchanged grins and Mike went back to scanning the crowd.

A case of his kept coming up in his mind and he doodled on his napkin while he thought about it. Maybe the judge, old family friend that he was, could help him. His client was a 3-time loser and was going to have to be thrown on the mercy of the court. Mike didn't want to do it, the brother didn't want to do it, but if he didn't plea bargain, the state would kill him. The case was lost long before Mike got it. Mike looked at the judge and half shrugged. It didn't make any difference. None of this volunteer work that he did made any difference. Just kept the system unclogged. His little bit for the people, he thought cynically, his mouth souring.

Mike's eye kept being drawn back to the woman in the pillbox hat. Stunning, he kept repeating to himself. He tried again to catch her attention by staring and again he gave up. Thembu laughed and made faces. Mike continued to scan the rest of the party. He caught the eye of an attractive blonde at the table next to his. Their eyes expressed interest. Mike gave her a wry jumping-the-border-is-problematical smile and broke contact. He looked around to see if any sisters had caught him playing eyegames.

Mike excused himself from his table and walked over to the judge's table.

Thanks for inviting me Judge, I'm leaving now.

The judge nodded and shook his hand, How's your father? he asked, spraying Mike with fine droplets of wine spit.

Fine, said Mike, haven't spoken to him in some time though, I've been busy.

Maybe he should make an appointment to speak to the judge about his case later. Mike hesitated and the moment passed.

Give him my regards when you see him.

Will do.

The judge leaned closer, speaking under the buzz of the conversation around the table.

Mike I'm running for office next year . . .

Mike noticed from the corner of his eye that the stunning woman was watching him with an idle aloofness. Closer now he saw that her skin was smooth and very taut, her face full of hollows and spaces. Her dark eyes were cool and restrained.

. . . and I can always use some good young blood on my team.

Mike repressed a smile.

The judge misread the smile and laughed aloud, Always plenty room for good young blood. I'm serious now Mike. You call me next week, okay.

Mike nodded, I'll do that Judge.

He stood up and glanced at the woman in the pillbox hat, their eyes held for a blank moment before she haughtily broke contact. Mike smiled approvingly. She didn't appear to be with anybody, if he were in a different mood he would go after her.

He nodded at Thembu and left. Thembu excused himself and caught up with Mike at the door while Mike waited for his car to be brought up.

Alma, said Thembu, lovely isn't she?

Mike told him about his case, his decision not to ask the judge.

Well done my friend. If the case is lost, save the favor. Ask only for favors of significance.

Mike's red Mercedes was driven up and Mike and Thembu shook hands, fingers snapping off the edges.

Come by the house next Friday my friend, said the bulky South African, there will be some people by, you will enjoy meeting them.

Mike waved and drove off. A dissatisfied, should've, would've, could've feeling followed him home and he couldn't tell if it was because he hadn't approached the judge about his case or because he hadn't approached the woman. At his apartment he dropped his clothes and left them where they lay. Naked, he lay back in his worn black leather lounge and put on headphones for a little Johnny Hartman and John Coltrane. They used to visit all the very gay places too, those come what may places. Those places where one relaxes on the axis of the wheel of life.

That Friday Thembu let him in with his customary grin stretched even wider. My brother, he said, I have a treat for you.

Thembu walked him through the small groups of American and South African Blacks to a large balcony window. Alma sat on a lounge.

Thembu's eyes sparkled in his broad face and he was unable to hide his pleasure.

Alma, said Thembu, this is my friend and brother

Mike Daniels, the one who so shamelessly ravished you with his eyes the other night.

She smiled.

I wouldn't go that far, said Mike in his best smooth, I was just appreciating the package.

Thank you, she said.

I noticed you at the judge's last week, I meant to speak to you then.

Oh, she said, but you didn't get up the nerve.

I wouldn't go that far either, he said with a grin. Her voice is pleasingly rough with oddly stressed syllables. She was, surprise, surprise, as attractive and stunning this time as the first.

Thembu came back and took his arm, Excuse me Alma, he said, I must take him for a moment.

Thembu guided him to a small klatch of South Africans, I have some people here I want you to meet, he said.

They don't have the clicking names like yours do they? said Mike, You know I can't get it right.

Thembu laughed, We don't hold it against you my brother, he said, it is something that you must learn at your mother's breast.

They were expecting the new administration to be much more receptive to the Boers. Constructive engagement, explained Thembu, and we're trying to limit the damage. We have been working with some groups like TransAfrica but we can use all the help we can get. Especially from our cutthroat American brethren. He shrugged, We learn, slowly perhaps, but we learn. We have learned at least the criteria of official American interest. The rest, my brother, is on us. It's only a matter of time, he said, his voice gone soft and tender, perhaps this decade. Azania.

He paused and savored the word, repeated it, Azania.

Once Azania is free, then Mike we will be able to turn

our attention to the real liberation of Africa. The unity of all Africa. Thembu's broad face seemed to widen even further. Think of it my brother, a United Continental Africa. In this modern complex world of ours there are only continental powers. U.S., China, Russia. Continental. Until we do that we won't be able to even feed ourselves. But a Continental Africa. Now that's something different.

Some people in the states, said Mike, have been speaking of a worldwide entity of the black peoples. A global state. A Black Federation.

Thembu laughed conspiratorially and patted Mike's shoulder, Ah my friend, some of our younger intellectuals have also speculated on such an entity, but we are not so arrogant as to try and structure it yet. Still the key is a unified Africa, so first things first. Azania. Next week we have an important meeting at State. Perhaps you will assist us as part of the delegation. With your fair skin, laughed Thembu, we can pass you off as the representative of the Coloreds.

What if I'm expected to click?

Perhaps I was wrong my friend, perhaps we can teach you after all.

Soon after being introduced to Thembu's friends and associates Mike excused himself and casually wandered back to the balcony. Alma was in conversation with another man. Mike started to walk off but he had missed her once, he wouldn't miss her again. He stood a respectful distance off to the side and waited for her to finish. She glanced over occasionally and soon froze her conversation short.

Mike took her home that evening. At the door he asked if he could come up. She hesitated but shrugged a yes. The walls of her spacious apartment were dotted with prints and paintings, itself a collage. She gave him a tour, a gallery, she explained, On the side really, I'm in fashion. A buyer.

She set out a tray of cut vegetables. An avocado dip. Wine.

Mike asked if he could stay the night.

What for? she asked, her deep brown eyes full on him, I don't fuck strangers.

For a minute he was angry then he had to laugh, he liked her style.

I just like to call things as I see them, she told him. I do like you though Mike.

At the door he turned to her, put his arms around her and nuzzled her. She stood unresponsively, letting him have his way but not participating.

With a grunt, he stepped back from her, You're mighty blasé, he said, One day you're going to learn the proper attitude.

Oh, she said coyly, and I won't be so blasé?

Precisely.

Mmmm, she said, closing the door on him, My how we fantasize.

Between working with the judge, his Acme responsibilities, his volunteer work, board memberships and ongoing business deals, Mike didn't have the time he would have liked to give her over the fall. It turned out to be for the best though because her affection was a seesaw, a mercury of extremes, come and go. Come into my life please, get out of my life now. By the end of the fall Mike just went with the flow. If it was on, okay, if it wasn't, just as okay. When it was on, it was good. He enjoyed it, enjoyed her, enjoyed kissing her hidden, vulnerable sides. As he dug deeper and deeper into the finer details and smudgier aspects of the politics with the judge, he found her perspective and grasp of issues irreplaceable. He often expressed surprise.

I do read, she said testily.

Mike spent so much time with the judge that the judge's people started calling him the judge's spear carrier. Mike found he had an affinity for the political.

Reagan's election caused the judge to shift his gears. He spent more time at the clubs, saw more people, forged alliances. Mike didn't get a chance to see much of Alma and had to fight for time to go see his boy down in Philly.

It's going to get hot Mike, said the judge over dinner one evening, Reagan's going to drive Blacks to the wall. They don't know it yet but it's a sure bet, you mark my words.

The judge stabbed his salad with his fork, We've got to be ready Mike, can't wait until the last moment, as we love so much to do.

The judge stopped eating, So whattayasay Mike? It's going to be as hot as the Sixties, just a different battleground. Get in now and position yourself. We can use you.

We?

No man is an island.

I'm already on board, said Mike.

Full-time Mike, I need you full-time.

Excuse me, the judge said, drinking a tall glass of milk down in one swallow, I've got to maintain my ulcer.

He put the glass down with a burp, You run that slot for me Mike we'll have a full ticket.

I don't know Judge, I've made an investment in Acme and I'm not vested for another three years. Maybe then.

Then is too late Mike.

Mike reached for his coat and his briefcase, I've got to run Judge, Alma and I are going to listen to some music, I'll think about it.

The judge fixed Mike with a stare, looking at him over the top of his hornrimmed eyeglasses, What you don't understand Mike, the country's lurching to the right.

The name of the game is cut the dead weight and we're the first ones up for sacrifice. Actually it's going to be a good thing for us. We've been on that welfare tit way too damned long anyway, it's sapped our damned spirit. Whatever, we're about to ride some rough water Mike. The Blacks are going to have to march. Throwing ourselves on the mercy of the whitefolks doesn't work anymore, if it ever did. It's about power this go-round Mike. Power. How do we get it, how do we use it. We gotta march Mike. And if we bid for power and lose, it's going to be our ass. We'll be punished for having the gall to raise our heads up in the first place. I'm not telling you anything new, but we're outnumbered Mike, five to one at least. We've got to work five times as hard, we've got to be five times as slick. Can't afford CPT anymore, unless we're changing it to Colored Precise Time.

I'll think about it Judge, seriously, I'll get back to you soon.

The judge napkined his chin. They shook. Mike took up his briefcase and pushed himself away from the table.

Ask Alma what she thinks, the judge said after him, You better snap that woman up while you can Mike. Young man in a hurry like you will move a lot faster with a wife, especially one that can keep up with him. And your father, ask him what he thinks when you talk to him, and be sure tell the old roaddog hello for me.

Mike waved, I'll get back to you.

The music wasn't very good and he and Alma left early. Walking across the street to the parking lot on the red light, she said offhandedly, Blackmen are weak.

What? said Mike, stopping in the middle of the street. A blue Jag honked to an angry stop.

What did you say? asked Mike, jaws tight, What did you say woman?

Get out of the street, she said, pulling at his arm.

He came stiffly. On the curb, he stopped her, What was that about?

Nothing, she said waving it off, just forget it.

At her apartment Mike sat on the bed with his back against the wall watching the late news on TV while she went through some gallery papers.

Alma, what where you talking about when you made that statement about blackmen being weak?

She didn't look up from her desk. Nothing Mike, I was just thinking about something so I said it, I don't really want to talk about it.

But I do, I . . .

Her attention was suddenly drawn to the screen. One Robert Wendal had been offered a job with the Reagan administration as an adviser on minority affairs.

Her attention was rapt.

I lived with him for over a year, she said with a curiously excited disdain, He's a little man and he'd be just right for that kind of little job.

The phone rang. She answered. Hello. Yes, she says, I was just telling Mike how perfect he would be for such a little job. Wouldn't he though? Haha. No, of course not. Why would I? He just might, you never can tell.

Mike half watched the TV screen and half listened to the conversation. He could feel her obvious excitement. Still pissed about her earlier remark, Mike watched her judgmentally. The brother may be a little man, but he just picked up quite a few inches. Wonder if this is what qualifies as a strong blackman. It didn't rate as power in his book. The same old yassuh boss colored power that we've always had. Only kind a blackman in America can get, he thought with suddenly surprising bitterness. She calls us weak and then rewards weakness. But it wasn't much more than what he was planning to do. Mike realized his contempt was tainted by jealousy.

When she got off the phone she apologized, A friend,

she explained, her eyes glued to the screen, we haven't spoken in a longtime. She knows Robert.

The judge wants me to run for office, he said, I told him I would think about it.

Her eyes were cool appraisal, her approval physical force.

Come on, she said, I'll buy you a drink.

Over drinks she told him that she had planned to go to the Newport Jazz Festival. Yesterday was her birthday but cramps sent her to bed.

Oh, they were awful, she said, they still hurt.

He hadn't known it was her birthday. Looking at her though, he could see the pain seeping through the thick mask of makeup she applied so adroitly to her hard urban features. Her practiced boredom remained undisturbed. Everything sunk into the deep waters of her Cancerian nature.

It would have been nice to spend such an intimate occasion with her. Even now, he sat back reserved, never really relaxed with her, fearing sensitivity or affection would be abused.

I intimidate men, she said peering at him over her glass, I don't think that men can deal with the women's new freedom.

Well I can, said Mike, does that mean I can have you?

You just want to fuck me.

I'm going to get you too, he said, ignoring that, And if you fall in love with me I'm going to make you pay for making me work so hard.

That's why I don't fall in love. A pause added sincerity to her words, Because I'm tired of being abused.

People give you only as much respect as you demand.

I just don't expect people to want to hurt me, she said.

Hurt you, he snorted, I can't even get a grip on you.

You know what I call you when I'm talking shit with my partners?

No Mike, she said, cocky again, What do you call me when you're out with the boys?

My bucking bronco bitch.

I don't buck.

Late that night, before they slept, she pressed herself against his chest.

At least you understand me, she said into his chest. She paused, her voice strangely taut. I've got whatever you want Mike.

Mike looked at her closely, looking for the catch.

That's a strong statement, he said cautiously.

Well it's true.

Good.

It won't be true forever.

I don't expect it to.

That night he watched her in her sleep, the carefully etched lines of her face softened and whispering her secrets to the early morning light. Did he really want her, he asked himself again, or was it the chase that excited? How long before the seesaw shifted and the icewoman emerged again?

She shifted in her sleep, seismically, much, he assumed, as the great plates of the earth do. He decided. He wanted her.

He got out of bed and went to his desk. He wouldn't run for office, he preferred to work in the shadows. He sat at his desk without consciously meaning to. A legal pad. He picked it up and wrote, *Plan*. He was tired of being kicked around by the winds of circumstance. He was tired of being swept up in every little game that came down the pike. He needed to decide what he wanted, Mike Daniels. He has been what his father wanted, what the army wanted and what Acme wanted, he had been what the people wanted and now the judge wanted to make him what he wanted, even Alma wanted, he looked at the bedroom. Well, what did he want, and how was he going to get it?

He rose to get a drink, no, he sat back down, no drink, are you serious about this or aren't you? He picked up a pen and put it down for a pencil. He wrote on the pad, *Objective*. He thought about it for a moment and wrote, *Objective: Power*. That's what he'd like, he thought, a little power of his very own. He looked at it again and laughed, too vague, a first draft. Whatever it was, he was going to have to make a lot of money. A lot of it. Or at least control it. Power cost. He rolled up his sleeves and got the drink anyway, it was going to be a long night. More like a long year. A life sentence. Whatever.

§§§§

LT. LAWRENCE CALLED SGT. GILL TO THE STAND.

Could you tell us Sergeant, just what you saw on the night in question?

Well, said Gill, I had been drinking with a couple of good old boys down at the NCO club and then we went back to the hootch to play some aceyducey. I had had enough 3.2 beers to get a buzz and I needed to take some weight off my bladder so I went to the officers' showers, cause they got this emergency urinal over there. I was a little buzzed but not so's that I couldn't find the shower. I stood there doing what I do, uh, and you know Kicks's hootch was like a piece of a click from the shower, right over that ridge there and I could see him in his tent.

What was he doing?

Uh, what was he doing, well I told you, he was sitting on his bunk.

And then what Sergeant Gill?

I don't rightly know for sure, cause I wasn't paying any attention till the explosion, I didn't know what had happened, I thought it was incoming and went running to the bunker with my little wee wee hanging and swinging.

Gill laughed, unbothered that he was the only one laughing in the courtroom.

Sergeant what did you see?

Well like I said I wasn't really paying attention, I was trying to get back to the hootch.

What did you see Sergeant?

Well sir, I saw him sitting there one minute, then boom, the frag grenade went off and I was hightailing it for the bunker trying to salvage my little swinging wee wee. I did think I saw one of the colored soldiers run by but sir, I aint sure, but that was the impression I had.

Obviously Sergeant Gill, you think a black soldier would have been likely to be involved. Why is that Sergeant Gill?

Well said Gill, glancing at them, you know, Kicks had a little problem with the colored guys. Everybody knows they stick together, it's a big thing with them, you know. Being Black I mean.

ᔔᔔᔔᔔ

A BRISK JUNE NIGHT. WILLIE AND LINDA HEARD THE MUSIC from the Jazzmobile's featured group at Grant's Tomb while they were still walking down Riverside. The Are and Be Ensemble, we Are here in the badtimes and will Be here when they gone.

> *If there is no struggle*
> *There will be no progress*
> *In our lives*

Sundiata on a sungun. 360°. The music eased through the trees, greeting them as they crossed the Drive and joined the crowd.

Linda bought plantains from the merchants congregated at the foot of the steps of the Tomb and Willie bought two of Aris's sunfried tabouli sandwiches. They threaded their way through the festive crowd until they found a seat on the grossly tiled bench that ran drunkenly around the huge granite tomb.

Want some? Linda offered him a plantain. She knew he didn't like plantains. He passed her half of one of the tabouli sandwiches.

Linda munched her plantains, enjoying the breeze, the darkness, the music, the milling crowd that they were yet not a part of.

A tall brother in a striped kofi detached himself from the crowd and walked over.

Mrs. Clarkesdale got cribbed, said Jacob, We think we know who did it. What do we do with them?

How is she? asked Linda

She alright, she got beat pretty bad and she's in the hospital but they said she's stable. She's a tough old bird.

Willie frowned. The block association meets tomorrow, he said, Hold off till we discuss it with them.

Jacob nodded. He stood there a moment until the heaviness of the silence made it obvious that he was intruding.

They resented Jacob's intrusion, another evening committed, another evening gone. They had another meeting later on this evening. The health coalition.

Okay, see you tomorrow. He blended back into the crowd.

Damn, muttered Willie, he would have to speak to Jacob before the block association meeting, find out what hospital, find out . . . he caught the train of thought and stopped it, not right now. He looked out over the crowd with a deep frown.

We're still too close to this crowd, he muttered, running his hands back over his dreads in an impatient motion.

Further back, said Linda, come on.

They were jealous of theirtime, what little they could snatch from their obligations and responsibilities. There was always more needed to be done, always more responsibility to take. Since moving out of the Bronx into the Gold Coast just north of 110, Willie and Linda had become involved in the Harlem gentrification battles, co-ops and auctions, lawyers and crime and community, this and that. The new frontier. All this in addition to the ongoing activities and Willie's sound tech jobs and Linda just about having made the decison to go back to school. Time. Time. Never enough time.

She picked up her plantains and headed toward the rear of the tomb. They found an unlit spot on the wac bench and sat. They still heard the music and the crowd's conversational buzz cleanly on the still night air.

Let's not go to the meeting tonight, said Willie, they can do without us one night.

She looked at him quizzically, her eyes bright in her face and accented by her dreads tied back from her face with a red leather ribbon. Willie? He who missed no meetings?

What about Abeki? she asked, absently pulling a strand from her dreads and twirling it in her hands before letting it drop back into place.

Let's leave her at the babysitter's. She doesn't expect us to pick her up till late. We'll call and tell her what's up and check in every couple of hours. Okay?

Fine with her. She nodded and settled back into a groove on the bench.

He didn't feel like going to the meeting anyway. They

didn't have a chance of saving the Sydenham Hospital the mayor wanted to close. The bottom line was money, and, as usual, they didn't have it. Mayor Koch did. Their protests were just street theater, amusement. There had to be something that they were missing, they were fighting and losing too many of these skirmishes. They had to broaden their thinking. Put all these skirmishes in some kind of order. Some kind of comprehensive strategy.

Willie realized he was thinking, scheme, scheme, scheme, and stopped, no dammit, not tonight Willie Brown, tonight was theirs, ourtime, Willie stretched his head around on his neck and let himself relax, looking at the trees around him, the tomb, the crowd. His arm draped around Linda's shoulders and he snuggled his face into the thick braids of her dreads.

You think anybody saw us leave? teased Linda.

Jacob won't tell on us.

They laugh and snuggle. Much too soon the concert ended, the music faded away, the crowd slowly dispersed. Many gay souls passed the quiet dreadlocked couple perched in a dip of the wac bench.

Everybody was gone when they finally left, walking home along the Drive, horsing around, having a good time still.

Let's eat, said Linda, I found a new place.

Where? asked Willie with feigned skepticism, We've tried them all.

Some years ago they decided to try all the little greasy spoons in Harlem, in hopes of finding the special places, the ones that made the best pancakes, the best ribs or chicken and waffles, or big wide greasy steakcut french fries, or pheasant-con-chitlins. Some had been rejected for sanitary concerns, bad service, prices, dangerous clientele, whim, etc., but otherwise they had tried every little Harlem joint north of 110th.

Where is this place? asked Willie.

She grabbed his hand and pulled him, Follow me.

He followed her up 125th, admiring the sway of her round Levi'd hips. Music coming from the speakers set on the sidewalk in front of a record store caused them to dance a few steps as they passed.

The spot was a new place, just opened, 137th and Frederick Douglass Boulevard.

No fair, said Willie, this just counts as half a find.

Since when? snorted Linda, tossing her dreads.

They made pigs of themselves, sitting at a little front window and watching the street life pass, hooting, hollering and having a good time still.

Our compliments to the chef, said Willie when they paid their bill, This establishment shall get a four star rating. You agree?

Quite, burped Linda.

They walked home slowly through quiet Harlem avenues on vast starlight galaxies of embedded broken glass chips. They skirted the bad corners and even still the sense of decay began to weigh on them, littered streets, vacant, boarded-up buildings and seedy little stores struggling to stay alive. Old Harlem felt down and out today.

On one quiet sidestreet two men crossed the street and walked toward them. He and Linda quit talking, both suddenly alert. They moved away from each other and Willie commanded his tensed body to go loose. He sensed Linda positioning herself beside him and he was glad again that she had kept up her martial arts training. She could take care of herself. He maintained his appearance of casualness but with every sense alert and zinging with adrenaline. He and the two brothers nodded as they passed. From the corner of his eye he watched the shadows thrown behind the two by a streetlight until they were out of range of a surprise attack. He walked a few more feet and looked over his shoulder, the brothers were down the street and moving on. He and Linda began talking again.

On their block they passed Mrs. Clarkesdale's apartment. Willie remembered Jacob. He would call him in the morning. He would have to remember to write that down. His mind clicked into gear on some other matters that he needed to make note of.

Linda put her arm in his. Not yet, it said. Still ourtime, at least till we get to the door. Okay?

He smiled and pointed, the Jacksons had put a flowering planter in their window, even in the darkness the bright yellows and reds caught the eye.

Linda thought it was nice, she might plant one too.

I've got to be gone for a few days, he said.

He felt her tense, felt the questions that came tumbling to her lips. But she didn't ask. They had agreed that what not involved in best not to know the specifics of.

I'm meeting Bailey in the morning.

What about Mrs. Clarkesdale? she asked.

He grunted foully, the grenaded map of his face shifting. Clarkesdale was a spunky old lady from Durham N.C. who had lived through almost a century of troubles and struggles, to be beaten and hospitalized by some young punk black kids with no respect. Our kids, he sighed. It wasn't right.

I'll take care of it, said Linda.

You have the time?

He knew that she had to have her papers in day after tomorrow, she was finally going back to school, after all these years of talking about it.

I'll have it, she said.

She sounded reflective, and he put his arm around her shoulder.

Come on, he said, it was a good move.

She wasn't comfortable going back to school. They

found themselves resisting a certain level of achievement as bougie tainted, but they had agreed that their effectiveness was impaired. They would have to move to a new level of operations. He was trying to turn his occasional sound tech jobs into clients and an ongoing business, she was going back to school. They weren't kids anymore. Street theater wasn't getting it. She smiled, her fingers affectionately twirling one of his dreads.

Their home. The first two floors of an elegant if old brownstone. They opened the wrought iron gate, and closed it behind them, their bodies molded arms around shoulder tight, greedy about what little was left of theirtime. No telling when they'd get more. They filled the moment with little neck pecks, cheek and forehead pecks, greedily milking pleasure, determined, when they could, to enjoy each other and life to its fullest.

֍֍֍֍

JETHRO AND TUCEPT WALKED INTO THE GHETTO AND FOUND Jackel sitting on Willie D's bunk stuffing Willie D's gear back into his footlocker.

I was looking for some toothpaste, he said, wide face oozing wellbeing.

Jethro took some toothpaste out of his locker and threw it on Willie D's bunk.

Use this, said Jethro.

Thanks, he said, as he got his toothbrush and went outside.

Jethro lay on his bunk.

Tucept frowned and went to the tent door to watch Jackel make his way to the shower. Then he went to Jackel's footlocker. It was unlocked. He raised the lid and looked inside.

Say man, said Tucept.

Yeah, said Jethro.

Tucept held up a small tube of toothpaste.

Come on, said Jethro, I wanna check something out.

They found Welch and asked him if Jackel knew about his place in Soul Alley.

Yeah, said Welch, I took him down about a month ago. He looked them over, What's up?

Don't know yet, said Jethro, we'll check back with you.

They wanted to be certain before they condemned a brother.

I got a idea, said Tucept.

That night he, Mike and Jethro got in a corner and talked real low.

The next evening they were lying on the bunker in the sun. Mike walked up. He's the one, said Mike, I waited until Top wasn't around and checked his personnel records. He doesn't have any. As far as the army is concerned he doesn't exist.

Yeah, said Jethro. We'll have to make sure of that. Spread the word to watch out for him but don't let him know we're on to him.

Jethro climbed off the bunker and went to find their hootchmaid. He found her doing business with Welch and stood off to the side until they were finished.

Hey, mamasan, called Jethro, la dai.

She came over grinning and showing teeth stained a glossy black by the betel nut she chewed constantly.

When Jackel cut hair tomorrow and you clean, bic, you bring me piece, little piece, titi, okay? Five hundred piaster. Bic.

Jackel cut his hair every other Friday, tomorrow.

Two dollars mpc I bring beaucoup piece, choice cut huh GI Jethro? She popped another betel nut into her mouth.

Okay mamasan, three dollars mpc, titi piece bic.

They were back on the bunker when mamasan passed Jethro a ball of paper.

Insurance, he said.

$$\mathcal{SSSS}$$

A STORM OUT OF THE GULF HAMMERED MEMPHIS. PONcho snapping in the wind, Tucept took the soul of the Tribe in hand and, centering himself, he conjured up the Board of Destiny. He sent his futuresight along it into the eons and traced the path of power. Soon he would be ready. Strange shadowed figures, dark brooding haints stalked the woods with him, relishing the storm, spirits of much power, this one in the top hat, and that one in the ragged cloth of a slave with a jackleg preacher's Bible, here a cripple and this one a basket weaver. Their presence drew the storm to him and spurred its intensity. Tucept threw his hood back and let the storm wash his face. Thunder drummed. Lightning wreathed him and he drew power in surging singing waves.

On the Drive, red embers of a lit pipe glowing in her palm, an old gingerheaded woman rocked and waited.

A SIGN WAS ATTACHED TO THE GREAT BAOBAB TREE THAT stood in front of Tucept's tower.

ROOTDOCTOR T. HIGHJOHN
Rootwork & Conjury
High Hoodoo My Specialty
Sliding Fees

A late model black Volvo drove smoothly up the twisting little road and stopped in front of Tucept's tower. A dark heavyset man got out, a thick man in a well cut blue suit and wide solid features barely loosened with good living. He looked at the stairs and shook his head. This had better be worth it, he thought, climbing the stairs with slow, heavy, resentful steps. At the top of the stairs, he stood and reflected. Why was he doing this? A damned conjureman? Is this 1980 or isn't it? He shook his head and looked out over the woods but he didn't see them. He was tired. No, not tired, weary. Weary. Battle fatigue, burnout, you name it, he had it. He had given his youth to the struggle, the Movement, to this organization and that organization. Paid his tax, he thought with a wry smile. His Black Tax, his mentor had called it long ago, when he harped over and over, Our only power is in organization. Organize organize organize. Your tax for being Black. Put some time in with the organizations of your choice.

Well he had done it. He had been a chief when a chief was needed and a flunky when they called for a flunky. But it was never enough, something more always needed to be done. I guess there really aint no rest for the weary. O lord when will I be able to lay my burden down.

Tucept laid Hands on the client's soul. He massaged the kinks out of it and softened old calluses grown thick. He toned it up and oiled it with ancient primal essences. While he worked with his Hands, he hummed deep Delta blues, them blues is just life trying to teach you a lesson blues.

After finetuning the client's soul, HighJohn fed it, letting mojo flow through his Hands in waves of power until the soul glowed with renewed lifeforce.

A different man walked out of Tucept's tower that afternoon. He stood at the top of the stairs and looked out over the mistgreen woods, whistling, zippi di do dah, zippi di aye.

It was good to be alive, to have the wind blowing against his face, to feel the sun warm on his skin.

My oh my what a wonderful day,

A green Chevy pulled up and parked beside his.

He stretched again and stood, Come on old hoss, got work to do. He had to admit he'd enjoyed it, he thought proudly that he'd fought the good black fight. Like Martin said, a committed life is my legacy. He started down the stairs with a spring in his step, Just a little bit longer old hoss, one more lap. You can do it.

A deep mahogany woman got out of the Chevy and walked up the stairs with a stately, fragile dignity. She looked familiar, they nodded as they passed. Her eyes were haunted. At the bottom of the stairs his face lit up with sudden recognition and he turned to stare, Well I'll be damned. God, she had done some beautiful stuff. He had copies of all her early albums. He wished he had told her how much her music had meant to him these many years, all the times he had gotten heart from her work, all the trying times she had helped him through. Even now, certain of her songs brought back whole periods of his life, people he had known and loved, battles he had survived. A black world resource, he thought. He considered waiting and flicked back his coat sleeve to check his watch. Maybe next time. The struggle waits for no man. He thought that was funny in a dry sort of way and chuckled as he got into the car. Putting the pedal to the metal, he drove down the twisting little road through the woods, still whistling, that plenty of sunshine was coming his way, zippi di do dah, zippi di aye.

〽〽〽〽

CHOPPERS DROPPED FROM THE SKY LIKE HAWKING BIRDS OF prey. Tucept crouched fetal in the belly of the flying beast and watched the ground rush at them. The landing zone was hot. He watched tracers blossom from the treetops below and rise toward him in slow motion.

Such lazy death didn't appear capable of killing anybody. But by the time the tracers whizzed by him they
were grownup bullets and they were killing. A familiar
knot in his stomach made him impatient to be on the
ground and fighting. It was only then that the gutclutching
fear would release him. The dropping choppers hovered
over the landing zone for the split second it took to
vomit out a load of grunts and take to the sky.

Tucept hit the ground running, firing his M16 with one
hand, the other holding his boonie hat to his head as the
blades of the rising choppers cycloned the air and washed
the muddy waters of the ricepaddy away from him in
ripples. Feeling naked before the whining bullets Tucept
ducked into the muddy grass and fired at the woodline.
Around him men dropped in bloody comedy. Jethro ran
past him with the pig. Tucept scrambled up and followed
him, splattering through the muddy ricepaddy, clumsy
clodhopper feet sinking into the mud with every step.
The sting of a passing bullet nicked on his arm caused
him to fling himself behind a dike and he took the
moment to catch his breath. Jethro was crouched behind
the dike in front of him and firing steadily at the woodline
with the pig. Craning his head Tucept placed Willie D.
He saw Jackel. He didn't see Mike and Prester John.
Welch was still AWOL. Lucky dog. The firing from the
woodline increased and Tucept ducked deeper without
bothering to fire back. Mud seeped through his jungle
fatigues as he watched the choppers dwindling in the
bright sky. Maybe his arm nick would get infected and
he could spend a couple of days at the rear in a hospital
being looked after by roundeyes. A man as shorttime as
he was shouldn't be out here on an LZ this hot anyway.
To his right a man screamed and died almost in his ear.

He heard Kicks's command to move out and, reluctantly heaving himself out of the mud, he worked his
way toward the woodline. Thick gunsmoke haze sur-

rounding him made him feel like part of a surreal shadow army of running ducking puppets.

Near the woodline a burst of fire pinned him and Jethro down. They watched Cruz try to make a dike and take AK rounds to the chest that hammered him to a stop and danced him down to the ground in crisp Hispanic moves. Chest pumping blood, his body crabbed the ground in tight little circles.

Willie D, Ortega and Prester John broke for him. Tucept helped them with moving lips, muttered words and two quick clips from his M16. When they reached Cruz he was still crabbing in a tight circle chased by little AKed puffs of dirt. Prester John threw himself on Cruz to stop him long enough for Willie D and Ortega to grab his legs. Prester John, fatigue shirt soaked in blood, took his arms and they boogied up out of there fast, Cruz's moaning head bobbing with each step.

Suddenly Prester John's head blew open, spraying blood and brains into Cruz's chest wound. Tucept saw it but he didn't believe it. He just couldn't. Prester John's headless body carried Cruz a few steps more before his knees gave way and he went down. Willie D and Ortega brought in a deadman anyway.

Tucept and Jethro looked at each other for a hot painful instant, unable to express the pain lancing through them. The Ghetto had beat the odds so long that Tucept had forgotten how easy it was to die here.

Tucept heard the little spotter plane before he saw it, numbly craning his neck up to stare into the sky and watch it pass slowly over. Before long they heard the whine of the far off jets growing louder by the moment. There they were. Two of them. Coming out of the sun.

One of the jets peeled off for a pass. Tucept watched the strafing jet machinegun the earth in a blistering run that he couldn't quite believe was coming right at them. A screaming, silver blip, growing like magic out of the sky and snarling at them. The grunts bogged down in the ricepaddy didn't believe it until the earth around them erupted, throwing men and earth into the air in a sensuous puppet show. Tucept squirmed deeper into the mud. When the second jet came at them, Tucept turned over on his back and fired uselessly at it with his M16. Jethro emptied the pig and cursed in tongues.

The silver blip of the first jet positioned itself for another run. Tucept burnt off an angry useless clip at the jet. The diving jet suddenly veered off, leaving a lazy canister falling out of the sky.

Oh shit. Tucept buried himself, smashing his face deeply in the cold muck. When the napalm went off he felt the heat lick at the back of his neck and burn the exposed skin. A sea of flame sprang into being and consumed the air that had been there. Air rushed into the burntout space with a thunderclap and a hurricane wind that tried to suck him from his deathgrip on the earth.

A couple of grunts fired on the dwindling planes with useless frustrated bursts. A more determined effort was made on the spotter plane and then they settled in to lick their wounds.

They were through for the day. They set up a perimeter near the edge of the ricepaddy and when the scorched earth cooled they gathered the dead. The cooling earth cracked and cackled as they walked through filling old bodybags with crisp new welldone manpieces. Choppers ferried out the dead and wounded.

Tucept found Jackel, fried. He spit on the mansized cinder and left it.

That night Tucept didn't sleep well. They had almost made it. He had really forgotten that they could die until Prester John showed him how easy it was. He spent most of the night staring at the night tent of the starpointed sky.

Early the next morning Kicks had them following Charley's trail. Jethro was point, Tucept behind him with the pig. Kicks was worked up and he whipped the demoralized unit deeper and deeper into the hot green embrace of the jungle. They fought their way through the thick jungle, through muck and clinging waitaminute vines until Tucept thought he would drop. He scanned the trail with dead eyes, plodding step by step, Jethro's back often wavering until Tucept blinked him back into focus.

That night they stood down boneweary. Jethro and Tucept were too tired to do more than lay their ponchos on the ground under them and stretch out. Jethro reached out and touched Tucept's shoulder. Tucept thought he jumped but he was so groggy he couldn't tell if he really did or just thought he did.

Here man, said Jethro in the darkness, I want you to take this.

Tucept reached out his hand and felt around until Jethro put something in it.

Tucept brought it close to his eyes so that he could see it in the darkness. Night birds chittered. Jethro's bag. He absently felt the shapes inside. Hard little somethings that clanked softly. He always wondered what was in it. Jethro had never taken it off before. The thought caused him to shake himself awake a little.

This your mojo bag aint it?

Keep it for me man.

You sure man?

What?

Keep it for me man, Jethro repeated, his voice detached in the darkness. Do that for me okay Tennessee?

Tucept was too tired to argue, or even try to figure it out.

Sure man, he said. Snuggling back into his poncho and laying his head on his rucksack pillow he started immediately drifting off to sleep, hearing Jethro as if from some great distance.

Keep it for me man, take care of it.

Sure man, murmured Tucept, I got you covered.

The next day Tucept meant to bring it up when he stuck the little bag in the deep side pockets of his jungle fatigues. But Kicks told Jethro to take the point.

Tree, point, move out.

The brothers protested. Fuck that, said Tucept, Jethro pulled fucking point all fucking yesterday.

But Jethro was already moving out, with an uncharacteristically pliant composure that threw Tucept off.

Tucept grabbed up the pig and took up a position behind him. Soon he was a patrol automaton, one foot placed carefully in front of the other, eyes scanning the jungle, raking the ground, maintaining contact with Jethro and tingling with anticipation when Jethro walked up to a bright gold bamboo garden.

A CHANGE IS GONNA COME. THE FILIPINO BAND LIKED IT and played it often. A subdued Tucept, Mike and Willie D sat listening at a front table. They listened without conversation. Just like that their luck had broke and boom—Prester John wasted, boom—Jethro wasted. Just like that. Like they weren't alive breathing and farting just yesterday.

Tucept glanced at Mike and Willie D. They were the only ones left now. Welch was on the books as a deserter. If he came back he would be courtmartialed, they didn't expect to see him again. The Ghetto was falling apart. Dammit, they had almost made it. Tucept wanted to cry.

So how do we do it?

We draw straws.

Straws?

No sense in all of us doing time.

Well let's get it over with.

They left the club. When Mike and Willie D went down the dapline Tucept went down with them. At the front of the line the burly brother hugged him with both shoulders, Aint nothing but a ticket home blood, he said, You and me brother, against the world.

They trudged silently across the field in the darkness. When they got back to The Ghetto, the light was on and Welch was lying on his bunk.

Hey hey, what's happening man?

They hugged and dapped him with loud undue exuberance.

Man we didn't think we were ever going to see you again.

Shit you can always come down to Soul Alley.

Not now man, you heard about Jethro and Prester John getting wasted?

Yeah, I heard, that's why I came by.

We taking Kicks off man, he got Jethro killed.

Welch shook his head, Taking Kicks off is not smart medin.

Hey man, you the one told us to never let a brother go down. Jethro went down on a zoom man, Kicks made him pull point again.

First off Kicks aint got the balls to make Jethro pull point, said Welch, but that aint the point. The point is that taking Kicks off is a stupid move. They gon come right here to you and you going to LBJ. And this time you'll stay till they transfer you to Leavenworth. Not smart. You'll never go home.

Fuck you man, Kicks dies.

We drawing straws to see who does it.

Where the fucking straws, Fuck Welch. Where does mamasan keep the broom?

Half drunk they stumble around looking for mamasan's broom.

Welch snorted his disgust with them. I'll be right back, he told him as he walked out into the brisk evening.

Drunken asses, he muttered to himself. He walked down toward the officers' quarters. Past the gun battery, he reached into the deep side pocket of his jungle fatigues and pulled out a fragmentation grenade. He flipped it from hand to hand as he walked. Kicks had gone against the code and Welch believed in the code. Simple as that.

He crossed the ditch to the path that led to the officers' quarters. Gripping the handle of the grenade in a tight fist he pulled the pin and started to stick it in his pocket. He changed his mind. What the hell, if Kicks wasn't there he would find him, not that big a post. He threw the grenade pin away. A man was coming down the path toward him in the darkness, bars glittering on his shoulder. Welch stuck the hand with the grenade into the side pocket of his fatigues and saluted the captain with the other hand as they passed.

Evening sir.

The captain nodded and saluted.

The night air was calm and he could smell moisture in it. Monsoon coming soon, he thought. He and Oop would have to find another place. Theirs hadn't kept the monsoon out last year. He passed the officers' shower, a man at the urinals, looked like Gill. Welch angled across the field so he wouldn't be seen. Kicks's tent. A light on. A figure sitting on a bunk.

Welch took the grenaded hand from his pocket as he walked past the open tent. Yeah, it was Kicks. He let the handle fly and held the grenade long enough for Kicks not to send it back to him.

Kiss the widowmaker he muttered before he flipped the grenade into Kicks's tent. He kept on walking. He didn't stop walking when he felt the almost immediate explosion at his back. He didn't stop walking when the cries and yells started, when the post siren gave the false incoming alarm. He didn't stop walking when he passed The Ghetto and saw Mike, Willie D, and Tucept standing outside the bunker with GIs from other tents asking, What happened?

TUCEPT SAT MOTIONLESS IN HIS HIGHBACK CHAIR. THE BONES lay on the floor in front of him, the 4 shouldered cross. Shadowed figures stood around him, their voices a low murmuring babble of languages and dialects that only he heard. The voices of Ol' Prophet Nat. Gullah Jack. O Balio. uMlenghi. Doc John. D. Walker. Boukman. O. L. Young. LaBas. And on. And on. Shadows in shadows in shadows. The Hoodoo Brotherhood. Sorcerers all. Our Games have been many. These are our victories, these are our defeats, these are your lessons as written in the Great Book of Hoodoo. Listen young hoodoo and grow in power.

Tucept listens and is born again. HighJohn stands. Hoodooman. I am The Way.

SECTION THREE

⟨⟨⟨⟨

DE POWER

CHAPTER 7

〰〰〰

HIGHJOHN WALKED THROUGH THE PARK WITH LONG jackleg strides, the big black flathead tom stalking beside him. They climbed to the highest point in the park. There, surrounded by a waving green treetop sea and thrust into a bluecast sky of darkclouds and still waiting air, HighJohn leaned back against a thick tree whose spiderwebbed roots veined the ground. The flathead tom faded off into the bush.

A bright yellow butterfly with black-bordered wings had trouble getting into the high wind. HighJohn stretched out his hand and the butterfly landed on it. He lifted it and it glided away on a current. He smiled. In the distance the darksky wrinkled with lightning and the faint rumble of thunder. The winds began to whine in his ear. He felt the gathering of forces and tingling with anticipation he got down to business, settling himself, cooling out, letting his perpetually knotted mind unclench. Pulling a flask from his pocket he poured a libation to the four corners of the earth, muttering as he did,

I curse this slave's existence with every bone in my body

I curse it

I curse it

I curse it

Taking up the Tribe's soul in his Hands he conjured up the Board of Destiny. With futuresight he studied the board, judging the probable destinic and evolutionary challenges that the Tribe would have to face.

What kind of people did he want?

He frowned. He needed a people capable of mastering any situation possible in the infinity of the future. He needed a people who would, no matter how challenging the circumstances, instinctively walk the path of power. He needed master players. He needed a race of rulers.

The saga of the Blacks began to shape itself in his head according to what he wanted to program into the soul of the Tribe. What first, he pondered. Arrogance. He wanted a proud, arrogant people. He conjured up the first monkey tribes to stand and struggle to humanity and called them Firstborn. Firstborn! To rule is your birthright! He chronicled the founding of civilization, the isolation and sloth of an elder race, the decline of a once mighty people. He built a commitment to the destiny of the race in the Tribe's soul by carving in its conquest and enslavement in hard brutal strokes. He showed the conquest and dispersion of the Folk to the four corners of the earth and called these the Leanyears. We survived.

And then the Longmarches. The Ascension of the Blacks. Tales of relentless struggle and ruthlessly strategic commitment to the destiny of the black generations. Tales of power. Because more than anything he wanted a people bred to the instinct of power. A race of rulers. And so he forged his myth accordingly. A saga of struggle and mastery. The Longmarches. Generations and generations of struggle. Working the Tribe's soul with swift sure strokes he programmed in traits like discipline and dignity, selfresponsibility and selfdirection, the ability to grow from both victory and defeat. With all the patience of a master craftsman pleased with his work HighJohn carefully weaved an inexorable Will to Power into the soul of the Blacks and exulted in the length of his game. I am HighJohn he howled, and this I swear, the Blacks will never again be enslaved. By the gods and all that's holy I shall forge a race of rulers.

And so into the heart of his myth he placed his survivor's vision. The Blacks still marching where others have long since fallen. Survival of the black generations unto eternity. The Promised Land. His myth came alive, its heart a burning sunheat thing, a beacon in times of both celebration and despair.

The storm around him grew in intensity and he felt its fire in the small hairs of his arm. As he worked he constantly checked his myth for alignment with the Board of Destiny. A good fit. A good Work. He was proud of it.

He checked it over for emotional impact, logical holes, vividness and texture, factors that would affect its life span, that would give or take away the fire that gave it life. He fussed with details like the professional he was, deciding here that the acid smell of despair should cling more thickly to the holds of the slaveships, and there making the sky over that Brazilian plantation a brighter crystalline blue, the one over the Calcutta ghetto a dingier azure. Here he evoked a sense of destiny and there nobility of spirit.

Noting the spiritual toll of forever war, of generations upon generations consumed in struggle, he added gut acceptance of life as unceasing challenge. He gave his people ironic amusement, the ability to laugh in fate's face, to demand of life its pleasures and to enjoy its struggles, for let it come rough or smooth you must surely bear it. Struggle on, oh you mighty race.

The winds rose. Blueswhining blooddebt wind, moaning cries of millions gone. The rains came slowly, whispering through the trees as lightning cracked the midnight sky. A forked bolt lashed the tree in front of him and his world lit up, a splitsecond nova enveloped in rolling thunder. The ground tingled and the hairs on his arm stood on end.

He unleashed his anger and the storm grew in fury around him. The wind slashed rain into his face and he felt it over his entire body, a massage of rain, a second skin, the distinction of himself and storm blurred, merged, and he was storm, boundaryless, living wind, storm, lashing the earth below him with his mighty rains, spitting lightning and laughing thunder shivering through his veins. By the gods I am HighJohn. His winds whipped the puny trees scraping his angry belly and he threw lightning with abandon, drunk with power and piling bright bolts on top of each other, fascinated with the wardrum thrill of his thunder, with the kaleidoscopic display of his lightning spiderwebbing the nightsky. I rage over a Memphis braced high on the bluff and open to my fury. The city cringes beneath me and I hear the oldfolks whisper of the anger of the oldgods.

I am HighJohn de Conqueror. Hoodooman. I walk in storm.

HIGHJOHN FOLLOWED SPIJOKO ALONG A RIVERBLUFF SILhouetted against the morning sun, breathing in air fresh with the rinse of afterrain.

It is sometimes difficult to release a good student, said Spijoko, his brow furrowed, There comes the time when the good teacher becomes the student. A difficult transition at best.

HighJohn waited.

So perhaps I overstep my authority, Spijoko started again, sighed and paused. HighJohn had never known him to be this disconcerted before, it almost embarrassed him. He knew what Spijoko wanted to say but he wouldn't deliver his head into the lion's den.

Your game is a hard one HighJohn, said Spijoko finally, It will cause suffering.

Spijoko allowed his concern to stand naked on his words and HighJohn's defiant answers faded from his mind. He walked in silence. He was aware of the responsibility of power. If his game was on, the generations would follow his path. His Way. If he was strong those that followed his path would be strong. If he was egotripping and bullshitting, they would follow him to defeat and go down hard, suffering more than if he had just left them alone and let them remain slaves. Is he for real, or just megalomaniacing? Was he just ghostdancing his people down a hardroad to genocide? HighJohn's nightmare.

He chose his words with care.

We already suffer, he said finally, I ask only that we suffer the hardship of being a strong people rather than the hardship of being a broken and conquered people. I ask only that our generations never again be enslaved. I ask only that we survive as a people.

And I question only timing HighJohn, said Spijoko, We are still weak.

They stood looking out over the river. Moonlight glinted a waving trail on dark restless water. Storm gathered in the distance and they felt the dampness of the air against their skins. HighJohn felt Spijoko intent on him in the darkness and spoke, his voice pained indecision striving for conviction.

My teacher, he said, as you have taught I am a longgame man. I have looked as far into the future as my vision can see and I see no other destiny. I have laid my tricks and this I swear by the tail of Moj, there will be no ambushes while I am point.

Spijoko whispered in resignation that the hands of he who would wield the thunder must be hardened unto claw. He who would war with the beast must become the better beast.

HighJohn walked on, his voice hard in the darkness.

There will be no ambushes while I am point.

Spijoko sighed, It is your decision Stormbringer, the ground has been prepared for your seed. You do well to remember, young hoodoo, that to rule is to serve. Power without compassion is a sin.

$$\mathscr{S}\mathscr{S}\mathscr{S}\mathscr{S}$$

THOUGH ON TIME I HURRY THROUGH THE BUSTLING STREETS of Oldcity to the Council of Elders' meeting hall and dart into the welcome shade of the building. I need a moment to compose myself. I have anxieties, the apprentice's curse. I place on my mask of cool so that by the time I am ushered into the Council Hall I have the appearance of absolute conviction that is our trademark and our power. Though only apprentice I am still hoodoo.

The 15 members of the Council of Elders sit half circle behind a thick wood and marble desk. They stop talking as I am shown in. The Chief of Council, a striking nutbrown woman of indeterminate age, rises briefly when she greets me.

Welcome hoodooman, she says in cool liquid tones, How was your journey?

Tolerable, thank you.

You are HighJohn?

I am HighJohn, grade apprentice. Order of the Ascension.

I give them sign by which my authority is recognized,

and then, my anxieties again, thrice damned demons, I ignore protocol and speak bluntly.

I bring the Call of Gathering.

The Chief of Council looks disappointed at my lack of grace.

We have expected you, young hoodooman, she said after an unsettling pause, It has come to our attention that the Hoodoo Brotherhood has been sending the Call to the Tribes. Yet the old tales say that the Call of Gathering will be given only when the survival of the Tribe is at stake.

I let then my words speak for themselves, I reply, It is written in the Great Book of Hoodoo that when the Call is given the Tribes will gather and the Firstborn shall know their birthright. I have brought the Call. Does the Delta stand with the Firstborn?

They buzz with conversation and conference. I am being perhaps a bit highhanded. They could not refuse. The Brotherhood had seeded the Myth of Gathering well. Too many generations have grown up in the true belief of the Gathering of the Tribes. When the Firstborn shall stand again. They will follow for the same reason that I come, survival of the species is the highest law. Yet I understand their hesitancy and sympathize with their fears. My people have made their precarious peace with this slave's existence. They survive, clinging to lives already crippled with insecurity and now I come to them with an ancient warcry: Up you mighty race. Destiny demands.

Is it any wonder that some curse my name? I am Stormbringer, the dark unknown exploding into their ordered lives, chaos in a world striving for order. I'm lucky they don't stone me.

A grayhaired oldman stands with stiff dignity. If you would please wait in the outer room young hoodoo while we speak on this matter. We will call you shortly.

I hesitate. Timing is the essence of command theater.

The last time the Brotherhood called Gathering, I say, the Tribes did not come. We have since been conquered and enslaved and now we are the despised of the earth. Our backs are against the wall. The Blacks bid for power. I bring the Call.

I nod respectfully and withdraw to the waiting room. Once out of the council chamber I sit and relax. Centering myself I draw power reserves from the air, refreshing relaxing power. And I think again about my mission.

I have still not grasped the game behind the Masters of the Order Ascension selecting me for this mission. True I am myself of the Delta but still I am only apprentice. Journeymen and above were sent to deliver the Call to the other Tribes. To entrust an apprentice with a mission of such import is unprecedented. Apparently I have become a factor in the Order's game, a game so much longer than mine that I found it incomprehensible. That's what I did not like, I am a player not a pawn. I am no mystic, slave to forces he doesn't understand, I am a hoodoo sorcerer and I acknowledge no power greater than myself. I will not be pawn in another's game, not even the Order's. The old farts thought to orchestrate me as they did all others. True, it was a good game and I was glad to be involved. After all these years the Call has gone out and soon the Tribes will march. I wouldn't miss it for the world. I will play but my eyes are open. These are portentous times for my people, red meat and wine for a young man in a hurry.

After waiting a couple of rather long hours I am called back to the Hall. I know the answer as soon as I walk into the room of unclenched eyes and loose easy smiles, I feel the quick flush of success! The Delta is down.

I smile and sit in the chair provided earlier for me.

The Chief of Council is less formal than before.

The Delta honors the Call, she says, We will be at the

Place of Gathering at the proper time. The necessary orders have been given, arrangements are being made.

She smiles with sudden warmth, Actually young hoodoo, she said, as we have expected you, the issue has already been placed before the Tribe. We expect assent. The Folk have long waited on the Call. The taste of servitude has become bitter to the tongue. We here, she indicated her fellow council members with a sweep of her arm, have achieved a degree of comfort and are of course more cautious than most. We would rather this burden be borne by a later generation. But if it is time then it is time. You may report to the Masters of the Order Ascension that the Delta stands with the Firstborn.

I salute her. After making all the necessary arrangements I leave elated. It's still a nice day outside, the sun high in the sky, and I walk briskly to my quarters, chastising myself for my earlier concerns. After all, renegades who would bet against the Folk have already been neutralized and isolated from power. Many of the council are Hidden Members trained by the Order. Ascensionists all. The Brotherhood left little to chance or circumstance. We of the Hoodoo Path have lost much face in the long years of our defeat. It has been whispered that our magic was not strong enough to withstand the magic of our many conquerors. This is so. A lesson well learned. This time we will not fail. We will not make the same mistakes twice, *The Blacks shall never again be enslaved.*

I am tireder than I realized and by the time I get to my place I am more than ready to rest. My place is on the southernmost edge of town. For I live apart from all others and walk in mystery as befits my calling. No one can know all of my faces. No one knows where my truths end and my tricks begin. I got tricks in tricks in tricks. I got tricks it'll take generations to unravel. My Game is always on.

Well most always. Still walking on a cloud of mission completed, I am almost at the door of my sanctum before my radar goes off. Someone is there. My radar flares out seeking danger. My order has made an art of survival. Cowards all, we let no possible danger go unmonitored. We do not walk this earth, we stalk it. My every breath is an act of war, I do not sit with my back to the door.

My radar senses no malignancy. Nonetheless I stalk, a fully armed sorcerer opens the door.

The ochawitch sits in my chair.

My radar still flares out into corners and crevices. We of the Brotherhood trust no one. But she is a warrior and we have fought together. My mission is done. I sense nothing malignant and my eyes unslit as they dig deeply into her two deep brown orbs. Our rhythms are compatible and I feel her every breath. I smile and open myself to her. There is no greater pleasure.

CHAPTER 8

〰〰〰〰

A STORM, WITH HARDDRIVEN RAIN. ON RIVERSIDE DRIVE the oldlady waited. A yellow cab came down Person and went into the park, tires splashing water. The oldlady noted the outline of a lionmaned man in the backseat. One down one to go. She relit her pipe and sat back to wait.

The cab's bright lights valiantly cut against the rain-shrouded trees on the little winding road into the park as the cab driver reluctantly followed Willie D's instructions.

Hell nobody lives in the park he muttered, looking again in the rearview mirror at Willie D's dreads and almost missing HighJohn's tower when it loomed out of the darkness, stilts throwing warped shadows in the car's rain-watered headlights.

This is it, said Willie D from the back.

I'll be damned, the cab driver muttered.

Willie D was only a little smug while paying the meter and the tip. After arguing with the driver at the airport, he had been none too sure himself when they finally entered the park. He lifted the hood of a military-cut nylon parka, grabbed his bag and stepped out into the rain. The cab pulled off with a jerk as soon as the door was closed.

I don't blame him, Willie D looked at the tower being battered by the storm. Looked right gothic. A light was on in the front window.

As he started to dart across the street, a red Mercedes barreled up in a spray of muddy water.

What the blessed hell?

The driver's window went down. Mike leaned out and yelled at him, You a little old to be playing in the rain aren't you, youngman?

Willie D whooped and slapped the steaming hood of the car, Mike Daniels, he yelled, you old dog.

He walked around and they shook through the open window. Mike parked, grabbed a bag from the backseat, ducked out into the rain and slammed the door.

Is this Tucept's place? he yelled over the storm.

Must be, yelled Willie D, glancing at the stairs, But I would hate to climb those stairs just to find out we on the wrong block.

He noticed the sign on the baobab tree.

ROOTDOCTOR T. HIGHJOHN
Rootwork & Conjury
High Hoodoo My Specialty
Sliding Fees

This is it, he said, looking at both the tree and the sign closely before starting up the stairs. Strange tree, he murmured.

They climbed the swaying rainslick stairs carefully. Gripping the rail, they ducked the wind that tugged at their clothes and blew rain slanting into their faces.

DE POWER

At the top of the stairs, in jungle fatigue shirt over old Levis, HighJohn waited with the door open. The rain chased them inside and he closed it out behind them.

They shook themselves dry, shouting, laughing, back-slapping and making clumsy attempts at dap.

Wooweee, said Willie D, shaking his dreads free of glistening water. This is monsoon weather.

You get storms like this often? asked Mike, stripping his jacket off.

Often enough, said a grinning HighJohn, Sho is nice to see you dudes. I didn't know if you would be able to make it.

He led them into the frontroom, genuinely pleased to see them, Can I get you something warm to drink? I've got some tea.

Tea sounds good to me, said Mike, sitting on a couch and taking off wet Italian loafers.

Fine with me, said Willie D.

Okay, said Tucept, just a minute.

He sat down in front of a terminal glowing with green figures and his fingers skipped quickly over the keyboard, CRT display doing visual acrobatics. On the box, the Dells spoke on what freedom means.

Willie D looked around HighJohn's crowded frontroom curiously. He went to a wall rack of small smoked bottles and picked one up. Nail clippings labeled with the initials *rdx*. He picked up another. Hair? Different initials? He made a rough count of the bottles. Fifty or more at least.

At the terminal HighJohn finally sighed satisfaction, turned the system down and stretched.

Okay, he said, going to the kitchen, Three teas.

Willie D looked over book titles. He picked up Siu's *The Craft of Power* and thumbed through it, snaky locks bobbing as he flipped pages.

Mike watched him for a moment, How did you get your hair like that man? he finally asked.

Let it grow without combing it.

Why? asked Mike with a frown.

I like it.

How do you keep it clean?

I didn't say I don't clean it, I said don't comb it.

Willie D's voice was testy.

That's what he told me when I asked him, said Tucept, bringing out a tray with 3 mugs and a steaming pot.

HighJohn put the tray on a coffee table and pulled up a chair. Mike and Willie D drew up chairs, Willie D put *The Craft of Power* beside him.

He sipped his tea.

That's good man.

Private blend, said HighJohn proudly, How's the family man, you still married?

I'd be a fool to lose this woman.

Willie D reached into a backpocket, pulled out his wallet and flipped through accordioned photos of what he proudly referred to as the crew. He pointed with a thick-knuckled finger to a roundfaced woman, staring mischievously at the camera from smoky halflidded eyes under a bright dread halo.

Linda, he said, my crony.

And this, he pointed at a photo of a serious little girl instead of the baby HighJohn remembered, is Abeki, the little lady.

He looked fondly at the photos before putting them away.

You married again Mike?

Mike shook his head, Engaged though for the fall.

They congratulated him, toasted many good years and dapped around.

How's your boy?

Mike shrugged, He's fine. Ah, I don't see him as

much as I should, I guess. He looked half defiant, half embarrassed, Always busy, you know.

Willie D shrugged, You do what you can man.

Mike flushed. Yeah, he said, grounding a halfsmoked cigarette stub out in the ashtray, How about you Tucept, any kids?

HighJohn shook his head.

The storm battered the house.

Remember monsoon? said Willie, It was like this all the time.

You remember all the times we laid around getting high in Nam? said Willie D, On patrols, even on listening post, monsoon or not.

The bunker outside, said Tucept.

And guard duty, laughed Mike.

You remember the time we got busted down in Soul Alley? howled Tucept, I'm sitting there with the opium pipe in my hands when the MPs come in and all I can think is, busted, let me get one more toke.

They howled and dapped, drowning out the rain and storm outside.

I was so fucked up that . . . said Willie D.

He was so fucked up, yelled Tucept, that he wouldn't get in the cell down at LBJ and ended up in the conexes.

Hey you know Welch sneaked a canteen of water to me in that fucking conex. I don't know how he did it, I never asked him.

Willie D's angular face softened, Hey whatever happened to Welch anyway?

Still in Soul Alley, I guess, shrugged Mike, He never came back after Kicks got fragged.

A pause marked the conversation.

Yeah ole Welch probably still laying up there in Saigon with that opium pipe in his mouth, cutting that paper.

They call it Ho Chi Minh City or something now.

They probably draft his black ass and send him to Cambodia.

They sniggled.

Welch wouldn't go to Cambodia, said HighJohn, Remember that time down in the Mekong Delta when that black Cambodian soldier came up and dapped us talking about me same same soul brother, me same same soul brother?

Heavy, wasn't it? yelled Willie D, Dapping too. And that sucker looked just like some brother back on the block, Welch and Jethro swore from then on that the Cambos were black. Hell Oop was black enough for me.

Talking about Nam loosened them up and the years dropped away.

I got some wine back here, said HighJohn. He went to the kitchen and brought it out, cold sweat beading the bottle. He pulled the cork and poured a libation to the floor four times. To the north, the south, the east and the west. He filled their glasses and toasted, For the fellas from The Ghetto. Welch, Prester John, Jethro.

They drank.

Strange libation, commented Willie D.

The four corners of the earth, said HighJohn, an old hoodoo thing that folks around here are into.

I noticed the sign on the tree next to the stairs, said Willie D, Rootdoctor T. HighJohn huh? That you?

HighJohn nodded, I do consultations.

You not serious are you man? Mike asked incredulously, You telling us you're the local rootdoctor or something?

HighJohn nodded, Or something sounds about right.

Are you serious man? Mike said looking around the room again, noting the herbs, the strange laboratory, the fetishes, the smoked bottles.

Considering how you used to turn your nose at Jethro, he said, I'm curious as to how you got involved in it.

HighJohn shrugged, It's a living.

Is there a lot of this hoodoo around here? asked Willie D.

Yeah, said HighJohn, the Delta is fulla hoodoo for those who see. According to folks around here, de first monkey to stand was de conjureman.

He told them the story of Moj. He told them about Spijoko and his studies. While he spoke he gathered his consciousness into his third eye and detached himself from his physical shell. Leaving it on automatic pilot he withdrew deep into himself and his hoodoo mind. He monitored himself for a moment, watching his body perform. It was a well trained instrument.

Finally turning to his game, he conjured up his myth and looked it over with small grunts of satisfaction. Not only had time not lessened its detail but some points had been sharpened and defined since the last time he worked on it. Good. That meant that he had worked the time factors so that it grew with time rather than dissipated. A damn good myth. Might have some stamina in it. A couple of thousand years at least. He checked the elements.

The rise and fall of the Firstborn. The Leanyears of defeat. The Longmarch of Ascension. Something was missing. It took him a minute to put his hands on it. The Leanyears didn't have enough impact. He wanted to evoke a sense of strength extracted from struggle. He looked at the Leanyears for long judicious moments before adding more pain, nagging pain rain on stone. Fatcutting, callusbuilding pain, long hard years forging an old people into a new mold.

The big black flathead tom glided into the room and stretched out on the mantel in one smooth elongated motion. Long black tail popping lazily, it stared at them through unblinking yellow eyeslits.

Outside the storm battered the tower.

Say man, asked Mike, stilling himself, Is this place swaying?

Probably; said HighJohn, I've been here so long that I don't feel it anymore. It gets worse during storms.

You get these storms like this often? asked Willie D.

Often enough.

You're lucky that your plane made it through, Mike said to Willie D.

It didn't start until we landed. How long did it take you to drive down?

Mike checked a thin Rolex on the inside of his wrist with a practiced precise manner.

About sixteen, seventeen hours.

Straight through?

Practically. Couldn't leave Washington until last night. We had a meeting just yesterday on an important new acquisition. A new company that should substantially enhance our productive capability.

You still with Acme? asked Willie D.

You better believe it.

Acme is one of the dogs of the earth, said Willie D sharply, Its productive capability doesn't need enhancement.

Mike smiled sourly. In a minute Willie D would be calling him a bougie opportunist, et al. Any dude with his hair piled on his head like that didn't have anything to say to him. Willie D couldn't be into anything but some old bohemian '60s shit that let him sneer at what guys in the trenches had to do. He hadn't really planned to come. He had too much to do to take time out for a bullshit session with old army buddies. But at the last minute he had thrown some clothes into a bag and gotten on the road.

I suppose you've got a better idea, Mike said with a dismissive wave of his manicured hand. Buried somewhere in that bouffant hairdo of yours.

232

Say fellas, drawled HighJohn before Willie D lashed back, I didn't bring yall down here to squabble over who's the better negro, house or field. I figured you could work something out. Both yall got good game. When you coordinate them it will make both of you stronger.

His tone was smug and Willie D bristled.

What are you talking about man?

The reason I got you two dudes down here. I decided it was time for you two to work together.

You decided? said Willie D.

I decided.

And who gave you the authority to make that decision for us my man? asked Mike.

I've read the Great Book of Hoodoo. I walk the hoodoo path.

Oh, said Willie D sourly, that does explain it doesn't it. Why don't you just hoodoo us and make it easy for yourself?

I am hoodooing you.

Willie D laughed, a short bark, You aint doing that good a job of it.

I'm doing alright, said HighJohn, I know most of your business.

Amused, Willie D waited to hear about his business.

For instance, said HighJohn, I know all about your organization and your operations.

Willie D was no longer amused, his face hardened, perceptibly accenting the old frag wound lines mapping his face.

I know your people and your programs, HighJohn continued, Personally I wouldn't implement phase three until your cells in the Caribbean and the South Pacific islands are more firmly established. But that's a personal, your strategic process is basically sound.

HighJohn sat back in his chair, eyes amused. It was

that damned playful streak in him that enjoyed throwing shit in the game.

Mike watched them both, mind going 50. It was becoming fast apparent that far more was going on here than just an old army buddies thing. He looked at Willie D curiously. Organization? Operations?

Willie D's eyes had slitted, You do know a lot about my business don't you HighJohn?

I keep my finger on the pulse.

Mike's eyes shifted to Tucept. What kind of game was Tucept playing here?

I suppose, Mike said smoothly, that since I'm here too, that I'm part of this, ah, pulse.

My congratulations, said HighJohn, on your recent promotion to the number two slot. The judge made a wise decision.

Mike held up his glass in a sardonic toast, My compliments on the quality of your information. That decision was restricted to the excom only. Not even the rest of the organization knows that.

Yes I know, said HighJohn, Also I know that you two could, ah, considerably enhance each other's productive capability. You can work it out on the ride back home.

Willie D looked Mike over with tight calculating eyes. Old bougie Mike? Number two of what? He would have never thought Mike had anything on his mind other than a good time and a paycheck. Tucept either for that fact. He frowned, wondering again how Tucept had breached his security. Willie D walked over to HighJohn's chair and stood over him, You still aint told me man, how you got so much information regarding my operations.

They knew enough of Willie D to know that he could be dangerous. HighJohn remained seated, I told you, he said calmy, I'm da hoodooman. I used my crystal ball.

He pointed at his computer terminal. Basic hoodoo law, he said, Knowledge is power. So too is information.

DE POWER

Willie D looked at the computer terminal, sitting innocently on the desk, screen blank and inoperative.

You aint telling me shit man, he muttered, Aint telling me nothing about how you got to my shit.

I'm getting to it man. Let me finish running my game and if you don't like it then you can reject it. Blood.

They stared at each other for a locked moment before Willie D grudgingly sat down, Okay, he muttered, but so far I don't like it. Blood.

Part of my hoodoogame, began HighJohn as he dug into the deep chest pocket of his jungle fatigues, is monitoring the games of black warlords.

He pulled two twisted little brown roots from his pocket and held them out in the palm of his right hand.

I have, he said, brought you power.

The wind rattled against the window in a sudden flurry accented by a flare of lightning and the deep rumble of thunder. The tower vibrated and swayed.

The two little twisted roots in the outstretched palm of HighJohn's hand were small curiously shaped things with serrated convoluted grooves.

HighJohn de Conquer root, he told them, the root that's named after me. Supposed to help you overcome all obstacles.

He passed one to each of them. And as they stared with curious fascination at the little grooved root he opened their minds and planted his myth.

Mike and Willie frowned uneasily as the root evoked a disturbing yet exhilarating parade of images, sensations, thoughts and emotions. From the distant past to the far future the saga of the Firstborn unfolded in their minds. They fought their way from a brutish fourfooted existence to the knowledge of themselves as men. They mixed paints with a bushman artist depicting a successful hunt and felt the hunger of an Untouchable denied fruit. They built the Sphinx and knew the pit of slaveships.

They felt the pleasure of a Haitian woman calling Erzulie and the bright sun of a Brazilian summer, the bonechill of a Tashkent winter and the bloodwarmth of island rain. They conquered the stars one by one. They knew the determination of a colonist on the Dog Star's second planet and the stump pains of a rearmed vet of the Sirius 6 Belt Wars and they wept with the loneliness of a scout on decadeslong patrol of the Outer Asteroid Belt. They saw the awesome terror of planet busters and sun poppers. They saw the rise and the fall and the reemergence of the Federation of the Thousand Black Worlds. Far into the future they saw generations come and go as HighJohn carefully weaved myth into the fibers of their souls. A saga of struggle. They lived the Firstborn's battles, their victories and defeats. They knew the Firstborn, the Leanyears, the Gathering and the Longmarches and they knew themselves links in a line unbroken.

Willie D sat motionlessly awed at the destinic panorama unfolding in his head. The saga of the Firstborn and the vision of black survival carved itself into his heart and there was a surge of pride and arrogance about being Black. He drew power and felt himself filled with a determination that he would do all that he could to ensure that what he saw and felt would come to be.

Mike too sat motionless as the myth lived in his head. He caught Willie D's eye for a moment and felt a camaraderie that he hadn't felt since the days of foxhole Nam and Firebase Sin Loi. Felt good. Felt damned good. Confidence settled in and he no longer questioned his decision to commit his life to the struggle. He believed in the victory and the importance of his contribution to the victory.

Da hoodooman smiled. HighJohn on the gun. He conferred upon them the power of conviction and armored them in a sense of destiny. With this amulet of power, chanted the shaman, you are invincible before the enemies of the Tribe. We shall win. Be confident in the victory. Good over evil. Do battle.

ひひひひ

I CLIMB TO POWER. THE SUN RISES, BRIGHT RAYS FLARING over the dark horizon. The rock of the mountain is unyielding under my boots and I stop for a moment to rest and look beneath me over the vast plain of the Place of Gathering. Already the Tribes of the Firstborn arrive and congregate at the base of the mountain. The peak of the mountain is the hoodoo highground from which the trained voice can be heard throughout the Place of Gathering. It is from there that I will give the Call.

The breeze is fresh here and I take deep, invigorating breaths, relishing the sting of the crisp air. From below the jumbled tongues of the Tribes reach me. Some have seen me and I hear them call my name. HighJohn de Conqueror. He who has been chosen to give the Call. I who do what must be done. I was as surprised as any when the Masters of the Order Ascension selected me to give the Call. True it is a great honor, already the generations know my name. But it is a sacrifice play. If I surface I will be known as a man of power. A target. I started to refuse but already power had begun to gather unto me and I knew that on this path lay my destiny.

Dare I bid for power?

Whoever heard of a hoodooman passing up power?

I will give the Call.

I must hurry on to the top. The necessary destinic forces will soon be in fertile conjunction for the seeding. The time of opportunity will be short. I climb quickly, my feet falling easily now into the rhythm of the ascent. As I climb, power gathers thickly about me and it is warm and satisfying. Strong destinic power. With this power even destiny is but a toy. It is a good feeling. The generations shall know me, my name shall be legion. I will live forever.

By the time I reach the peak I am exhilarated. The wind bites at my face and snaps my robes like wings from my body. I taste storm in the air and I am pleased. Storm is a totem of much power for me. I look out over the Place of Gathering and my breath catches in my throat. The sight is awesome. As far as the eye can see the Place of Gathering is covered with the Tribes of the Firstborn. A milling mass of humanity with still more coming, millions and millions of them, a sea of black brown and yellow faces. Tall thin Ibos come with wiryheaded Goran, Bantus sit next to Dravidians under the shade of colorful umbrellas and Harlem checks in with the Black Belt South and earthtoned Latinos from Rio and El Barrio. Trenchtown Rasta argue theology with Cairo Sunni, wooly headed South Moluccans and lean Khmers laugh with cousins from Paris and Holland. From the Sahara to Azbekistan they gather. One people. Old feuds are forgotten. Tribes that have warred for centuries mingle and age-old enemies recount old battles. Merchants of different lands barter their goods and cousins talk in foreign tongues. So many millions, and still they come, in ones and twos, families and groups they come, faces alive with anticipation of the Gathering, babies riding above the crowd on the shoulders of their parents, laughing in many tongues. So many of them! I exult! From the four corners of the earth the Tribes gather and my heart is full. Long will the songs be sung and the tales told of the Gathering of the Firstborn. A once mighty people strong again. As far as the eye can see, a milling sea of the Firstborn, millions and millions. By the gods, we cover the earth!

My laughter rings wild against the heavens and dark thunder rumbles in the distance. It is time. The moment of destiny is now. I must grasp it or it will be only a sour memory. I take a moment to center myself. I am ready. I am HighJohn.

I raise my hands. The milling crowd slowly quiets and all faces turn to me. The wind snaps about my lone figure and the rising sun behind me throws long shadows from me. I sing out, my voice an undulating fieldholler into the heavens.

I am HighJohn de Conqueror, I bring the Call!

The answering roar of the Firstborn fills me with power. I shiver with the sensation and start my conjuration, weaving before them a blackworld reality. I start easy, gathering them slowly into my myth, the saga of the Firstborn leaping from my heart to theirs. I fire their imagination with the tales of heroes and sheroes, with visions of what could be, with the honor of our legacy, with the power of arrogance. Up you mighty race. My words touch them and they stir restless beneath me.

I fill them with a vision of us as a powerful, respected people, of our generations strong and prosperous. Survivors. I open their minds and feed them words of power. My voice throbs throughout the Place of Gathering and before my very eyes I watch the sleeping giant waken. I feel the click when it happens, when suddenly the Tribe and I are one and I have them, a sea of black brown and yellow faces all turned to me, listening to my words with all their hearts and souls and I have them by the gods I have them in the palm of my hand I have them and I feed them power in great mighty waves.

I AM HIGHJOHN, I call out, I BRING THE CALL!

Time hangs in motionless expectation and suddenly the Call leaps fullgrown to my mind.

Demoja!

I CALLL HOLYWWAAAAAARRRRRRRR! DE-MOJAAAAAAAAAAAAAAA!

For a split second the Call wavers between reality and

illusion. Suddenly the sky lights up as lightning slashes it into an angry wardrum of thunder. A murmur sweeps through the Tribes. I'm hot. My mojo is on. Power races through me, I am the power, HighJohn de Conqueror. I can do anything.

Again I give the call.

DEMOJAAA!

Those at the base of the mountain pick it up tentatively. De mo ja! De mo ja!

The chanting voices of the people feed me in rhythmic waves. There is no high like riding the wave of the people's passion, power such as I have never known, I grow in leaps and bounds, filled to bursting and drunk with power. My concerns fall away and there is a sensation of settling and I am the power, the center of the universe, a burning radiating sun. Around me the storm gathers and I am mighty beyond belief. I am rulemaker. The reins of destiny are firmly in my hands and I exult! My entire being sings with song. I am alive! Others merely exist but I live! By the gods I live!

DEMOOOOJJAAAAAAAA!

Words of power are music on my tongue and the chant grows.

DE MO JA! DE MO JA! DE MO JA!

More and more voices pick it up and it spreads throbbing throughout the Place of Gathering, hammering at the heavens. From the four corners of the earth the Firstborn speak with one breath of Holywar.

Demoja.

The word came to be.

I felt it when it began to live in the hearts of the people and the soul of the Tribe. When I no longer needed to nurture it. It lived. I stop and smile with satisfaction as the chant demoja continues to rise about us.

Demoja.

DE POWER

It is done.

I have named the thing and it is done. I am a mighty sorcerer and reality shall yield to me. My seed shall grow into a mighty tree. A galactic horde that shall rule the stars. Every Black, man woman and child, shall be unto self an army. Masterplayers. A race of rulers. And then shall the Blacks dance, yes, even on the graves of galaxies. This I swear by the tail of Moj.

Demoja.

And now I must withdraw. Quickly. My game has been exposed and my enemies have the scent. It is a bitter joke to be warlord of slaves.

Before I leave I drop the twisted root that bears my name and stamp it into the rocky ground. I step down. As I hurry back down the hoodoo path I hear behind me the chant demoja become the whisper demoja and smile proudly. Oh you mighty race. Oh sly, slick, and wicked. Yes we are still weak and our enemies are legion. Yes we must war from the briarpatch, grabbing destiny by its armored throat and whispering softly, amongst ourselves, *Holywar against all.* My heart is full and I am so proud that tears roll from my eyes. My people. A fighting instrument forged on the anvil of adversity. My horde.

I leave the Place of Gathering with a small arrogant chuckle. Holywar of the Blacks. Demoja. A good conjuration if I do say so myself. Reality shall yet yield to my will. My people shall survive. For when the Blacks must call on the will to survive and conquer know that I am the Way. HighJohn de Conqueror. Hoodooman. My magic is powerful. My will is law. My name is Holywar.

Demoja.

SUCH IS MY MYTH AND SO IT IS WRITTEN.
   Believe or be damned.
   That is all.

＄＄＄＄

And Shine said: There's fish in the ocean
and there's fish in the sea
but aint none of these fish
gon outswim me.

About the Author

Arthur Flowers, a blues singer, writer, Vietnam veteran, and native of Memphis, lives in New York City. He has contributed to several magazines, been awarded a PEN grant and a New York State Council of Arts Fellowship, and serves as Executive Director of the New Renaissance Writers' Guild.

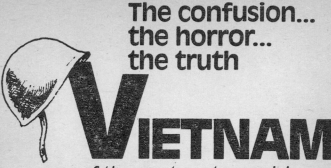

The confusion...
the horror...
the truth

VIETNAM

one of the most controversial periods of U.S. history